Chrystal is a 188-year-olc [obscured] rom that, she's just your aver[obscured]

London, 1851. A young [obscured] for dead, but rescued by a g[obscured] don for the Great Exhibition. Their intervention is so successful that she's still alive in the 21st Century where she passes as a Steampunk to explain her idiosyncratic taste in clothing and old-fashioned speech. Educated in clockwork, steam power, and what modern science dismisses as "ætheric mysticism", she may be the only person who can save our 21st Century world.

Steampunk is a genre that combines science fiction with nostalgia for a past that never was. Set in worlds where history diverged from our own during the Victorian era, it often makes use of original gadgets and innovative engineering devices or scientific principles.

Chrystal Heart

because Steampunk can be more than whimsy

Meg Kingston

Jay Walker Writing

First published in Great Britain 2013

This edition published by Jay Walker Writing, 2013

A catalogue record for this book is available from the British Library.

ISBN 978-0-9552602-4-7

Printed and bound in the UK by Antony Rowe Ltd.

Writing may be a solitary profession, but even writers are gregarious creatures and need good company.

With thanks to my support team: Martin, Smotyn and Meme;
My fellow members of CRAG: Sue, Bob and Paul;
All my beta readers, unofficial consultants, Splendid Steampunk friends and everyone who contributed to my crowdfunding project.

Thank you all.

For Eugenie,
Thanks for your support,

Prologue

October, 1851

Philomena Mercedes Carstairs slipped away from the crowds leaving Hyde Park, straightening the hat pinned over her neat chignon. She twitched her short cape into place over her tight, grey jacket and turned into an unlit side street, away from the throngs of merrymakers flooding towards purveyors of refreshments on more fashionable streets. Although the coffee houses claimed to welcome ladies as well as gentlemen, she knew from experience that the more popular ones would not serve a woman on her own. Especially when more rewarding customers were queuing for places at their tables. She would avoid the crowds, following the back streets to her lodging-house and brew coffee on the stove there.

Unbeknown to Philomena, her passage did not go unnoticed. Three shadows detached themselves from the heavy darkness beneath an overhanging wooden building. One figure turned down an alleyway, hurrying to get ahead of her, whilst two wraith-like others slid silently in her wake, careful to prevent her discovering them.

" 'Scuse me, Missus," said a voice in the darkness beside her.

"Oh," Philomena stopped, her hand rising to her chest where her heart thudded against her corset.

" 'M sorry, Miss. Didn't mean to startle ya," said the man.

Now that Philomena had turned, she could see the man more clearly. He would have been almost as tall as her, had he not stooped so. His coat was well-cut but worn at the cuffs and stained in many places, while his rough accent spoke of life in the murkier parts of the city. She gathered her scattered wits enough to smile at the stranger.

"Can I help you, Sir?" she enquired.

"Wondered if you might spare a few coppers for an ex-army

man down on his luck?" said the man, moving closer.

"Oh, of course," Philomena lifted her bag for her coin purse. A sudden sound from behind made her turn. Seeing another figure reaching for her, she ducked and spun about, backing away until the back of her bell-skirted dress touched the dirty brick wall, her bosom heaving with fear.

Footpads. And I let them trap me, she thought. Someone tore the velvet cape off her shoulders. A hand reached for her bag and she grabbed the wrist, twisting to throw her slender weight against it. She heard a satisfying yelp and released the damaged limb, looking around for the second assailant. He blocked her escape but made no attempt to engage. As she looked for an opportunity to break past, a third figure came running and Philomena found herself, once again, backed against the wall with her two opponents facing her more warily this time. The man whose wrist she had injured was pulling himself to his feet, a knife in his left hand.

Made of stern stuff, these bandits, she thought as she searched for a way to evade their tightening circle. She pulled the purse from her bag and threw it behind the men, where it fell with a loud rattle.

"That is all I have. Take it and be damned," she shouted.

The nearer two men hesitated, glancing towards the purse, but the injured one never took his eyes off hers.

"I think we'll take more than yer purse, Missus," he said.

"I have nothing further!"

None of the men spoke, but the knifeman moved in, the other two flanking him and thwarting any possible egress for her. He lunged with the blade and she barely managed to knock it away with her right arm. There was a loud crack, her frilled sleeve tore and blood spurted as she ducked under their advancing hands, trying for the open street. A fist struck her shoulder, throwing her towards the man in the centre. Shouts and running footsteps sounded as if they were several miles away and she got a clear view of the attacker's face as his knife penetrated her ribs. Her knees buckled and her vision failed as she heard a group of men attacking the thieves who'd struck her down. There were shouts from the robbers and softer words in a foreign language and then nothing but blackness.

Several voices were talking in sing-song tones; a language of short sounds bubbling over each other, rising and falling in odd ways. Philomena opened her eyes and saw richly-coloured cloth hanging a few inches above her face. The air was thick with sweet-smelling smoke and she found it oddly hard to focus her eyes. The haze made her cough, and a young man's face came into view. He lifted his hand away from her chest and she saw blood trickling from a neat wound below his thumb. Philomena swallowed hard, trying not to look and instead focused on his curious, embroidered hat, as bright as the cloth hanging. Everything felt distant, dreamy, and she had the strangest feeling that she'd seen his weathered, brown visage somewhere before.

"You speak Engliss, Lady?" he asked, his words so heavily accented she could barely comprehend his meaning.

"Y-yes," her voice came out as little more than a whisper. "Yes, I speak English. Where am I?"

"You in our lodging," he replied. "You badly hurt."

"The footpads!" Philomena tried to sit up, but he pushed her shoulders back onto the bed.

"No, you mus' not spill," he said. Confused, she subsided and another figure moved beside the bed, with a thurible that spilled green, sickly smoke over her.

"You need to go sleep," he said. "We leaf you now. Here you safe."

"But, but..." unable to think of an argument, Philomena stopped trying to say anything.

"You mus' remember," he went on, holding up his hand so she could see the dripping cut more clearly. "The Chrystal need blood. Human blood."

"What?" She thought about sitting up, but her body was becoming heavy and lethargic again. "What crystal?"

"Not crystal, Chrystal!" he corrected, a guttural sound. "We go soon, but the Chrystal keep you alive. Remember, Chrystal need..."

"Blood. I remember, but I do not understand," replied Philomena. She realised her words were slurring but couldn't bring herself to try again as the world went hazy once more.

Philomena woke with a parched throat and a terrible headache. The heavy, colourful cloth still hung near to her face and she pushed its embroidered weight aside to sit up, feeling lightheaded. After a moment, the world stopped spinning and she looked around. An ornately-engraved carafe sat on a small table, a glass over its mouth and a towel neatly folded beside it. She had barely noticed the metal bucket on the floor before a wave of nausea washed over her and she doubled up.

Laying the soiled towel on the floor beside the bucket, she rinsed her mouth out and stood carefully. The world wavered a little before it settled enough for her to take stock of her situation; she was dressed in an unbleached cotton shift, whilst her own clothes were nowhere to be seen. Dress, new jacket and even her corset had all disappeared. Her right forearm was bandaged, feeling heavy and awkward. She staggered her way to the window, opened it one-handed and flung back the shutters, revealing nothing but an empty alleyway. Fresher air rushed in, making her head spin again and she leant on the wall for a moment until it passed. In the sunlight, she could see that the room was largely empty, save for the cot she had lain in, the fabric draped like a tent on a framework above, the little table and a small dresser against the wall. Closer inspection of this revealed a bowl of water covered with another length of the embroidered cloth and a large looking-glass. She bent to look at her reflection and gasped.

What has happened to me? Her dark blond hair hung in greasy rats' tails. Her face was gaunt, comprising of shadow-filled hollows crossed by sharp planes. Her lips were so pale as to be almost invisible against her white skin and the green eyes that stared back at her looked a thousand years old and darkly underlined with shadows. The silver-backed glass reflected something white on her chest and she looked down. *The wound!* She slipped out of the shift-dress and began pulling at the bandages, gently lifting each layer, half fascinated, half terrified of what she might see.

I will not faint like some helpless milksop, she muttered when the strange vertigo threatened to overwhelm her again. She steeled herself to look and eased away the final wad of bloodied dressing, craning her neck to see the wound that she thought had killed her. It took a moment for her mind to register that yes, there was a partly-healed wound; but there was something else. Embedded in the centre of her chest sat a metal structure of intricately-engraved brass-coloured pipes and what looked like valves. And in the middle of this was a crystal, almost as large as her fist, faceted like an uncut gemstone. As she stared, the crystal brightened to a clear, bright green and then dimmed again, just like the pulse of a heart.

This time, she did faint.

Philomena came round slowly, the discomfort of her limbs increasing as she dragged her mind back to consciousness. Disoriented, she watched a blur of bright colours wavering across her vision. She blinked, rubbed her eyes and the embroidered cloth came into focus. As her memory flooded back, she pulled herself to her feet and fingered the metal construction buried in her chest. It hadn't vanished, as she'd half-expected. Her skin appeared to have grown back over the metal frame, but not completely over the stone in the centre. She stared at it for a moment, watching its slow rhythm. Tentatively, she pressed the fingers of her left hand into her right wrist, searching for the heart-pulse. She found it as the crystal brightened. **Lub-dub.** She held her breath, counting silently, *one elephant, two elephant, three elephant*. **Lub-dub.** The pulse in her wrist came exactly as the crystal brightened. Philomena picked up the mirror and stared at her emaciated visage, thinking, *What have they done to me?*

Her wide-eyed gaze focused on the bandages on her heavy right forearm and she remembered the wound she'd received trying to deflect the knife. Hesitantly, she began to untie the dressing.

Chapter 1

In which a thief gets more than she expected

Summer, 2012

The tube station is crowded, people hurrying in all directions and I'm just another commuter hurrying home. They'll never know it was me, and I'll be gone long before they call the police. The perfect place to work.

I had a narrow escape last week, had to drop a woman's purse and leg it. So I'm being careful today. My hoodie, jeans and trainers are old and battered, my unwashed hair in need of a cut and my cheap handbag empty of anything that could identify me. No-one who knew the be-suited office-working Samantha would recognise this grey nobody standing at the edge of the throng, watching for an easy target.

Him – carrying a raincoat over his arm with something heavy swinging in the pocket. My feet start walking and my brain flounders after them as I cut across the tiles at an angle towards him. A quick jostle and I stumble back, letting him push past. He barely even registers my existence, just shoves the obstruction away as if I was a piece of litter blown in his face. But my hand is full. I dash up the stairs and into the shadow of a vending machine that hasn't worked as long as I've been coming here. My heart pounds, but no shouts follow, so I can check what I've got. A nice, fat wallet, heavy with promise. I push my prize into an unlined fleece pocket to bump against my leg as I run up the last flight and onto the street. I nip into a quiet alley to inspect my prize. A dozen credit cards drop from my hand as I hunt through its pockets – they're no use to me, not without his PIN numbers. Lots of paper – receipts from the look of them. A driving licence and ... nothing! No cash – not even an emergency taxi fare in the zippered pocket. All that trouble for a tight wad bastard who lives on credit!

If I don't get some cash, I'll be hungry again tonight and probably out on the street. There's no way Tony'll accept another excuse for his rent. It's been lean pickings for weeks and I have to find some money! I pull my hood forward again, take a deep breath and head back towards the station.

This time, I choose a woman. I like these people with loose, long coats, especially when there's a weight pulling one side down. She's an eye-catching sight, although no-one in the crowd is paying her any attention. Londoners are so determinedly blasé about life that they'd die rather than be seen gawping at anything! It's like she's so visible she's become invisible.

She'd be tall, even without the funny hat she's wearing and her face is too severe to be pretty -she'll look even worse when she discovers her purse has gone! Her whole outfit is kind of old-fashioned, not just the hat. Under her coat I can see a figure-hugging waistcoat and dark blue skirt flowing down to her leather-booted ankles. But I'm not here to criticise her dress sense. This time, I don't even need to bump into her, just time my grab carefully for when the coat flaps away from her leg. I come up behind her, brush my hand along the flowing fabric and into the pocket. My fingers close on something and I draw it out quickly. But my wrist is seized in an unyielding grip. Startled, I drop the wallet and try to jerk away. She holds on! Panicking now, I struggle to get free but find myself swung round to face a pair of emerald green eyes, glaring down at me from under that ludicrous hat.

"Looking for something?" hissed a low voice.

"I, er...," my brain couldn't tie enough words together to answer her.

"Because I do not think you will find it in my coat," she continues harshly.

"I was just..." I still couldn't form a proper sentence. Those hard, green eyes drilled into my brain and withered the words before I could say them.

"Just picking my pocket? You need to do better than that, little thief." She's staring at Kerry's brass pin on my fleece, the only bit of jewellery I haven't sold yet.

"No, I wasn't..."

The half-shadowed face creases and a throaty laugh turns my blood to ice. I struggle again, but she just holds on and waits for me to give up.

"No, you certainly were not. Pick-pockets used to learn their trade and not get caught. Perhaps you should come with me!"

Her voice is low and she's speaking quietly enough to attract no attention from anyone else. Why isn't she yelling for the police? Is she just trying to scare me before letting me go? I try to hold on to that hope, but she starts walking towards the exit and I stumble to keep up, my arm still clamped in that vice-like hand. I get my feet underneath me, reach up with my free hand, then jerk backwards and twist, thinking to surprise her and pull my wrist free. I only succeed in tearing her sleeve, so I get a glimpse of her arm – and the metal rods buried in her flesh. I twist harder but can't help seeing the rods moving like pistons as she lifts me off my feet. I'm so startled, I stop fighting and hang limply in her grip. Then I see a glass tube in her other hand, moving towards my face, and begin to panic.

"I said you were coming with me," she says as I black out.

I come round lying on my back, an unfamiliar yellow light shining through my eyelids. Without thinking, I open them and turn my head, only then realising I wasn't at home. A room cluttered with odd tools and science-lab stuff, like nothing I'd ever seen before. I recognised my fleece among the coats hanging on a wooden stand by the door. And I'm lying on a leather sofa with a brown patterned blanket thrown over me. Where the hell is this? The room was so chaotic it took me a moment to notice her, standing beside the window and looking at me.

"I expected you would be awakening about now," she said without any greeting and I realised who she was. Memory flooded back - the crowd, the woman in strange clothes, her incredible grip.

"What? Where am I?" I ask, twisting to look around the strange room, but stopping as my head starts to spin.

"You are in my workshop," she said, calmly.

"Your what? But why?" I'd been kidnapped. By the woman who caught me picking her pocket!

As I tried to get my head around that, I felt the first heaves of panic and fought them down to look for a way to escape. I watched her walk to stand between me and the door, arms folded. She wasn't wearing the hat or that long coat, but the fancy blue dress with its tight, grey waistcoat was almost as outlandish and added to the unreality of the afternoon. I couldn't miss noticing her amazing hour-glass figure and wondered what she'd look like in normal clothes. *Or out of them,* whispered a little voice that shocked even me.

"Um, how long have I been out?" I asked, remembering where I'd been when I blacked out and suddenly worried I might have hit my head when I fell. Was that why I felt so dizzy?

"A brief while. It would have been complicated to convey a struggling companion, so I used my sleep-jar to discourage you from offering such resistance," came the reply. "Until I could bring you here and talk to you." I realised I should keep her talking, play for time while I worked out what to do. But so much was strange about this whole scenario that I couldn't take it all in. At random, my terrified mind latched onto something she'd mentioned.

"Sleep-jar? What's that?"

"Something I carry when I need to venture into crowded places. A small vial containing crystals that release an ætheric compound to discommode footpads and other miscreants long enough for me to make good an escape," she replied. "Though I do not usually bring them to my workshop afterwards."

I remembered the glass tube and realised she must have knocked me out with that. What kind of weirdo carries chloroform in case they're robbed?

"You keep calling this place your workshop," I said. I remembered someone in a film saying it was important to talk to your kidnappers, to make it harder for them to hurt you. "What do you do here?"

She just shrugged. Definitely not one for casual conversation!

"But why have you brought me here? What are you going to do to me?" I heard my voice getting higher with each question and missed her answer while I tried to calm myself down.

"I mean, what is all this equipment? We didn't have stuff like this when I was at school," I persisted, sitting up and pushing the blanket off me. The room swayed a little and I tried not to sound as scared as I felt while I looked for a way out.

"I think you would describe it as a mixture of chemical equipment and engineering tools – if you wish to divide the sciences in the modern way."

I wasn't exactly sure what she meant, but I got her drift. I stood up for a better look around and she caught me as my legs folded, returning me to the sofa. I slumped and she guided my head down between my knees.

"You should take a moment to recover from the effects of the sleep-jar before you try to stand," she said roughly, although her hands were gentle as she supported me.

After a moment, the worst of the dizziness passed and I sat back up, but carefully. My captor let go of me and I heard her cross the room and pour something, stirring it with a spoon that made a strangely glassy sound. When she returned, she held out a cup to me.

"Tea," she said. "It will help."

I accepted the cup and sipped. Luke-warm and horribly sweet. I tried to put the cup down on a little table beside me.

"No, drink it," she ordered, pushing the cup back. I did as I was instructed, although my stomach heaved threateningly. I held the empty cup out and she took it, placing it on its saucer. Then she stood over me, playing with something small that I couldn't see. Suddenly I noticed the plaster on my arm, inside the elbow.

"What have you done?" I gasped. "Did you inject me?"

I pulled the plaster away before she could stop me, revealing a little red mark as if someone had injected the big vein there.

"No, I did not inject you. I just extracted a small vial of your blood," she replied calmly.

"What the hell? But why?" I wasn't sure if my head was spinning because of her bleeding me for god-knows-what, the knock-out drug or from the increasingly weird situation.

"I needed a little blood."

"Needed? What for? One of your experiments?" I shouted.

She shrugged again. "Something of that type."

"So – you drugged me, kidnapped me and stole my blood? You're mad!" I yelled, righteous anger was starting to replace my fear at waking in this strange room.

She seemed to consider the possibility for a moment, then shook her head slowly.

"Not mad, I was merely very tired," she said.

I reached for my handbag on the floor and rummaged in it for my phone. It was a cheap prepay one I'd got from a bag yesterday. Tacky pink plastic, but safely anonymous. Much to my surprise it was still there. I thumbed the [ON] key.

"I'm calling the police," I said. "They'll have you for this."

"For what?" she asked, her voice icily calm.

"For, for kidnap. And drugging me... and assault. They'll throw the book at you!"

The phone lit up and played its silly switch-on tune. Belatedly, I realised I should have waited until I was out of her reach before calling for help. I didn't even know where I was, so how could I tell them?

"At me?" If her voice had been icy before, now it would freeze an Icelandic volcano.

"Of course. You can't do stuff like this!" I could hear my own voice rising but couldn't stop it. The familiar little pictures played across the phone's screen and I hurriedly punched in 999.

"Or at the one who tried to pick my pocket?" she continued.

I hesitated, my thumb hovering over the green key. "You can't prove that," I said, but wondered if she did have some sort of proof. She seemed so certain.

"No, I cannot," she said, moving away from me towards the bench in front of the window. "But what would the constables find if they searched your home?"

She had a point. There were a couple of handbags under my bed. They were decent knock-offs of designer labels and I'd been hoping to get a few quid for them at the pub later. Could the police prove they were stolen? I didn't know. Was there anything else? I racked my brain, trying to remember if I'd ditched the last wallet yesterday or taken it home.

While I was thinking, she'd walked back over, carrying a folding wooden chair, which she placed on the floor in front of me. She sat down neatly, closer than I would have liked and effectively blocking my escape route - although I wasn't sure I could stand up, let alone run away. She reached out, grabbed my wrist and calmly took my phone.

"Your telephone would not work in here, even if you tried," she said as she switched it off and laid it on the table where I snatched it up, dropping it back into my bag.

"Now," she continued. "If you are over your hysterics, may we discuss what you are doing here?"

"You brought me here!"

"Yes, I did. And if I had not, the constables may well have arrested you by now," she continued in that level tone.

"They couldn't have..." I interrupted.

"Oh, but they could have. And sooner rather than later, I believe. You are not a very good pick-pocket, you know," she said.

"Really?" I snapped. "I took a policeman's wallet last week and he didn't even notice me. Is that *good* enough for you?"

"It may be that these constables and commuting people are more careless than they should be, but there are no skilled pick-pockets today. You have been lucky so far. But your luck would have run out and unlucky thieves get caught and taken to the cells."

I felt my face going red and didn't trust my voice to answer her.

"And what would your friends think if you were charged as a common thief?" she asked.

"What? You know nothing about my friends!"

She sat back, regarding me for a moment. Then she held up her left hand and began counting off her fingers as she commented.

"Your clothes are of good quality, although they have seen better days. Your speech is too refined for one of the criminal class, even though you try to hide your upbringing. You are a rather amateur pick-pocket who does not seem to understand how lucky she has been not to be caught. In short, you are a Gentle who has fallen on hard times. And I presume you have friends whom you would prefer to not know how wretched your situation has become."

My head had been drooping as she listed my failings but snapped up at the odd way she pronounced *gentle*. As if the word meant more in her mouth than in mine.

She held up her hand and I saw what she'd been toying with. It was the pin off my hoodie. She was holding it by the fastening on the back of the top hat, turning the little brass gears with her fingernail.

"That's mine!" I reached for the trinket, but she stood up again and I subsided onto the sofa.

"This is a most unusual item," she said. "Why do you wear it?"

Once again, there was some sort of meaning behind her words that I couldn't grasp. She continued to stare at me as I wondered and I realised she wasn't going to let me off without answering.

"It's a Steampunk pin. Just a bit of jewellery," I explained.

"Steampunk? And what is its significance to you?"

I glowered up at her. "It was a present. From someone I used to know."

Her dark eyes seemed to bore into my soul and I struggle against an urge to hide from her stare.

"And you know about this 'Steampunk'?"

"A little." I didn't want to talk about Kerry. Not with this strange woman.

"So. You are in a difficult position. And I need someone to help me with an important matter." She paused, waiting for an answer I wasn't going to give so she continued, "Someone who understands this 'Steampunk', is prepared to assist me for fair payment and who will not worry about the situation's legitimacy. Someone, frankly, like you." She turned towards me, her black eyes glinting oddly as she stared with that strange intensity.

I swallowed hard, understanding her words but not quite

making sense of it all. And fascinated by her eyes - I had thought they were green when she grabbed me earlier. I snatched at the one bit of her speech that had made sense.

"You said payment. You're offering money for me to do something. When?"

She just looked at me for a moment, a slight smile playing on her lips. "So you are desperate. I suspected as much."

"No, not desperate. Not at all," I flustered. "I'd just like to know the terms you're offering, before I agree..."

I stopped in confusion because she'd started laughing at me. A rich, throaty laugh that sounded more genuine than anything she'd said so far. Eventually she stopped and took a couple of breaths before speaking again.

"My terms are that you have no choice. You will agree to help me because you do not want me to give your details to the constables. But I can give you a little money in advance, if you need it so much."

I hesitated. I didn't want to tell this strange woman how bad my situation was. But if she gave me some money, it could keep Tony quiet for a few days. While I thought, she poured another cup of tea, stirred in a ridiculous amount of sugar and put it on the table next to me. I picked it up to give myself another moment to think and took a sip automatically.

"Bleugh!" I nearly spat it out. Not only was it too sweet, but it was stone-cold and tasted horribly stewed. But under those terrible, dark eyes, I forced it down my throat. She smiled grimly and took the empty cup and saucer.

"I presume your silence indicates your agreement, however reluctant," she said over her shoulder.

"Well, I could do with some money now. Yes." I said, trying to sound nonchalant but feeling certain she wasn't fooled for a moment.

She pulled a worn leather wallet from a pocket inside her skirt where I would never have spotted it. "You are in arrears with your landlord?"

I nodded, suddenly wondering if she'd been spying on me.

"How much?" she asked.

"Um," I paused, unwilling to admit the severity of my situation, but truly frantic for the money to pay Tony.

"It is a simple enough question." she snapped. "How much rent do you owe?"

I tried to think of an answer that wouldn't make me sound too hopeless, but still persuade her to give me the cash I needed. But my brain had frozen again. Her eyes seemed to have taken hold of something deep inside my brain and stopped it working.

"Um," I started again, but couldn't go any further.

She glared at me, but pulled out a wad of notes, folded it and held it towards me. I took it without looking and pushed the bundle to the bottom of my bag.

"That will keep him at bay for now – you may tell him he will get the rest next week," she said, then handed me the little brass pin and turned her back.

"I will see you here again promptly at half after nine in the morning," she continued, speaking to the window. "And wear a hat."

I dashed out of the door without further comment, down a flight of uncarpeted stairs and out of the house. On the street, I turned left and ran for a few blocks, dodging down side streets until I was sure she wasn't following. I stopped to catch my breath and looked around for landmarks, recognised one of the street names and realised I was only about half a mile from home. When I reached the junction, I checked all the approaches but there was still no sign of my kidnapper chasing me. My knees threatened to give way again as I realised I'd got away from the strange woman without telling her my address. There was nothing in my bag to identify me, in case I'd been picked up by the police, so she wouldn't have found anything if she'd checked while I was sleeping off the effects of her *sleep-jar*. I'd got away with her money! I turned to the wall while I checked the cash she'd given me, counting the notes by thumbing through the pile in my bag. There were nineteen and the first one I looked at was a fifty. Quickly, I shoved it back into my handbag and flicked through the others, checking the corners rather than pulling them out. All the same. I'd got nearly a thousand quid and all it had cost me was an hour with the weirdest person I'd ever met.

And a little blood, of course.

Chapter 2

In which Sam realises she didn't get away with anything

I woke late, with the sun full in my face through the thin curtains. It took a moment to work out why I'd slept so long, then I remembered the weird day I'd had. After getting away from that bizarre house, I'd bought a pizza for dinner and gone to bed with a full stomach for the first time in months. Tony had been waiting for me, surprised I had money for him. I'd given him four fifties and still had enough left to last me a few weeks if I was careful. And all from a stranger who was never going to see me again. I knew how to find that strange room she'd called a workshop, but she had no idea where I lived.

I checked my watch, to see how late I'd slept, but it had stopped. Crappy Chinese tat. A new battery'd cost more than the watch was worth, but at least I could think about buying one! My now-working phone said it was 10 11, though. I ate the last slice of cold pizza, washed down by tea with no milk as I dressed in old black jeans and an almost-clean t-shirt. I might as well go shopping for proper food to stock the cupboard today, 'cos it was already too late to catch the morning commuters. Anyway, I could afford a day off from the tube station and the shopping centres. I folded one of the fifties into my purse, hid the rest in the laundry bag in my wardrobe and pulled a jumper on as I yanked the door shut behind me. It was a typical London day - grey and dreary, although for once it wasn't raining. First to the mini-mart for milk and to get smaller notes in change, then see what I could pick up at the so-called farmers' market. They'd be packing up after the morning's trading and I could usually blag some cheap pies and stuff. I might even have lunch in a pub, as a treat.

I was so busy thinking about the things I could do now I'd

got some money, I didn't pay attention to anything else and it must have been a minute or two before I realised someone was walking with me, half a step behind. I slowed down, but they didn't come past – just kept that creepy half-pace distance. So I turned to say something rude about weirdoes following ordinary people and found myself looking up at a familiar face with dark green eyes, half-covered with a black veil. I stopped, staring at the stranger who'd been so insistent about my helping her. She was dressed even more outlandishly today, in a dark red skirt that exaggerated her bottom in some odd, sexy way and swept along the ground behind her. Today's matching jacket was tight and made her waist look so tiny that I expected the wind to snap her in half. She wore a sort of top hat, like Isambard Kingdom Brunel in that famous photo with the big chains. Only it had red silk flowers stuck on it. And that veil - and black fluffy feathers! There was a dull silver chain slung between one of her jacket buttons and a pocket. I noticed she carried some sort of cloth bag, with a folded lacy umbrella through its leather handles.

"Oh!" For a second I hoped the ground would open me up and swallow me, then I thought about running for it. But I dithered, noticing that she was effectively blocking me against a garden fence.

"Good morning," she replied. "When I realised you were not going to arrive by half after nine as agreed, I decided I should come looking for you."

"But, but..." I was amazed she'd managed to find me. How on earth?

"I was wondering when you would arise, as the day is already half-gone," she continued.

"But how did you find me? You don't even know my name!"

She pulled a face. "This is true, we have not formally introduced ourselves." She held out her hand, "You may call me Chrystal."

"Crystal? Um, er – I'm Sam," I replied.

"Pleased to make your acquaintance, Sam," she said, shaking my hand in her firm grip. "But my name is Chrystal – it is a sound made in the throat, not the softer *C* in common usage."

"Krystal?" I tried, knowing I wasn't making the same harsh sound that she used.

"Near enough," she answered, nodding. "My manners teacher always insisted on the importance of pronouncing a person's name correctly."

"M-manners teacher?" Every time this weird woman said anything, she seemed to twist normal words so they made no sense anymore.

"Yes, Miss Featherstonehaugh. A frightful dragon, but she certainly knew how to train young ladies in the proper decorum."

"Oookay," I said slowly, no less confused than before.

"And your own name, is Samuel not a name for a boy? Surely a strange manner by which a girl should be named."

"N-no. It's short for Samantha. I don't use my full name."

"Really?" she looked surprised. "So be it. Sam you are!"

As we'd been talking she'd taken my elbow and started walking us in the opposite direction from the mini-mart. I tried to free my arm, but her grip was far too strong for me to break free and I didn't think I could have got away however hard I'd struggled. We passed the chippy, looking sad with its shutters down even though I could smell them heating the oil inside. My mouth watered but I didn't think this was a good time to suggest stopping for an early lunch.

"Where are we going?" I asked, hoping to steer the conversation onto a subject I could understand properly.

"The British Museum," she said, as if that were obvious.

"The Museum? But why?"

"Because they have something of mine which I need to have restored to my possession."

"What? But can't you just ask them to give it back? I mean, how did they get something of yours, anyway? They're only interested in antiques and really old stuff," I said.

She laughed, a short sound without humour. "It is somewhat old, most likely an antique by their standards. And they obtained it when I moved away from London for a while. I did not foresee a need to secure my house properly. Someone must have presumed it had been abandoned and they cleared everything out before finding that no-one else can live there. I expect they sold the valuable items where they could – and the Museum bought at least one of them."

"So why not just tell them it's your stuff? Surely they'd give it back if they knew you owned it."

"Ah, that is the difficult part. I cannot prove that this item was mine, so they will retain it unless I, er, remove it in an unorthodox manner."

I stopped walking, catching her unawares and she lost her hold on my arm.

"You mean steal, don't you? You're going to rob the museum!"

She actually looked shamefaced. "I hardly think it reasonable to call it theft when it is my own property in truth."

"But if it's yours, why not just ask for it back?" I asked, then realised how guilty she had to be. "You never owned it honestly, did you? No wonder you can't ask for it back – it was stolen property in the first place. And you're going to steal it all over again!"

"No, not at all," she replied, although her expression was too complicated for her to be telling the simple truth, even if she wasn't actually lying.

"So what, then?" I asked. I guessed that I had her on the back foot, so I pushed for an answer. Maybe this was the moment when I'd learn something that made sense of this whole ridiculous situation.

"It is something that was made for, er, a relative of mine. A family heirloom, but I cannot prove ownership, if you understand my situation," she answered.

"And what do you need it for?"

"That is also difficult to explain. Suffice it to say that the consequences of my not obtaining this device and adapting it for a different use would be too terrible to contemplate," she said.

"For who?" She didn't answer and I pressed the point. "For you?"

"I do not rightly know, perhaps for the whole world," she whispered.

"What? How?"

"Because there is a slow clock that turns and there are forces in this world that would prefer chaos to such steady turning," she said.

"I don't understand!" I said, wishing she'd give me a straight answer instead of this mystical mumbo-jumbo.

"Nor do I, fully," she said with a sad smile. "But I have become aware that this clock is winding down and may need help to start again. Or chaos may reign over the order we humans have come to prefer."

I could tell there was more to this than she was admitting, something fishy was definitely going on, but I couldn't see how to get any more out of her. I decided to try another subject that had been bugging me since I'd realised she was following me down the street.

"So how did you manage to track me down, anyway?"

"Ah, now. That is another difficult subject. Suffice it to say that I will have no trouble finding you over the next few days. I have this, well, locating mechanism that will know where you are at any given moment. I consulted that to determine the direction in which you lay and waited outside the building until you emerged."

"Sort of like a GPS? For people?" I asked.

She didn't answer and I bit my lip in frustration. Her explanation left me no clearer about how she had found me, but it didn't seem likely that I would be getting a better answer anytime soon.

"Did you bring a hat?" she asked, confusing me again with another sudden change of subject.

"Erm, no," I admitted. I hadn't even given it a thought, as I'd never meant to meet her today.

"So you didn't arrive on time and you didn't bring a hat, either," she said, looking at me with a hard expression. "You had no intention of assisting me at all, did you?"

"Well, I didn't really understand what you wanted. And I thought you didn't know where..." I trailed off, realising I'd said too much.

"Did not know where you lived?" I nodded, reluctantly. There wasn't any way I could deny it, after all.

"So you were not about to help as promised, even after taking my money?" she asked, although it wasn't really a question.

"Um," there wasn't any way I could defend my actions. Once again, I wondered how she'd managed to track me down. Then I realised she was still looking sideways at me with those strange eyes of hers.

"So. You try to pick my pocket, you accuse me of stealing something that already belongs to me and you take payment from me with no intention of earning it. And they speak of honour amongst thieves," she said, her voice curiously flat as she stopped walking and turned to face me.

"Well, you didn't tell me what you wanted. And after seeing your workshop, I thought you were just..." I'd done it again. There was something about this strange woman that seemed to loosen my tongue. Or was I so desperate for company that I'd blab anything, just for the sake of talking to someone?

"A lunatic? A madwoman?" she offered, helpfully. "And if I were insane, would that justify you stealing from me?"

"Well, er, no."

"So are you hoping to steal from me again today?"

I didn't have any way to answer that. Truth be told, I *would* steal from her in an instant, if I had the chance. And I wouldn't lose any sleep over it, either. As I thought that, I realised how low I'd fallen – the old me would never have stolen anything. I even used to go back if I hadn't been charged for something in a shop! Had I really become so hard?

"Are you proud of yourself, Sam-of-the-boy's-name?" she asked and I had the strangest feeling that she'd followed my entire train of thought.

"I suggest that we come to an accommodation," she continued. "You help me as we have discussed and I will see you well-paid for your time and trouble. Once I have recovered my property from the Museum, then we shall go our separate ways and neither will have taken anything from the other except that which is due from our agreed transaction. Does that sound reasonable to you?"

"Um, yeah. I guess that's fair," I answered. But I was so confused by her odd way of speaking I wasn't quite sure what I'd agreed to.

"Good. Then we are in business," she said.

We rounded a corner and hurried across the main road, narrowly missed by a taxi that hadn't stopped with the rest of the traffic. I stepped off the pavement to avoid a couple of large, black birds that were eating something splattered on the ground. But they took off as we approached, cawing loudly and flew straight towards Chrystal. She didn't flinch, just raised her right arm to fend them off and they landed in a tree behind us.

In the shadow of a building, she stopped and opened the large bag she'd been carrying. She pulled out an old-fashioned hat with goggles fastened Steampunk-style around the brim and a dark net fixed to the front. She passed it to me, together with the umbrella.

"Put the hat on," she said. "And keep it on whilst we are in the Museum."

I did as she instructed and then watched her shake out a waist-length black cape that had been folded in the bag. She reached out, unfastened Kerry's pin from my jumper, drew the cape around my shoulders and fastened its brass buttons. I shivered inside at the touch of her hand on my breast and bit my lip to stop any sound escaping that she might notice. She folded her bag and turned it inside-out, making it look more like a leather handbag. Finally she fixed the pin in place on the front of the cape and stepped back a pace to inspect her handiwork.

"No, no, not like that." She turned the hat, glancing between the shiny goggles on its brim and my face, apparently lining them up correctly. Then she tugged the net forwards and down. "You need to cover your face more – we would not want the closed-circuit television cameras to get a good look at us!"

"But why?" I asked. "Are we going to steal it today?"

She made a noise that was almost a snort. "Not during daylight. We will return after dark – but I wish to get a good look at the layout and security measures beforehand. And we would not like anyone to realise what we were doing and identify our faces afterwards."

I nodded, hoping I'd understood her properly. She wanted to recce the Museum while it was open and come back later to steal whatever it was she was after. But she didn't want our faces to appear on the CCTV tapes in case they realised what we'd done when they spotted the theft.

And I'd thought yesterday was confusing!

Chapter 3

In which a threat is acknowledged

The massive Hall was dim, with metal braziers of glowing coals spaced along ragged stone walls, spilling their light grudgingly into the vast space. The walls themselves seemed to hang unsupported, their upper reaches lost in shadows, the floor below the coals equally vague in the dim light.

But from that floor came a rustling, a hint of movements more heard than seen. Something was moving in the darkness - many somethings that hissed and shuffled, as if the floor itself were alive, crawling but trying not to be noticed.

A yellow-green flame leapt up at one end, killing the noise and freezing the scene in a single flash. Behind the light was another roughly-hewn wall, in front an intricately carved stone chair sat on a dais. Odd machinery covered one side of the platform, as if the insides of a giant clock had been exposed by the dancing light of the flames and frozen mid-motion, one huge gear cutting into the dais like a circular saw-blade. The room held its breath - silent, expectant. For a long moment, the very Earth seemed to stop turning. The wait stretched painfully, heart-stoppingly, interminably; Father Time himself dragged his feet. Suddenly another flame leapt for the unseen ceiling to one side of the dais, then another, opposite. The frozen clock-gears were thrown into stark relief as they began to turn slowly, passing through slots in the dais, clanking and glistening darkly. More fires sprang into life along the length of the Hall, illuminating loose rows of figures flinching away from the smoky, oil-fuelled blazes. Heads turned to follow as the lights flared up along the hall, the firelight reflecting reluctantly off occasional pieces of unpolished metallic armour and helmets worn over dark clothing.

Quickly, the flames shrank back, less threatening but still glaring harshly into hundreds of upturned eyes. The ceiling retreated into shadows and the crowd swung round to see a figure seated on the throne.

His hooded robes glistened purple and green, made from the skin of the last known dragon; his long hands hung over the ends of the seat's arms. Strange, unearthly figures with animal heads writhed beneath his fingers, their fire-lit stone bodies intertwining suggestively. His cowled head swayed oddly, turning to observe the crowd.

A slight figure in a black robe that hid its face came round the side of the dais. She seemed to glide, her head dipping in an odd rhythm that didn't match any human pace. Her sleeves hung empty, but around her neck hung a short, heavy staff on a chain. She twisted oddly and her staff swung to strike the floor in front of the raised platform.

"Silence for His Eminence Geb, the Great Ruler whose name is First." She lisped a little, but still her voice boomed larger than her small frame should be able to produce and seemed to come from somewhere lower than the hood of her robe. She struck the floor again and the whole room fell silent. She swung the staff a third time and then the black robe collapsed, pooling onto the floor and sliding towards the front of the dais.

The enthroned man raised his head, his hood turning to look across the assembled crowd.

"The world winds down once more," he said. His voice was deep, melodious but oddly sibilant. As if a great snake had learned the art of human speech. He repeated himself,

"The turning of the world slows as the old Calendar draws to its close again."

The assembled ranks stood, transfixed and silent. None moved, they barely breathed as they listened to the hypnotic tones.

"And this time, there are no humans to shed the hearts,

none who understand the power of the One with no heart," he went on. "They no longer make the Final Sacrifice. There are no priests to wash their altars with blood."

A moan, sounding like anticipation, escaped from a few throats below the dais.

"This is the year of the Calendar's end," the moan was louder now, flowing across the room and back.

"The Calendar will end and chaos will reclaim its place!" This time, the moan was almost sexual in its intensity.

"The very Earth will switch his poles." Moan.

"Mountains will burn and planes will fall from Mother Sky." Moan.

"The ice will melt and the oceans rise up to swallow the land." Mo-annn.

"Plagues will afflict both human and beast." The moan was louder than ever, and a dull, drumming thud came from a far corner of the Hall. It built slowly, spreading through the crowd and becoming a steady beat. The beat of booted feet on stone. A rhythm echoed in the moving of heads as each stomp sounded.

"The Great Mother's bees will die and crops will fail." Stomp, moan, stomp.

"The shell of Earth himself will shake and devour the cities of men." The stomping grew faster, less controlled, wrapped around by the rising moan.

"The balance between Isfet and Maat shall be restored!" He shouted triumphantly as the noise crescendoed.

The hooded figure gripped the arms of the throne and pulled himself to his feet. Even without the stage he would have towered over his armies. He slowly raised his hands, sleeves falling from stick-thin, leathery arms. Stomps and moans came faster, louder until they hurt the ears, shook the rock walls. At his gesture, the smoky oil-flames leaped upwards, a flash of light that once again swallowed the sound. When the light dropped down again, the stage was empty. Soldiers shook their heads, awakening from a shared dream. Or a nightmare. They turned and began to file out through doors set in alcoves along the long walls where men in red clothes handed a small, mottled pink biscuit to each soldier. Every man clutched it closely as he hurried away from the hall.

A dark shape appeared from under the platform, flowing back into its cloak. She hissed once after the departing men, turned and glide-walked to the door behind the throne.

"The Roman Emperors had it right, Renenutet," the tall figure greeted her as she passed the doorway. "Bread and circuses, bread and circuses."

"And yet Rome fell," she hissed in reply.

"Because their Emperors did not have true control over their armies. A human Empire can always fall to the might of its own force."

"But the army of the eternal Geb will never rebel," said the smaller figure. Her robe dropped to the ground and she lifted herself to her full height. She had a snake's body with human legs and small hands on thin arms. Her sinuous body curved as if to hint at human-like breasts beneath the scales.

Geb threw back the hood of his dragon robe, revealing a head that would never be mistaken for human. From sinewy brown shoulders grew a thick, supple neck topped with the head of a snake. He stepped out of the cloak to embrace his mate passionately. In the centre of his chest, a brass framework surrounded something which glowed sullenly and brightened before being smothered by their embrace.

Chapter 4

In which the British Museum is visited

Once again, I found myself half-running to keep up with her long strides, but this time I also had to keep the stupid hat on! Not to mention thinking about what she'd said, wanting to be sure I'd understood her properly. I guess she talks that way to go with those strange clothes - kind of Steampunk like Kerry, but somehow she was different. She must be one of those historical types who like to dress old-fashioned and shoot each other in mock battles on Bank Holidays. Still, she was paying, so who was I to complain? I'd seen people wearing much odder clothes at the Steampunk fair I'd been to when I was going out with Kerry, although they'd all seemed positively normal compared to Chrystal. I couldn't put my finger on it, but there was something about her that just didn't feel *right*.

Lost in my thoughts, I nearly ran into her back as she stopped suddenly. I'd been walking on autopilot and hadn't even noticed how close we were to the Museum. She checked my hat one last time and swept up the steps, lifting her long skirt out to one side. I got surrounded by a bunch of schoolkids and only caught up with Chrystal as she arrived at the information desk.

"One of your guide books, if you please, Sir," she said to the startled young man behind the counter. "And could you spare a list of your current exhibitions?"

He handed her the booklet and a photocopied list of galleries.

"Six pounds, please. Will there be anything else, um, Madam?" he asked.

She handed him a twenty-pound note. "No, that is all. I wish to conduct my niece around some of your fascinating exhibits," she answered. When he handed her the change, she simply tipped it into the "Friends of the Museum" donation box beside the counter and slipped an arm around my shoulders to lead me away. I swallowed hard. I could eat for days on the money she'd just given away!

"Niece!?!" I hissed, once we were out of earshot of the desk. "What made you say that?"

She shrugged. "It seemed appropriate. I could scarcely tell him you were a failed pick-pocket I had enlisted to assist me in robbing this veritable establishment."

"But – why did you have to explain me to him at all? It's as if you wanted him to remember us!"

"Which I do. I would like him to remember two harmless ladies who were dressed in the style of Steampunks, behaved a little oddly and even courted his attention. That way, he will insist that we were not suspicious characters, should anyone ask at a later date."

"Wouldn't it be simpler just to behave like everyone else? Or maybe just dress less conspicuously?"

"Ah, but you have already demonstrated that you do not blend into a crowd well – I could tell you were planning to pick pockets from the way you watched the daily travellers. I doubted that you could pass muster as an innocent tourist at the Museum, so I decided a more visible form of subterfuge would be a better disguise for us today," she replied. "And besides, there are often Steampunks in the Museum - they appear to gravitate to such environs. Surely you must be aware of that?"

She was looking at me, expecting an answer. So I nodded and that seemed to satisfy her. I caught a glimpse of our reflections in a window as we passed and I was struck again by her startling figure, so I stared straight ahead, trying to ignore the warm feeling growing in the pit of my stomach.

Groups of people wandered around the huge indoor courtyard, crossing from one door to another and I would have stopped to stare around the massive space if she hadn't been steering me towards the far corner. A crowd of camera-wearing American tourists enveloped us and we were swept along in their jostling, noisy midst until their guide waved her umbrella to gather them together outside the curved wall in the centre of the great hall and we slipped away. Chrystal pushed at my arm, steering me towards an open doorway and the stairs beyond.

She took my arm and held her skirt out to the other side again as we climbed the stairs, effectively blocking the stairwell to anyone else. No-one tried to come past and I saw people stop in their tracks and turn to go back up, rather than squeeze past us parading up the steps.

On the first floor, Chrystal led me through a display of Middle Eastern stuff into a room full of prehistoric pottery and pictures of cave paintings. Then through several galleries of Roman artefacts. She stopped occasionally to look at a display cabinet, check something in the guide book or point out some remarkable detail of a particular exhibit. She talked on through the display of mediæval tapestries and into a room of strange old clocks and watches. I'd stopped listening when I realised that all this was just for the benefit of the cameras and uniformed security staff scattered about the museum – part of our disguise as a couple of normal visitors. So I wasn't paying attention when she turned to face me and said,

"Over my right shoulder."

"Sorry?" I asked.

"That is the ætheric resonator. In the display behind me – look over my right shoulder."

I found myself staring at some copper-coloured pipes, tangled around one side of a wooden box with a glass-covered dial on the front and several short glass tubes fixed to its edges. It stood on a pedestal inside a glass case surrounded by smaller, similarly-obscure objects.

"Don't stare," she hissed. "We must not be seen to pay any

more attention to this exhibit than any other!"

An idea sprang into my brain, seemingly out of nowhere.

"I'll tell you what, Auntie," I said in a loud voice. "Why don't you sit here for a few minutes and rest your legs. I'll go and find us a nice cup of tea."

She looked at me, confused, then I saw her eyes widen slightly.

"Oh, thank you, dear. I would benefit from a brief respite," and she smiled at me. "But I feel a coffee would be more restorative, if you please."

As we talked, she made her way to a nearby bench, seating herself between a moustached older man wearing a bowler hat and a young couple more interested in each other than any of the exhibits. She positioned herself carefully to look away from the strange item she'd pointed out. I left her there and went in search of a café, glancing back from the doorway to see her staring around the room, apparently aimlessly, but undoubtedly clocking the many security cameras.`

It took a while to find my way to the café on the ground floor, but at least there wasn't much of a queue. One of the ladies behind the counter looked up after serving a gaggle of pensioners.

"Can I help you dear?" she asked.

"Erm, yes please. Two coffees to go, please," I replied.

"Oh, I'm sorry, love. We don't do take-out. There's a café just down the road that could help you – one of those big American ones," she said.

"Ah. I wanted to take it for my Aunt – she's having a sit-down in one of the galleries."

She shook her head. "You can't take refreshments into the Museum, dear. You'll have to bring your Auntie here, I'm afraid. There's plenty of room," she gestured at the almost-empty room with its jars of rough sugar lumps on the tables.

"Right! Sorry - should have guessed," I replied, turning back into the Museum proper.

I found Chrystal in the gallery where I'd left her, although she was now chatting to the grey-whiskered man next to her. I overheard part of their conversation as I approached.

"... than we realise," he was saying.

"Absolutely," replied Chrystal. "It is simply ridiculous for one to assume that the predecessors of modern scientists were naive and ignorant simply because they did not have silicon chips or internal combustion engines."

"I'm sure we could learn a lot from proper examination of these old contraptions, instead of locking them away in museums as curios," he said.

At that moment, Chrystal looked up, met my eyes and said to the man, "And here is my niece. I presume you have been informed that you cannot bring refreshments into the galleries?"

"You knew?" I asked. "You sent me off to fetch drinks I'm not allowed to bring in?"

She stood up and glared down at me, offended. "Of course not. Mr Peterson here was kind enough to inform me of that fact. But you were already gone by the time we started talking."

While Chrystal was speaking, he had taken a watch out of his coat pocket to check the time, draping its chain carefully as he replaced it. "It's Major Peterson, actually," he said, smiling at me. "Retired, of course – not seen active duty for years, now."

He stood up as he spoke, gestured towards the display of curios and went on, "I was just telling your Aunt that I'm certain many of these exhibits were working machines of some kind. I feel we are doing our ancestors a disservice by assuming that such things are merely follies to ornament drawing rooms or whimsical attempts at failed sciences."

"And you did not mention your rank to me, Major. Although I should have deduced a military career from your bearing," Chrystal tutted at him.

"You are too kind, my dear," he answered before turning back to me.

"And your Aunt is a remarkable woman. Such a delight to find a young person actually interested in history – even dressing in the Victorian style to visit the Museum."

"Now it is you being too kind, Major," responded my so-called Aunt. "It has been many a year since I could rightly be called 'young', I'm afraid."

He shook his head, "Nonsense! You're in the very prime of your life! If only I was twenty years younger, m'dear."

I wouldn't have believed she could actually blush, but something that looked suspiciously like it crept up her face towards her hat. "Oh, Major Peterson – you flatter me."

I really couldn't understand this mutual appreciation society that had sprung to life in the ten minutes I'd been away. *Why was she flirting with this old bloke, anyway?* I breathed a sigh of relief when Chrystal wrapped up their conversation.

"Well, It was a true pleasure to meet you, Major. I hope our paths may cross again some happy day. But for now, I need some honest refreshment. And if the mountain will not come to Mohammet..."

"Of course, of course," he replied. "You must go to the mountain. I recommend the ginger cake, by the way," and he bowed before turning away and walking towards the next gallery.

"What a charming, Gentle man," said Chrystal. "One of the greatest delights in visiting museums is to meet characters such as he."

"Um, quite," I answered. "Even if he was talking complete bollocks!"

She gave me one of her stern looks. "On the contrary. He

may have been closer to the truth than he will ever realise. Undoubtedly much closer than the person who labelled my resonator as an *idiosyncratic but flawed attempt at innovative clockmaking!*" She turned on her heel and led the way back towards the stairs leading back up to our overdue cups of coffee.

I noticed she had a slice of the ginger cake, as the Major had recommended.

Chrystal made sure more of the Museum staff would remember her as a slightly batty woman, who dressed in old-fashioned clothes and liked to be the centre of attention. I gave up trying to fade into her shadow, but kept my face turned down as she did and spoke as little as possible. I just couldn't square her behaviour with the idea of checking the Museum out before burglarising it. And the way she'd insisted on me wearing that cape and hat - not to mention the stupid lacy umbrella I was carrying! At last she'd had enough of flouncing around the café and Museum shop and announced in a loud voice that it was time to leave, as she was feeling a little tired. She turned towards the main entrance and I followed along in her wake, carrying both bags of her purchases.

"I thought you were in a hurry," I accused, once we were outside.

"As true as that is," she replied, turning to face me. "We cannot do more until the dark of the moon in three days' time. So we may spend our time browsing their excellent store or conversing with a good man like the Major without any detriment to our main purpose."

"And you don't look very tired," I retorted.

"I do not feel it, either," she answered without slowing down. "But we had achieved all of our objectives and it was a suitable excuse to leave. No-one questions a lady when she says she is weary."

"Really? You should have been in the office I worked at. My boss seemed to think we should all take CVs home to read after our twelve-hour days. I don't think it would have cut any ice if I'd told her I was too tired to do it."

"And so it is in this world we have built," she commented. "Folk are not Gentle any more."

She also went quiet for a while and I found myself wondering again about her bizarre way of saying 'gentle'. Just as I thought I was getting the hang of her odd way of speaking, she'd say something really weird that I couldn't get my head around. But – she'd promised to pay for my time and that was a good enough reason to put up with a few odd habits.

"It is strange, isn't it?" She interrupted and for a moment I wondered again if she'd been following my actual train of thought.

"Um, what is?"

"The Museum's preconceptions about what is a curio from a failed attempt to keep time and what might be an actual, working machine. One wonders who makes these decisions and on what grounds."

I breathed a sigh of relief that she hadn't been reading my mind.

"Well, I assume they have experts in all sorts of..." I began.

"Experts!" She spat the word out as if it offended her. "Narrow-minded fools who cannot look beyond their own petrol culture and see a more elegant world, with a different approach and achievements that are beyond their blinkered dreams."

She walked even faster as she went on.

"They are so arrogant, so certain that their machines not only work in the best way, but in the single way that *can* work. And anything else a mere frippery, an idle dalliance or a failed experiment. But they secure the evidence under lock and key as if it may suddenly rise on its *ornamental* legs and pursue them out of their *soi-disant* Museum!"

"Are you saying that thing can walk?" I asked, struggling to make sense of her rantings.

"What? No, of course not," she answered and I was pleased to notice her slowing her steps to a pace I could manage once again.

"No, the resonator does not walk, although it might for all their *experts* know about it. It is merely a device for detecting fluctuations in the æther – it does not do anything more than that."

"And why do you want it back?"

"I, um, wish to harness its ætheric detecting properties and tailor its use to permit the sending of a message over the æther. I have been unable to produce the effect that I require and I decided to recover this machine to resolve the issue, rather than working it all out from base principles."

"You mean you want to see how something's already been done, rather than re-inventing the wheel for yourself?" I asked.

"Precisely," she said, smiling grimly.

I decided to take advantage of her unusually chatty mood to get answers to some of the questions that had been driving me out of my head.

"And what exactly does this, er, ætheric resonator thingy do? If it doesn't walk?"

She thought for so long that I decided she was not going to answer, so I was surprised when she started talking again.

"It detects changes in the æther, both natural ones and those resulting from human activities. It can be tuned to a particular disturbance and then display several properties of it, such as its magnitude and pitch. From taking such measurements in different orientations, the user may deduce the direction of the perturbation and even an approximation of its range." She watched my bewildered expression. "Is that explanation clear to you?"

"Erm, not really," I answered, wondering if she was making up half the words as she went along.

"If you would explain to me which parts are unclear, then I will attempt clarification. But you must understand, I am no expert in ætheric principles. If I were, I could build my apparatus without recourse to a previously-manufactured model."

"Well," I hesitated. "Pretty much all of it, I'm afraid. I've always thought ether was a gas dentists used to use and I've never heard of it fluctuating, so the rest of your explanation was kinda lost on me."

She snorted. "What do they teach in these schools today? Is your science so blinded that it cannot determine the fundamental nature of the world unless it makes use of something powered by aeons-dead flora and fauna?"

"Um, you mean petrol?" I asked.

"I mean petrol and oil and gas and coal and everything else that manufactures more damaging smog and disturbance than it does power for those thrice-damned machines," she answered.

Stunned by her vehemence, I couldn't think of a reply. Fortunately, she didn't seem to need one.

"I apologise. I have not spoken so openly for a long time and have forgotten how to restrict my frustrations to the inside of my own head," she said, humbly. "Such an outburst is inexcusable in Gentle company and I beg your forgiveness for my outspokenness."

That word again. I mumbled, "Don't worry about it," and that seemed to satisfy her. I hunted for a safer topic of conversation. Chrystal seemed quite happy to let these uncomfortable silences drag on, but I felt awkward spending time in someone's company without talking.

"Um, do you always walk around town?" I began. "Why not catch a..."

I was cut short by another bird. It launched itself from the wall beside the path and flew straight at Chrystal. Once again, she reached up as if to bat it away and, once again, it veered off at the last moment. It landed back on the wall it'd come from and kept cawing as we walked away.

"That's weird," I said. "D'you think it's the same bird?"

"I doubt it, crows are territorial. And the two we saw this morning were half a mile from here," she answered.

"But I've never seen them attack anyone before. And that's twice in one day," I said.

"They will defend their territory as they think best," said Chrystal. "Even solitary members of the corvidae will gather together to deter what they perceive to be a predator."

"Members of the what?" I asked.

"Corvidae - the family of birds known as crows. Also rooks, jays, ravens and others. They are highly intelligent. For birds."

"But why...?" I stopped when I saw her expression – something between impatience and anger. I couldn't decide if it was the birds she was annoyed at or me for asking questions.

We walked in silence the rest of the way to her workshop and Chrystal led me upstairs. She held the door open for me to enter first and took her shopping bags, placing them on the little table. Walking over to a rack of metal shelves, she picked up an old-fashioned stove-top espresso maker and brought it to sit on top of a flat-topped tripod thing. She spooned-in ground coffee from a little wooden box and filled the bottom part with water from a jug. I saw her fiddle with something under the tripod before she walked over to the coffee table where she began to unpack her purchases.

"It takes a moment to boil, I fear. But it makes excellent coffee."

"No kettle?" I asked.

"I have never seen the point in buying something which performs only one minor function," she shrugged. "I have all this apparatus which boils liquids perfectly well. I may as well use it to make the coffee."

"Makes sense, I guess." I commented.

"I ensure I always have a way to boil water. Whatever I'm working on," she said, laying out two tiny cups and their saucers, an unmatched sugar bowl and a glass rod stained brown at one end. "And there is no electricity in the building."

"What? You've been cut off?"

She smiled sadly. "No, it has never been connected here. I told you, I am no believer in burning fuels for power. Not if there is a better way."

"But electricity doesn't burn – it's not like gas!"

She turned to stare at me.

"You actually believe that? You think electricity just appears out of nowhere?"

"Well, no," I said, realising I didn't actually understand the details of where it did come from. "But they're not burning anything, are they?"

"Of course they are," she answered, sounding like a primary school teacher I didn't much care for. "But at one remove. The power stations burn the fuel to generate the power they send down the wires to your home. It is exactly the same, really."

"I didn't know..." I petered out. I didn't know, so I couldn't argue with her.

"Coal-fired power station, gas-fired power station, why else do you think they are called that?"

"But what about nuclear? And there's all those windmills!" I countered.

"Atomic power is simply a different form of burning. You still consume fuel – and the ashes are even worse than city smogs. And how many of those windmills do you think there are? Just a handful compared to the number you would actually need to run this over-lit nation." She shrugged. "As I alluded before –

this is a world burning itself to keep going nowhere. And anyone who says differently is considered a crank."

"You're one of those eco-greenies, then?" Every time I thought I was getting a hold on how this woman worked, she threw me sideways. Every time!

"Maybe. Although I do not know what they propose as an alternative. I cannot say I have ever inclined myself to ask them," she said.

"So how do you light your workshop? And doesn't that coffee maker need power?" I asked.

"The light comes from a voltaic pile – it is in that cabinet in the corner. Both that and the foil that heats my coffee are charged by simple ætherics. It is power for free – if you know how to harness it."

"What? That's not possible – you can't get something for nothing. Can you?" I replied.

"One may, if one knows how. I am no expert, but even the basics are sufficient to harvest enough power to boil water and light my rooms. Strictly speaking, it is not truly free – I merely make use of the disturbances in the æther caused by more wasteful processes."

"But what is this æther?" I almost shouted, frustrated at her for not explaining properly.

"It is the matter which forms the basis of the universe, through which everything else moves. The Eastern philosophers call it the *Akasha.*"

"But that's nonsense," I said. "Everything is made of atoms – and those are mostly empty space. Even I know that!"

"No," she said, talking slowly as if to a stupid child. "Atoms are made of smaller particles and those are separated by the æther."

"So why haven't scientists found this – æther?"

"But they are trying to. Have you not heard of the research

in Switzerland? They have built a titanic racing track underground to capture æther. A ridiculous waste of time and energy, of course. All they need is -" and she gestured at the pot on its stand. I realised that what I'd thought was some scrunched-up foil under the stand had unfolded itself and was turning about a mast in the centre, as if blown by a breeze.

And I could hear the water starting to bubble.

Stunned, I listened to hot coffee spluttering up inside the percolator and out of the spout. By the time she'd offered me one of the little cups with a neat shortbread biscuit on the side, the moment had gone. I couldn't see a way to reintroduce the subject, so I just kept quiet. Whoever she was, Chrystal made a great cup of coffee.

Chapter 5

In which a pirate is despatched

The dim light served merely to darken the shadows in the extremes of the long Hall. Stone columns, carved with age-worn human and animal figures climbed upwards from the gloom into full dark before reaching whatever ceiling lay out of sight far above. The massive stone chair loomed over one end of the expanse, lit by muted lights set in the dais on which it crouched. The front legs of the throne were carved into naked figures with evident traits of both men and women but the heads of lions. Smaller, human forms bowed beneath their feet, offering up ornate bowls and caskets. Muffled clanks and rattles of distant machinery underlay the whispering of corridors and galleries that led to unspeakable secrets.

At the foot of the steps that led up to the seat, a long, brown finger traced a circle around a spark shining green against a grey screen set into an old, wooden human-style bureau. Other lights twinkled intermittently and once a flare trailed from one side to the other. But only that single point glowed constantly. Suddenly it flickered and was gone. The finger withdrew, its broken nail scratching the screen as it reached to press a brass button and then closed into a fist. After a moment, the hand unfurled, flicked a few switches, scribbled numbers on a scaly-looking piece of paper and the tall operator stood away from the wooden bureau. His black tongue flickered in the air and a hiss escaped the open mouth. Leathery hands lifted the cowl over his head, then closed the bureau's doors, allowing the shadows to creep even closer as the wooden panels covered the glowing screen, leaving only the few lights before the throne to light the room. Hooded once more, the snake-headed figure straightened in the gloom as a door opened in a shadowed alcove.

The man that entered would have passed unremarked in any modern city, except for his clothes. He looked about thirty, average build and height, with shaggy dark hair and a scar on one cheek. He wore a heavy white shirt and patterned waistcoat over baggy black trousers tucked into knee-high leather boots. A red bandanna was tied around his head, gold hoops hung from his ears and a heavy gold cross with a loop hung on a chain around his neck. His unshaven face wore a surly expression.

"You summoned me, Your Eminence?" he asked.

"We have a location for the disturbances. You will be going to London, Farran." The sibilance in his voice was more pronounced that it had been during his announcements that morning.

"London?"

"Alert the spies - we need a more precise fix on their location."

Farran bowed slightly. The emaciated figure half-nodded and turned away, his dragon cloak swirling as he left through the door behind his throne. The pirate shrugged and seated himself at the wooden bureau. He opened the front and keyed the switch below the microphone.

"Get me ætheric surveillance," he said.

Chapter 6

In which the Museum suffers a break-in

I spent the next three days moping round my bedsit, thinking about the whole, incredible situation. I seesawed between trying to forget the whole thing and daydreaming about that strange, fascinating woman.

It was obvious I couldn't get away from her and I really needed the money she'd promised, so I'd agreed to help her break into the Museum tonight when she said there'd be no moon. I was meant to be at her place for midnight, wearing warm, dark clothes. I didn't often arrive anywhere early, but I'd been so keyed up I couldn't wait any longer. I grabbed my little rucksack with a change of clothes and walked to her place.

I stopped across the road to look at the building. It was old – I don't know much about architecture, but I know this type of three-storey redbrick terraced house hasn't been built since before the war. I was surprised to realise that the only light on the whole row came from Chrystal's window. Londoners are notorious night-owls and I would have expected a few neighbours to be awake even at this late hour. Come to think of it, I couldn't see the tell-tale blue flicker of a TV screen anywhere, either. As I looked around, I recognised Chrystal making her way back towards the house. She wore a surprisingly ordinary coat over dark trousers and I wasn't sure it was her at first. She had on a soft hat and looked as if she was coming back from somewhere in a hurry. I crossed the road and fell into step with her just as she arrived at her front door.

"Hi," I said.

She jumped and turned to face me.

"Is everything alright? I thought I was early," I continued.

"Ah, you are. I merely slipped out for a brief errand before you arrived," she said, sounding a little awkward.

She opened the front door and led the way up to her workshop.

"Now, since we're assembled nice and early – would you like a coffee to waken you before our exertions?" she asked.

"Well, yes. But can you explain to me how that water boiling thing works? It looks like magic," I said.

She filled the coffee pot with cold water and coffee grounds, and placed it on its little stand, beckoning me closer.

"It is really quite simple. The foil is made of layers of rare earth elements, which respond to the ætheric fluctuations I mentioned before. To waken its latent sensitivity, you stimulate the foil so," she flicked at the base of the scrunched-up foil, sending a tremor along it. "Then it begins to pick up wasted energy from disturbances in the local area."

Sure enough, the foil was straightening out, like sails lifting in the wind.

"And once the foil has extended to its full expanse, it begins to turn." The metal sails were as smooth as if they'd been ironed into curves and the little windmill did just as she described.

"It is shaped to target the energy it collects towards the stand above it, which heats up as it cannot dissipate in any other way – and you soon have fresh coffee."

I watched, fascinated, hearing the water begin to bubble and steam its way through the grounds. The smell of fresh coffee spilled out, making my stomach rumble.

"Oh, excuse me," I said. "Anybody would think I hadn't had a huge dinner this evening!"

"Your belly is confused," she said. "It is not accustomed to being awake at this time of night." She pulled a packet of cakes out of a little cupboard with a wire mesh front.

"I'm sorry if I'm being dense," I said. "But where does the energy come from? What is this æther you keep talking about?"

She paused and looked down at me.

"Did I not explain previously? The æther is that which fills a vacuum and the so-called empty space in your science's atoms."

"That's just gobbledegook!" I sounded frustrated, even to myself.

"No, it is not," she smiled oddly. "Although your scientists teach that it is so. Even they will admit that sound cannot travel through a vacuum as it needs matter to carry it. In the same way, light needs æther to travel through. A vacuum may be a space devoid of matter made of the elements, but it still holds the æther, as this cannot be removed by any human means."

"But I Googled it at the library – and they've proved that æther doesn't exist. It was just a silly idea Victorian people believed in. Einstein said it was nonsense."

I was afraid she'd be annoyed at my comments, but she just looked at me condescendingly.

"Not all Victorian ideas were as silly as your scientists claim and it is far harder to prove something untrue than you may believe."

"But..." I started.

"Coffee?" she interrupted, setting out the cups.

I certainly couldn't argue that she'd boiled the water somehow, so I decided to give up. At least for now.

The Museum looked very different with its big wooden doors locked and no people on the stairs. I turned to cross the paved square towards the doors, but Chrystal took my elbow and kept us moving along the pavement. I realised it had been a stupid thing to do – we were hardly going to break in through the front door. But she hadn't shared the details of her plan and I'd been running on autopilot. I pulled level with her again, falling back into step, and she dropped her hand from my arm.

We both wore trousers and flat boots, with bulky hooded coats from Chrystal's wardrobe. She carried an empty sack made of rough, brown material. She'd warned me repeatedly to keep my face hidden and I was starting to like the feel of the generous hood which gave me the freedom to see sideways even while it obscured my face from any CCTV cameras looking down on us. It used twice as much material as any hoodie I'd worn before and it was far more effective.

We walked past the first side street and she nudged me to turn down the next – more an alley than a street. If I'd been on my own, I wouldn't have gone down there in the dark. We left the road and I noticed a street light with its cover shattered and wires hanging out. A second broken light hung its damaged head in shame and then it was too dark for me to see much of anything. I tripped on something and would have fallen but for that grip miraculously materialising just as I needed it. Once I'd found my footing again, she laid her arm around my shoulders and guided me silently with gentle pressure to one side or the other.

Chrystal led me along more alleys, switching and turning until I was convinced we'd gone round at least one complete circle. In the middle of a dark passage that didn't look any different to any other, she stopped and looked up at a wall.

"Would you give me a leg-up, please?" she asked as she turned my back to the bricks.

I bent forward, clasping my hands together and helped her lift herself up the wall. I wasn't sure how much I could help – I'm not that strong and I didn't know what she was reaching for or how high she needed to go. To my surprise, almost as soon as she was off the ground, her weight lifted away from my hands. By the time I'd turned to look, all I could see was the outline of her boots against the sky as they disappeared into the wall. A moment later, a knotted rope snaked down, jerked a couple of times and hung still. Swallowing hard, I began to climb, realising

Chrystal must be pulling on the rope at the same time. Just as I was pulling myself onto the flat roof beside her, I felt something brush past and saw a black shape tumble away, cawing. I recovered myself and coiled the rope up.

We were kneeling on a narrow strip of roof with skylights set in it, where Chrystal knelt, tugging at a cage of wrought-iron bars that protected the glass of a window in the wall in front of us.

"Almost there," she muttered as one bar came away in her hand.

"Wow – how did you do that?" I asked.

"Not as remarkable as it may look," she replied. "These old bars are already rusted most of the way through. I weakened this one two nights ago so that it required no more than a brief tug to admit us tonight."

As she whispered, she slid the bar downwards, ignoring the complaining noises its rusty surface made against the cross-bars that were designed to hold it in place.

She handed me the freed bar. "Bring that – we may need it inside."

I took the rusty metal pole and she produced something like a longish, thick pen from an inside pocket. I couldn't see what she did, but there was an odd whooshing sound and she pocketed it again.

"Follow me," she said as she lowered herself through the window frame which didn't appear to have any glass in it.

Not sure how far I had to fall, I slid through the frame on my belly, kicking slightly to find secure footing. I felt her hands grab my legs and I let go, falling slowly as she steadied me down the last few feet. I stumbled and there was a dull clang as the metal rod in my hand struck her right arm.

"Do not worry, it did not hurt me," she whispered and she held onto me as I found my balance again, then pulled my hood forward over my face a little more.

I noticed we were in a gallery full of huge carved-stone pictures that we hadn't seen on our recent visit. Chrystal turned to her right and whispered, "Quietly now. It is unlikely anyone will be here, but a security company is paid to patrol the displays at night. They rarely pass this way, but it is better to be careful."

We moved from one gallery to another, up a different flight of stairs and following a route that had me completely confused until we reached the gallery she'd waited in a few days earlier. She approached the display cabinet of "Victorian Curiosities" and I noticed the little wand thing in her hand again.

"This may be alarmed," she whispered as she set the wand against the glass of the cabinet.

The glass shimmered as if reflecting a set of disco lights and I heard the whoosh-noise again. Chrystal pocketed her gadget and reached for the ætheric resonator while metal fittings were still skittering to the floor.

"What! Where...?" I began, but she shhhhed me and I obeyed. No alarms had sounded yet and for the first time I began to think we might actually get away with this insane robbery.

She lowered the resonator onto the sack she'd laid ready on the floor, pulling the sides up until she could draw the top together and lift the whole thing.

"Okay, now to make good our egress," she hissed.

"Is that all we're taking?" I asked.

"I will not remove anything that does not belong to me," she replied and I had to hurry to keep up with her as she left the gallery in the opposite direction from our entrance.

"Isn't that the wrong way?" I asked as I caught up.

"We would not be able to get the resonator through the remaining window bars," she replied. "We will have to risk setting off the alarms."

"Um, which alarms? How are we going to get out of here?"

But I already knew. We were heading straight for the main

entrance.

She led me up the last wide, marble staircase, keeping to the edge and then peeking past a pillar before sliding around it, the resonator in its sack resting against the small of her back. I followed as quietly as I could. She stopped on the landing before the foyer, crouching down and signalling that I was to keep quiet. We waited for what seemed like an hour before she stood and began to make her way silently up the stairs, keeping close to the wall and moving one foot at a time. In the foyer, she paused again before edging her way quietly past the bookshop entrance and along the wall. The big glass doors stood solidly in front of us, the lions on them catching the light of the occasional car driving past and I realised the outside wooden doors weren't locked-up as they should be.

Chrystal mimed someone smoking and I guessed the security guard had opened the door to step outside. We crept closer, but could not see him outside. She pulled the sack further up her back and leaned close to whisper,

"Prepare yourself to run across the road."

I saw she was holding the wand-thing again and watched her tap it to the glass door. I could have sworn I saw the lion swirl towards her hand as I heard that odd noise for a second - before a very twenty-first century alarm siren drove every other thought from my head. Chrystal grabbed my arm and pushed me through the doorway in the same motion. Then we were clear of the building and running across the square, past the white security van, straight across the main road and into a side street. With the siren still ringing in my ears, Chrystal dragged me under a metal fire escape. She pulled me off-balance and shoved me into what looked like a cellar door. I didn't have time to catch my breath before she grabbed a lantern that was hanging from a hook near the door and lit it. Then we were running again, this time down a brick-lined tunnel that dropped steadily downwards as it zigged and zagged through the earth.

The floor under our feet was covered in a thick layer of mud that squelched in a particularly suggestive way, the curved walls were slimy and I tried not to touch them as we hurried past. I could hear water running somewhere below our feet - at least I hoped it was only water! The roof had pale spikes of stalactites in places, reflecting wetly in the lantern's light. It smelt disgusting and I had to fight for control of my stomach as it rebelled at the filthy air I was gasping into my lungs.

At last we slowed to a walk and Chrystal held her light up next to her face, illuminating her grin like the worst gargoyle in the world.

"Almost home," she said, startling me as her voice echoing around the brick-clad tunnel.

"Where, where are we?" I asked between gulps of air.

"In an old sewerage tunnel," she replied. "Some of these surface ones are only used to drain away storm water nowadays. They are meant to be closed-off securely, but many of the gates are broken and the remaining ones do not resist for long."

I saw a dim light ahead of us and we stepped out of a culvert onto a little stone platform on the side of the Thames. Chrystal pushed a railing back into place after us and pointed to a ladder leading up the bricks towards streetlights above.

"A few yards of climbing and we are only two streets from home."

Sure enough, I recognised the shop across the road – closed now for the owner's five-hour sleep before the morning papers arrived.

Chapter 7

In which Sam and Chrystal explore their relationship

Back in her flat, she asked me to clear away cups and lifted the resonator from its sack onto the little table. I expected her to check it immediately and took the opportunity to inspect something odd on her workbench.

I'd noticed a wire framework standing on the bench earlier, like an old-fashioned birdcage, but without the bird. Now, a large, transparent ball floated inside it, glistening like a soap bubble but looking much more substantial. For some reason it reminded me of the way the glass lion had swirled like bath water going down a plughole. I couldn't see what was holding it up and I was trying to decide if I dared poke it through the wires when Chrystal appeared at my elbow with the pen-wand-thing in her hand. She dropped it into a holder in the side of the framework and touched my sleeve.

"First things first. We need to remove this malodorous clothing and make ourselves clean again."

As soon as she mentioned the smell, I was shocked to realise I hadn't already tried to do something about us stinking of that awful tunnel.

"You may go first," she said, nodding towards the little bathroom I'd changed in earlier. "The shower is fully wound and there are clean towels waiting. Leave your dirty clothes in the basket."

I wasn't sure I'd heard her correctly, so I simply went into the bathroom and pulled off my hooded cloak. I thought I'd forgotten about the smell because I had got used to it – but the stink from my disturbed clothing was so intense I nearly gagged again. I held my breath and stripped off completely, stepping inside the shower cubicle before I had a look at the controls.

There was a shiny brass wheel where I'd expect to find a neat, white control knob and some sort of lever on the side of the also-brass-coloured water pipes. I hesitated for a moment, unsure what to do, but my hair swung into my face when I bent to inspect the lever and the smell of it made my mind up for me. I tried turning the wheel, but it wouldn't move. I pressed the lever and tried the wheel again. It was stiff enough to need both hands, but I was rewarded with a rapidly-warming spray of water from the shower head. I luxuriated in the water for a moment, then uncorked a glass bottle to find a thick liquid that smelled of herbs and rubbed a dollop of it into my hair. The bar of speckled soap on its little shelf smelt of the same herbs and something muskier, but lathered up quickly and the combination soon left me smelling a lot sweeter. While I scrubbed, I wondered how my hair had grown so much. When had I last had it cut?

I could have stood there in the warm stream for a lot longer, but remembering Chrystal would also need to shower, I turned the wheel back again, pushed the lever up and stepped out. The promised towels were large, fluffy and plentiful and I wrapped my hair up in one before fastening another round my pinkly-glowing body.

Chrystal was adjusting something on the wire apparatus as I came out. She just nodded at me and disappeared into the bathroom while I settled on the sofa. The clean clothes I'd brought from home sat in a neat pile next to me, where I'd placed them earlier after unpacking my little rucksack. But I wanted to relax and enjoy the luxury of feeling clean again for a moment.

I stopped to consider what we'd done, surprised to realise it felt very different from picking pockets. I'd expected the same feelings of guilt, tinged with fear at being caught. Instead I felt elated, as if we'd put something right, rather than simply stolen the resonator. I shook my head. This was silly – was I justifying the theft to myself because the victim was a Museum, instead of another person? I wasn't sure and that uncertainty bothered me vaguely, though I was finding it hard to care. I felt a little light-headed, almost intoxicated after our adventure and realised I was sucking on a strand of my hair - a bad habit I thought I'd given up when I started going to the big school.

Chrystal stepped out of the bathroom dressed in a couple of towels as I was. She looked fresh and pink – younger than she had before, as if she'd washed the years off with the dirt and smell. My heart skipped a beat and I reminded myself forcefully, *she's just a stranger who's hired you to help with one little robbery*. But my treacherous heart wasn't convinced. She lifted her arms to pull the towel from her hair and I caught sight of the metal rods I'd seen before. They really were embedded in her right forearm – I hadn't just imagined them.

She noticed me looking. Not that it was hard - I must have been staring. She lowered her hand and offered it towards me, palm upwards, so that I got a clearer view. She moved her fingers as if she were playing an upside-down piano and I could see the movement in her arm, somehow similar to the way my own tendons would have moved. The rods were covered with translucent skin and looked as natural a part of her arm as the freckles.

"It is complicated to explain," she said. "To cut a long story down, I was given these adaptations by some men who saved my life. Do they cause you concern?"

"N-no," I replied, feeling very concerned. "Not at all."

Without thinking, I found my hand moving towards that unlikely combination of flesh and mechanics, but drew it back without touching.

"Does it hurt?" I asked.

She pulled a wry face. "It itches sometimes – deep inside, where I cannot scratch. And my arm is heavy. But no, it does not cause me pain."

"I've never seen anything like that before," I said. Understatement of the year! I'd never even heard of anything like this.

"Nor have I. But it works. And without this, I believe I would have lost the use of my right arm."

"Was it some sort of... experimental surgery?" I asked.

She laughed shortly. "I suppose so. I did not have time to ask them many questions."

I realised the significance of something she'd mentioned. "You said adaptations, plural. What else did they do?"

In reply, she looked at me, capturing my gaze with her dark eyes. For a moment she looked uncertain, her hand reached for her towel where it fastened around her chest. I thought she was going to turn her back on me, but instead she held me eyes, loosened her towel and let the front drop a little. She dropped her eyes and I looked down, too. There were more of those pipes, although these were engraved with strange patterns. They surrounded an irregular-shaped lump in the centre of her chest which brightened and darkened rhythmically as I watched and I stood, unsure what I was seeing.

"Is that...?"

"Yes," she answered.

"So you're...?"

"Yes, I do believe that I am," said Chrystal. "And I am something else, as well..."

She left the sentence hanging, looking at me with those strange dark eyes of hers, almost daring me. This time, I did reach out one finger to touch the skin over that peculiar, beating thing, only to have her hold my hand to her chest. She let go of her towel, which dropped to the floor as she pulled me close and I felt her demanding lips on mine. I only hesitated for a heartbeat before releasing my own towel and wrapping my arms around her naked body.

Chapter 8

In which Sam examines her life

I woke to the smell of freshly-brewed coffee and rolled over in bed, confused and disoriented. It took me several long seconds to remember the night's events. I was in Chrystal's workshop, had been all night. In fact I was in Chrystal's bed and we'd...

"Good Morning," she greeted me as she sat on the bed and held out a steaming mug.

"Um, morning," I answered.

"You may shower if you wish," she continued. "But then I must work on the resonator and I will need you to leave quickly."

So she'd had what she wanted from me and I was unnecessary again. I decided to shower when I got home and dressed quickly in the clean clothes I'd brought. I slurped the coffee, accepted the cash Chrystal gave me without counting it and left.

For the first time in months, I didn't have to worry about money – for a while, at least. I could take it easy, instead of hanging round the tube station, scanning the commuter crowds for careless people with fat wallets. I could afford to eat proper meals and even treat myself to some new boots. I'd seen a leather pair in the Heart Foundation shop that looked very Steamy but never thought I'd have the money to buy them.

I stared at the fat roll of £50 notes but didn't unroll it to count how much Chrystal had thought my assistance to be worth. I did wonder if it would have been a smaller roll if I hadn't stayed the night. Was I now a whore, as well as a thief? I really didn't like that thought and pushed it to the back of my mind.

I looked at the mess of a bedsit I'd been living in, wondering if it had always been so awful and why I hadn't noticed, and it slowly dawned on me just how far I'd fallen since the company - Rosalind - had decided I was *surplus to requirements*. And now Chrystal had the nerve to treat me in the same way! I took a long, hard look at myself in the mirror and understood for the first time what that phrase actually meant. I'd never thought about it before, but today I learned how critical I could be about my own reflection. Looking back at me was a thinner, harsher version of Samantha than anyone in the office had ever seen. I'd not only lost the roundness from my cheeks, I'd somehow mislaid the soft edges of my personality too. So much had changed in a few short months.

So I tried to look at the woman glaring back at me without meeting my eyes, and decided I didn't like her much. The first thing I noticed was the crooked front tooth and closed my mouth quickly, trying to be objective about *her*. Hair hanging messily over her collar, so dull it looked mousy brown, hardly showing the red at all. Her face was as grey as old underwear, her blouse buttoned unevenly over tits that had shrunk to nothing, her collar bones standing out like a coat hanger. Looking at my reflection, I was amazed Chrystal had even spoken to me, let alone seduced me. If that's what she'd done. But I didn't want to think about that. I tried turning sideways on, hoping I wouldn't look so bad from the side. But the hollows in my cheeks made my nose appear longer. And I'm sure it used to look straighter.

Chrystal's money would keep Tony off my back for a while. I decided this was a breathing space, a chance to pull myself together again and make a fresh start. And probably a dozen more clichés, if I wasn't careful. I'd start by sorting out the bedsit, at least.

A trip to the supermarket meant better food for my cupboard, a roll of black bags and a whole pile of cleaning stuff. I also bought a copy of the London Evening Standard when I saw the headline

Daring Night Raid on British Museum

The article was more speculation than information and made it clear that the police thought the theft had been carried out by two men. There was no mention of what had been stolen, or of the missing windows which must have caused a lot of head-scratching at New Scotland Yard.

"Well, the police won't be looking for two women, at least," I murmured out loud, trying to convince my heart it didn't need to pound so hard. "But they may not have watched all their CCTV footage yet."

I started with the little sink in the corner of my bedsit, scrubbing off geological strata of stains left by previous occupants before moving on to the so-called kitchen unit and microwave.

By the end of a day scrubbing my way around that little room, I had five black bags full of used cleaning materials and accumulated rubbish. Plastic packaging from the chippy round the corner took up one whole bag, but I kept the cheap beer cans and empty cornflake boxes separate for the recycling bin. I even went through the box of clothes I'd never unpacked after leaving my flat and folded some of them neatly to go to the Heart Foundation shop. I kept the Steampunk clothes thinking I might start wearing them again now I didn't have Rosalind complaining about my *childish dressing-up habit.* But I wasn't going to be working in an office for the foreseeable future – and most of the pseudo-mannish jackets and matching skirts wouldn't even fit me now. A crow was scavenging through the rubbish when I took the bags out and its cawing reminded me of Chrystal, but I pushed that thought away, annoyed that she was intruding into my thoughts so much. Having added my rubbish to the bins behind the flats, I ran back up the stairs, feeling as if I'd dumped a much heavier load than a few black bags.

I stopped off at the shared cupboard to borrow the iron and its board. I couldn't remember the last time I'd made an effort with my appearance.

After returning the iron, I stood in the doorway of my room. It felt much bigger now I'd tidied and cleaned. There was a smell of freshly-pressed clothes as well as the lemony scent of clean surfaces. Tomorrow I'd buy more local papers and scour the *Sits Vac* as thoroughly as I'd scrubbed my sink. So long as I wasn't fussy about what I did, I'd find something to pay the bills before Chrystal's money ran out. If I had time, I wanted to look a few more things up on the library computers, too – and I realised I hadn't even opened a book in months. But I needed to find out more about this æther Chrystal kept mentioning. Even if I wasn't going to see her again. Which I wasn't! I was intrigued by the idea of the æther, that was all.

Standing in front of the mirror in my wardrobe, I pinned Kerry's Steampunk pin on my freshly-ironed blouse. I looked at my reflection again and decided I might be able to like this woman again, even if nobody else did.

Despite my best efforts, jobs really were hard to come by.

Even though I'd lowered my expectations, it seemed that employers weren't prepared to believe me. Time after time they said I was *overqualified for the post* they'd advertised. It didn't seem to matter how much I insisted I was happy to wash dishes or mop floors, the bosses kept telling me they couldn't afford to spend time training staff who'd be gone in a few weeks. I'd printed copies of my old CV at the library, but first I had to edit it, taking out most of my qualifications and dumbing down my previous responsibilities. But I couldn't completely hide the fact that my experience was in a different league. I finally found someone prepared to pay me to deliver leaflets, but at the end of my first day, he only paid me half of what he'd promised. He claimed he had to deduct tax and National Insurance – but mysteriously didn't offer me a pay slip showing these figures. As I walked out, he shouted at me not to come back again – as if there was any chance I would!

So it was back to the Job Centre again, trying to convince them I really was making an effort to find a job and wondering how people could bear to live like this all their lives.

I'd thought about splashing out on a hair cut, to match my smarter appearance, but I decided to save my money. I washed it three times, applied one of those deep treatment conditioners and fastened it back in a pony tail. It felt neater, but I knew I wasn't likely to get anything close to an office job for the foreseeable future.

The money the welfare gave me every fortnight would pay for me to eat or to stay in the bedsit, but not both. Once Chrystal's money ran out, I'd either have to find another way to pay the bills or leave. I didn't like either alternative and I couldn't think of another way out unless I went back to picking pockets.

On my way home after yet another disappointing day of walking round shops that weren't hiring, I realised I was only a few streets away from Chrystal's workshop. Almost without thinking about it, I found my feet turning down a street to walk past the house, half-hoping to catch her leaving or arriving home again. But as I approached the tall, red brick building, I felt stupid and hurried past with my head down, hoping she wouldn't see me after all. Although I'd thought of her many times in the weeks since we'd parted, the whole business felt almost dreamlike, as if it happened to a different person, or in another life.

Back in my room, I counted my dwindling cash and desperately combed the *Sits Vac* pages again. I'd expected it to last a bit longer, but my rent arrears and overdraft had turned out bigger than I'd thought. I sat with my phone, working through the names stored in it and wondering if I could swallow my pride enough to ask one of my old friends to let me stay in a spare room for a while. But everyone in there had known me as the successful career woman I used to think I was. I remembered casual comments about "benefit scroungers" and snide remarks over the head of a beggar on the streets and I couldn't bring myself to press the green key. Would any of my friends want to help me now I was one of those despised welfare cases? I remembered the contempt on Rosalind's face when she explained that there was no room for me in her life now, any more than there was in her company. Had everyone been using me for their own shallow benefit? Had anyone ever cared about me for myself?

Then I thought about the phone itself. It was a good model, bought new a few months before they made me redundant, though I'd changed to a pay-as-you-go SIM because they'd stopped paying my bill and I couldn't afford even the cheapest monthly tariff. Maybe it was time to give up even that small expense. After all, no-one ever called me and the only calls I'd made were in search of jobs I never stood a chance of getting. I'd get a good few quid for it at the loan shop, too. I stared at its little keypad, feeling as if it was somehow the last piece of my old life, my office life. I slid the back off and pulled out the SIM card. Quickly, before I could think too much about what I was doing. I shoved the phone into my handbag, added its charger and pulled on my coat. At least I could haggle with the shop about what it was worth. If I was lucky the man who fancied me would be at work. A little harmless flirting always seemed to get me the best price for whatever I was trading in. It was like a dance – we both knew I was never going to reclaim my property, but we still called it a loan and pretended I would be buying things back in a week's time. Pride feels like such a little thing when people look up to you, but it really matters when you've got nothing left to be proud of. If I'd believed in God, I think I would have been praying for the right assistant in the shop, to give me a slightly better deal than he was meant to.

Stepping outside, I turned left towards the so-called village centre with its cluster of pound stores, theme pub and the loan shop. It was windy and I pulled my coat collar higher, wishing for one of Chrystal's silly hats to keep the litter from blowing into my face as I battled my way down the road.

I hadn't even reached the first corner when someone grabbed my arm. Instinctively I clutched my handbag in both hands and ducked away, shouting "Thief". But the hand didn't let go. Instead it pulled me round to face my assailant and I suddenly recognised her. Bright green eyes bored into mine as a familiar voice said,

"Well, I did not expect a warm welcome, but I have never been mistaken for a common footpad before."

"Chrystal!"

She smiled wryly and bowed. "None other. I wonder if I could impose on you again, Sam-of-the-boy's-name?"

Chapter 9

In which a young man joins the army

The small windowless room was dimly lit by a lamp shaped like a tall plant with metal fronds opening out at the top. The lamp shed a sullen red glow over the tall figure standing with his back to the room, his hooded robes covering his head and pooling behind him on the floor. The figure swayed slightly, emitting a soft hissing noise that sounded oddly like a tune.

A metallic bell rang out from the other side of the door, which opened slowly as two men approached. The taller man marched confidently, followed by a bespectacled youth who stared openly at the fantastical carvings on the walls. The soldier, his face part-covered with a copper-coloured mask, stopped in the centre of the room. He waited for the young man to stand next to him, placed a hand on his back and pushed him down, bowing at the same time himself. They held that position for a moment, then the cloaked figure spoke over his shoulder.

"Thisss isss the new recruit?"

"Yes, Your Eminence," replied the masked soldier.

Turning to face them, Geb addressed the young man. "Your name?"

Released from the hand that held him bent, he replied, "Paul, um, Your Eminence?" His voice wavered and he glanced from his companion to the tall man under the odd leather cloak.

"And how many yearsss have you, Paul?" The sibilant voice spoke slowly, struggling to pronounce the words.

"Eighteen, Your Eminence. I'm not much of a fighter, but your men said I could be very useful in your army. That you

needed men like me..."

His voice faded away and he stared openly at the swaying figure in front of him.

"You left your family to come to me?"

Paul's arms fell to his sides as body began to sway.

"Are you a man, Paul? Have you known a woman?"

The young man nodded, his swaying now in time with the cloaked figure.

"And do you take drugsss, Paul? Sssmoke the weed? Chew the qat?"

"N-no. But your men say they eat the, er, wafers."

"Make a man of you, those do," said the soldier, leering as Paul nodded eagerly.

"Leave," hissed Geb and the soldier turned for the door that swung closed silently behind him.

Geb lowered his hood and reached out to lift the young man's head to meet his black eyes, holding the youngster there as he tensed and went slack again, still swaying.

"You want to be ussseful in my army, young Paul?" whispered Geb. "You're not much of a fighter *but you ran away to become a sssoldier?"*

Paul didn't answer. His body swayed as he stared into the snake's face that loomed over him.

"You want the wafersss that make you a man?" the snake-man asked softly.

Paul's eyes were wide in his slack face, but they clouded with fear as Geb's mouth opened and two huge fangs dropped into place. He took hold of the young man's arms.

The strike to his neck was so swift that Paul didn't react until Geb stepped back. The teenager's mouth opened as his hands flew to his crotch, clutching at a sudden urgency, panic filling his eyes. Then one hand flew to his chest, fighting back a desperate pounding as his mouth opened in a scream. He fell forward onto his knees and pitched onto his side on the dusty floor. Geb stepped back, one last drop of venom dripping from a bloodied fang as he turned away from the writhing shape. The screaming had stopped as the black, swollen throat closed, but the young man's struggles grew more frantic. Then weaker as the dragon-cloaked figure turned away through the opening door. By the time he'd swept past the red-clothed men standing by with a stretcher, the swollen, blackened body on the floor behind him lay motionless.

Chapter 10

In which Ætheric technology is discussed

Her room was even untidier than before. The workbench was littered with odd tools, coffee cups and strange things I couldn't even begin to identify. There was no sign of the glistening sphere inside the wire cage, but the wand-thing hung in its little bracket and there was some sort of clamp on the other side, away from the window. The wooden box we'd gone to so much trouble to steal from the museum sat in the middle of the chaos and Chrystal beckoned me forward to join her, gesturing at the resonator. She'd taken the back off, so I could see the case was largely empty - with metal fixings inside the top and some sort of wheel on a spike in the base. There was a little shelf inside, fixed below the dial on the front, with glass bulbs or something underneath. Cog wheels were fixed inside where the brass pipes connected to the outside of the box. Daylight came through the little glass tubes set into the side, illuminating the dust floating inside with little beams at angles to each other.

"I have removed the mount for the ætheric foils," she said, "but the foils themselves have deteriorated badly and it will be necessary for me to manufacture replacements. In order to do so, I need to analyse the composition of the existing foils and for that I require your assistance."

"You want me to help? I'm no scientist!"

"Thank heavens for that," she replied. "I would prefer not to work with one who is hidebound with the preconceptions of this century."

"So what do you need me to do?" I asked.

"I have here," she gestured at a tray with a sheet of plywood lying flat inside. "The foils I removed from the resonator. Although in a poor state of repair, I will be able to ascertain their precise shapes and thus to replicate them anew. But before that, I need to deduce their composition and I have been unable to do so by working alone."

"Oooo-kay."

"Incidentally," she went on. "I find your new hairstyle most fetching."

"Oh, thank you."

"I was a little surprised initially, as I thought it a little severe for you," she went on. "But now I can see how well it emphasises your cheekbones."

"You don't think it's too harsh?" I asked, looking up at her through my eyelashes. She just smiled and turned back to her workbench. She lifted the plywood from the tray and I saw several pieces of foil lying underneath where the wood had been keeping them flat. They looked dull and some of them were torn. Chrystal lifted out the most crumpled one, using a pair of whitish tongs.

"I have been cannibalising this one to provide samples, but I have been unable to burn it and observe the resultant display in sufficient detail to be sure of my results," she said.

"Does it matter that you use the same stuff? I mean, you know it's metal, so what difference does it make?"

I half-expected her to be annoyed at me for such a stupid remark, but she didn't seem at all offended.

"Different types of metal have different ætheric properties," she said. "Just as some will conduct electricity more readily than others."

"And you know what was used for this?" I gestured at the resonator.

"No – as I mentioned, this is not my area of expertise. The master who built the resonator understood the properties of his materials very well and would have chosen each element for maximum effect. I am merely a novice in ætheric studies, so the best I can do is to duplicate his choices and hope that my poor efforts will result in a working machine. This needs to be a more precise machine than the one which merely heats the water for our coffee."

"So what do you need to do?"

"I must learn which metals were used in its construction, then procure foils of the appropriate constituents, meld them, cut the resultant compound foil to shape and then attempt to restore the apparatus to a working state."

She looked at me expectantly and I searched for something sensible to say.

"And that's before you can begin work on your own apparatus?"

"Yes, indeed. I hope to build an equipment which will operate as an ætheric sender, based on the mechanics of the resonator."

I thought about this for a moment. I'd never been any good at science in school and used to spend lessons in the lab messing around with my friends and then copied the results from someone who'd actually done the experiments. I didn't like science and the science teachers didn't like me, so we'd got on just fine. I was used to switching off when they explained anything because it was easier than trying to understand all those foreign words and squiggles in the text books. And yet, here was Chrystal explaining something radically different to anything I'd ever come across and it was making sense! Sort of, anyhow.

"So you need me to watch the display for you?" I asked.

She looked up at me, smiling properly for the first time since she'd appeared outside my home that morning.

"I cannot safely burn the foil and watch the flash on the display at the same time. I have made several attempts, with no better result than a waste of foil material. Consider this your first lesson in the science of ætherics."

I reached out to touch the scrap of foil, but she pushed my hand away.

"It is important that the foil not suffer any further deterioration," she explained. "It must not be touched by anything which may influence the results of my analyses. That is why I am using the bone tongs."

"Bone?" I asked. "I thought they were plastic."

"Ah, the modern obsession with oil and its products," she sighed. "No, these tongs were made from ox bones and have served me well for many years."

"I've never heard of tongs made from bones before – where did you buy them?"

"Only a few streets from here. Although I suspect you would not find them anywhere but antique shops now."

"Do you buy much from antique shops? I've noticed you have a lot of really old stuff," I commented, gesturing vaguely around the room with its old-fashioned, heavy-looking furniture.

She looked thoughtful.

"A lot of these items were not antiques when I bought them. I am much older than you think," she said deliberately.

"Surely you're not much older than I am – maybe five years? Ten at the most!"

"Ah, Sam. I am much older than that. The Chrystal that functions as my heart has prolonged my life and my appearance has changed but little over the years."

"What? But how?"

"I do not understand the mechanism – I was understandably not awake when they implanted the Chrystal and I am naturally unable to remove it for examination," she replied.

"So – how old were you when they implanted it?"

"I was twenty-seven. A few years older than you are now, I believe?"

"Um, yes. So when was that?" I was struggling to make sense of this. I could just about accept that she had an artificial heart and parts in her arm, odd though they were. But the idea that she was much older than me seemed ridiculous.

"I was attacked and given my new heart back in 'fifty-one," she said slowly, watching my face as I absorbed this revelation.

"That was," I hesitated. "Sixty-one years ago!"

Then I completed my calculations. "And you were twenty-seven. So you're telling me you're eighty-eight years old!"

"Not exactly," she replied.

"Um, where have I gone wrong?"

"Your arithmetic is correct, but you are not aware of all of the facts," she said.

I just stared at her, wondering how much more of this I could take.

"You see," she said, locking her green eyes on mine. "I *was* born in 'twenty-four. But not nineteen twenty-four, as you assume."

She paused for a long moment.

"I was born in the Year of Our Lord Eighteen Twenty-four. I am *one hundred* and eighty-eight years old."

"No!"

"Yes," she assured me. "I did warn you that I was older than you thought."

"But – almost two hundred years...!"

"Yes."

"And the Chrystal stops you getting any older."

"No, it does not halt the ageing of my body. It merely makes the process take longer than it does for other people."

"You can say that again!"

"I am certain you heard me the first time," she replied and in the moment it took me to work though the oddness of her comment, I calmed down a little.

"So – you could be my ancestor. My great-grandmother or something?"

She smiled sadly. "No, I am not your ancestor. I am merely someone who has lived a long life. Although it is possible that I did meet an ancestor of yours."

I asked the first thing that came into my head, "Did you know this would happen? When they gave you the Chrystal?"

"No. I thought the footpads had killed me – I was so surprised to wake up, I did not think to ask many questions of my rescuers."

"And they didn't tell you anything?"

"I do not believe they spoke much English. One of them told me it is a Chrystal – not a crystal, but little more than that."

"And you didn't ask?"

"I passed out again out shortly after regaining consciousness. When I came round properly, several days later, they had gone," she explained.

"They just left you there?"

"I think they returned to their own country. The Exhibition was over, you see."

"Exhibition?"

"The Great Exhibition. People came to London from all over the Empire – and beyond. I have since deduced that my rescuers were from Tibet, judging by their mode of dress and the few artefacts they left behind with me." She gestured towards a wooden trunk which sat against the wall with a brightly-coloured cloth draped over it. "I never saw them again."

"Have you never tried to find them?" I asked.

She shook her head. "Travel was not so easy in those days and I had only limited means. By the time I was well enough to consider leaving London in pursuit, they would have reached their homes again and I had no clues to their names or precise whereabouts."

"So they saved your life and just left you to recover?"

"Yes. Although I believe they understood the Chrystal's ability to restore my health and trusted in its power to complete my recovery. They left me to sleep after implanting the Chrystal and I woke to find myself alone. Five days later."

It was my turn to shake my head. The whole tale was ridiculous, unbelievable – and yet, I had seen the Chrystal beating in her chest. And I'd heard the strange way she spoke – as someone who had been born in the nineteenth century might talk.

"Hang on," I said, suddenly making a connection. "You said the resonator was made for an ancestor of yours. Was that...?"

She smiled. "Yes, a small untruth. It was made for me. But if I had told you so, you would not have believed me."

"When you smile like that, you remind me of the Stables Manager I used to work for when I was a student," I said, feeling a heat in my belly as I remembered those summer weeks.

"The Manager was a Lady?"

I snorted, embarrassed. "A woman, yes. But she was no lady, I can assure you!"

She didn't answer, just looked at me quizzically.

"She taught me a lot more than riding," I blurted out, my face scarlet. "Not that I'm complaining - but no-one would ever have called her a lady!"

"And so it is under the new Queen," she said.

"Was it so much better in your day?" I asked.

She paused, her head on one side as she considered my question.

"Our society was different," she said. "But was it better? I am not certain."

I could feel my stomach turning somersaults, while I wrestled with the problem of this sexy woman who said she was older than anyone I'd ever met.

"And I thought you were just one of those people who dress up like Victorians," I said, trying to cover my embarrassment.

"But maybe I am," she replied, her face lightening up. "And maybe I am one of those people who would rather be undressed for a while."

She reached for me and I leant towards her, eager to be in the arms of this woman whose words were so strange, but whose body spoke to mine in ways I had never imagined.

Chapter 11

In which foil is analysed

Chrystal had asked me to trace some of the foil pieces onto a piece of card. There were nine altogether, three different shapes, and she set me to produce a neat outline for each one. I cut them out, ready to make the replacements she was planning. She busied herself about the workbench, clearing stuff away, replacing tools in drawers and washing coffee cups in the huge metal sink under the window. Finally she loaded the coffee maker with grounds and water, setting it on its stand to wait. Once we'd both finished, she went over to the foils on their tray, lifting the plywood cover and taking out the most damaged foil.

"We will continue to use this one for our analysis," she commented.

"I'm fairly sure it's the same shape as two of the others," I replied, coming to stand next to her.

"I believe so, too. There appears to be a tripartite symmetry to the arrangement, which is consistent with the stand to which they were affixed."

She cut a very small piece off the damaged foil, clamping it in a smaller pair of the bone tongs fixed to the side of the 'birdcage'. She then opened a shallow drawer, removing a bright red glass lens and dropping it into another stand.

"Now, the first stage of our analysis is to identify the metals used in its preparation. We need to filter the flame of its burning through each lens in turn."

She directed my attention to a white sheet pinned up on the wall. "We should not look at the flame directly, but at its projection on there. Now, observe!"

I nodded and turned to watch the sheet. I heard a click and saw a flash of colour appear on the sheet. It looked like an archery target in red and orange, but had a large, blank circle in the centre.

"What colours did you see?" she asked.

I described the pattern that had flashed up.

"Vanadium, I suspected as much!"

"Okay – how can you tell?" I asked.

"Every metal burns with a characteristic colour," she explained. "This lens will focus the different colours in centred circles and filter out the light from any vanadium which burns in the flame. In this way we can determine which metals are present in the sample."

As usual, I didn't quite follow her explanation, but it became clearer as we worked through the lenses, with clear centres or circles appearing for some of them. She had thirteen lenses in total and we ended up with a list of five metals that the she said were present in the foil. As she wrote the last one down, she sighed.

"So we have five elements to experiment with. Complex ætheric foils are often made with three distinct layers, so two of those layers are likely to be compounded of two elements each. If it follows the rules that I know, these will be symmetrical, with the simple layer being the middle one." She spoke as if to herself and I didn't interrupt her for clarification.

"But, we have more important matters to attend to!" she announced.

"Um – what's that?"

She flicked the foils under her water-heater with a mischievous grin in my direction.

"Coffee, of course. Would you?"

I was happy to oblige and collected mugs from their cupboard. She sat on the sofa with her list of metals and a pencil.

"Now, I know that germanium is often used with silver and that platinum is usually prepared on its own. So I suggest that we use that combination for our first two layers, with the vanadium and titanium compounded for the third."

"Why does it have to be so complicated? Why not just use simple kitchen foil?" I asked, thinking that a stupid question may be the best way to an answer that I could understand.

"No, I have already explained that that will not work at all. Aluminium has entirely the wrong ætheric properties. I can use a simple foil – with only one metal in its construction – for basic devices," she waved at the water heater which was turning steadily under the now-boiling water. "But this device is far more subtle. A Master in the Science of Ætherics may know how to construct this machine with fewer elements, but my understanding is limited. I will have to deduce the original constituents in order to replicate its workings."

"Okay, I understand you need to work out which metals are in it, but what are these layers and why do they matter?"

"The interaction between the layers of foil is key to the operating of complex ætheric foils. Fortunately there are standards and conventions that the maker is likely to have followed, even though I have not met this particular combination before. We will experiment with various possible combinations until we match the ætheric properties of the original."

"Do we have to melt the metals for the foil layers?" I asked.

"Fortunately not. I know a jeweller who is only too happy to produce foils for me, using the metals I specify. He is a talented metalsmith who is grateful for the opportunity to work with more unusual elements – although that gratitude is not sufficient to persuade him to waive his not-inconsiderable fee. We will visit him today and make our request. Once we have the basic foils, I will use the glass baton to meld the layers together."

There was so much in that explanation that I didn't understand that I didn't even know where to start. While I thought, she reached out to lean on the workbench. I stepped forward to help but hesitated, uncertain. Her face was even paler than usual and I stepped to her side, supporting her with one arm and helped her to the sofa where she almost collapsed. I sat next to her, wondering if I should make her sit with her head between her knees but worried that might make things worse. Was it her corset that was making her faint like this? Should I try to loosen that? I settled for just holding her with one arm and she leant against my side. After a minute she stirred, taking her weight but still leaning on me a little.

"Are you alright? Shall I get you some water?"

"Not water." Quiet, hard to hear and I bent my ear as close as I could to her lips. She was quiet for a long moment then,

"Sam, can I request your assistance?"

"Of course!" The answer was automatic. I didn't know what was wrong with her, but I wanted to help.

"My heart - the Chrystal."

"Oh - I see. What can I do?" I hadn't really thought about it before, but I guessed it would need some sort of looking after. "What can I do?"

"There's a box..." She nodded towards the nearer end of the workbench and I saw a small wooden box on it. Keeping one hand on Chrystal's shoulder, I stood and reached for the box with the other, then sat, the box on my lap with its metal clasp towards her. It was inlaid with an intricate geometric pattern in a combination of wood, brass and coloured chips. A swirl of green-blue stones seemed to formed a symbol, a complicated letter that looked vaguely familiar but I couldn't place where I'd seen it before.

"Sam - do you remember when I first brought you here?" Her voice was so quiet I struggled to hear the words.

"Yes, of course," I breathed.

"I took a little of your blood."

"Yes - for an experiment, wasn't it?"

Her head shook slightly against my shoulder and she

reached for the wooden box.

"It was for my heart," her voice was so faint I could barely hear her.

I opened the clasp of the box, pushed back the lid and found myself staring a syringe. A little larger than the ones doctors used, and made of brass, but a syringe nonetheless. In the lid of the box were fixed a number of very modern sterile needles, individually packed. I swallowed hard. I didn't know how to take blood from anyone - let alone myself. I wasn't particularly squeamish about needles, but all the same!

Chrystal slumped against me, either unconscious or very close to it. I eased her down so she was lying on the sofa, with me kneeling next to her. Rather than work out what to do with the syringe, I focused on opening her blouse and the front of her corset, exposing the heart in its metal frame. It was paler green than I remembered and I could hardly see its pulse. The whole assemblage was covered in skin, but my exploring fingers found a hole in the lower corner, where it would be most hidden by her clothes. Hopefully this was where the blood was meant to go.

Quickly, before I had time to think about it, I tore open the packet and used the sterile needle to stab my thumb, then wiggled it a little until a trickle of red ran down onto my hand. I held it against Chrystal's chest, squeezing and watching the blood vanish into the little hole.

I was concentrating so hard on keeping the blood flowing and trying to spill as little as possible, I didn't notice the Chrystal getting darker. Until a voice said,

"That is sufficient. Thank you, Sam."

I turned and met Chrystal's eyes. They were almost black, like her Chrystal. I moved back and she sat up, her face back to normal, looking as well as ever.

"I do not often allow the Chrystal to get so starved," she said. "But I was distracted by our work. And your presence."

"Are you alright now?" I asked.

"I am restored, thank you, Sam," she smiled. "I thank you for the gift of your blood."

"You're, um, welcome."

"You should know that the Chrystal responds to the blood it receives," she went on. "This is how I was able to find you - because my Chrystal leads me towards you while it is nourished by your lifeblood."

"Um," I said. *So that was how she did it!*

"But I must teach you how to use the syringe."

She looked so happy that my own heart melted. She may be six times my age, she may have a lump of rock beating inside her chest and she may need my blood to survive. But I realised I was falling in love with this strange woman.

Chapter 12

In which a message is unwelcome

"Your Eminence?"

The hooded figure seated on the carved seat inclined its head slightly. Long fingers rested on the knobbly ends of the chair's arms and a hiss made the fat human standing in front of him flinch. His left arm wore a sleeve of overlapping metal scales, articulated armour with a dull, reddish sheen. The same side of his face was covered with more of the metal, melding into his skin and leaving only the smallest hole for his eye.

"I, I'm truly s-sorry to disturb your meditations, My Lord." He paused, watching for a sign that he should continue. "Um, Your Eminence?" He tried again.

"Oh, get on with it," hissed the figure on the throne.

"Only you said you wanted to know right away, Sire," said the fat man hurriedly. "If we found out anything about those disturbances..." He hesitated, watching as the long fingers drew a stiletto knife from its sheath on the chair arm.

"And...?" Toying with the knife, testing its point against a near-skeletal hand.

"Well, it's an informant, one of the network, see. In London. England." He dodged slightly to the side, not wanting to meet the black eyes that stared unblinking from the shadows under the dragon-coloured cowl.

"Ye-es?"

"He, like, he says someone's been ordering special foils. Like they was making ætheric devices." He pulled a dirty cloth from his

pocket, twisted it between his hands.

"Someone?" snapped the hooded figure.

"Well, like... He said it was a woman, Your Excellence."

The figure on the throne hissed again.

"What sort of a woman?"

"Um, he said she was tall. And wearing, like, old-fashioned clothes. And she spoke kind of old-fa..."

The stiletto quivered as it stuck in the fat man's throat. For a moment he stared at his master, then his knees folded under him and he crumbled to the floor in a rapidly-spreading pool of redness.

The gangly figure stood, paused for a moment, then moved to the edge of the blood-pool, retrieved his knife and wiped it on the dead man's clothing. He walked over to the wooden bureau, hissed as he opened its doors to reveal the grey screen. A leathery hand reached out to click a switch and the hood leaned down to speak into the caged microphone on its little projection.

"Get me Farran," he hissed. "And send for the dogs. Those whelps of Anubis can clean up this little mess."

Chapter 13

In which a signal is observed and pencils are used

The jeweller turned out to be a grey-haired man who looked at the two of us in a way I wasn't at all comfortable with. His shop was a dark little space, with small windows and a solid wooden counter dividing the inside. He came out from behind a curtain when we entered, wearing a leather apron and a smell of burning. He reminded me of a teacher who'd been pensioned off in the middle of a term when I was at school. We were never told why, but the rumour mill in the playground had all sorts of details about why he had to leave. There was something about the way this guy looked at us when he thought we couldn't see his expression...

Chrystal took me back to collect the foils from him on Monday morning. We hurried out of his shop and back to her workshop, where she smoothed the three foils between two glass sheets in what we hoped were the appropriate layers. She applied her wand device, the glass-baton as she'd called it, to the sandwich and the glass swirled into nothingness, leaving a single, thicker sheet of foil from which we cut the nine pieces we needed and mounted them in the framework from the ætheric resonator.

Chrystal slotted the resonator's back into position and turned the box round, so the dial was facing her. She checked the little glass tubes, tapped the dial's glass cover and the needle swung round, settling at about eleven o'clock. A quick flick opened a panel below the dial, exposing three little knobs and a pattern of lights flickering with an eerie blue glow behind a brass grill.

"This bodes well," she said. "The foils must be responding

properly, or we would not see a baseline reading like this."

"Baseline?"

"The resonator is reading the æther and displaying readings that indicate normal disturbance. Think of it as similar to the background noise that is always present in the city."

I nodded.

"So, if I now set it to focus on animal resonances only," she said, turning a knob one click to the right. The lights dimmed for a moment, then a single one lit up again.

"Um," Chrystal turned another knob and a second light flickered on.

"Excellent, it is reporting the presence of two animals – that is the two of us," she smiled at me.

"Doesn't it count things like rats? I mean, this old building is mostly empty, yeah? So there are bound to be rats in here somewhere. Or does it only work close up?"

"In the first case, there are no rats in this building – they dislike the disturbances caused by my ætheric devices, so they tend not to come here," she said, smiling at me. My heart leapt and I swallowed hard to disguise my sudden reaction.

"Secondly, I own the whole building, which allows me the privacy I prefer and simplifies much of my life. And in the third case – the device's range can be adjusted, but I have it set to the minimum distance. On this setting, it will not reach beyond the house, but will include most of the rooms inside."

I stared at her. "You own this whole building? I assumed you were renting just this apartment. It must be worth a fortune!"

She shrugged. "I presume it is. There are certain advantages to great age. I bought this building when it was first built, using the money I was given by a benefactor. London was not so expensive in those days."

"All the same, that must have been a very generous benefactor. Was it a rich relative?"

"No, he was a visiting ambassador – he rewarded me for saving his life when he was attacked on a back street in London. I happened to be nearby and felt obliged to assist, as I had once been attacked in a similar situation myself. Indeed, I would not have survived that original encounter were it not for the generosity of strangers - as you know."

"So when was this? When you saved this ambassador?"

"Long before your grandparents were born, Sam-of-the-boy's-name," she smiled.

"I still can't get my head around the idea that you're as old as you say. I still feel like you're just a few years older than me," I replied.

"Whatever you are most comfortable with," she smiled.

"But doesn't it feel weird – being older than everyone else?"

She laughed, "I feel the same as I did yesterday. And the day before. When should it start to feel, as you say, *weird*?"

I hesitated. I'd never really thought about my own age in that way, either. I still felt young – although many girls my age were already married with kids of their own. An odd thought, but I felt as if I understood something very important about Chrystal in that moment. I struggled to think clearly, ignoring both the thought in my head that she was some kind of inhuman monster and I should keep my distance and my treacherous heart which had an entirely different view of Chrystal.

Wanting to decide which of these views might be correct, I decided to try a different question, while she was so chatty.

"I'm not sure how to put this," I began.

Something about the way I said it seemed to surprise her and she took her hand away from the resonator, turned to look at me and her green eyes focused on mine.

"Well, um," I continued. "You say you were born in the nineteenth century," she nodded for me to go on.

"But, er wasn't Queen Victoria very um, y'know," I took a deep breath. "Wasn't it illegal for women like us? I mean who prefer to sleep with other girls?"

She stepped toward me, smiling. "No, never illegal. Some scurrilous rumours even claimed that the Queen herself indulged with her ladies-in-waiting after the Prince Consort passed away, although I never believed that."

"Were there many girls like you? Back in the nineteenth century?" I asked.

She took me in her arms. "I honestly do not know, and frankly do not care. When I was young, two of my two aunts lived together in what gentlefolk called a *female marriage*. All of my life, I have known there were women who preferred other women. And in my long life I have tried most, ah, diversions at one time or another."

I just stared at her, realising I could be just the latest in her list of *diversions*.

"It is a fallacy that people in the nineteenth century were less accepting of individual choices than they are now. Society has not always frowned on individual preferences."

Diversions? Preferences? I still couldn't think of a suitable reply, so I kissed her. She returned the kiss briefly, then lifted her hands to my shoulders.

"But right now, we need to assess how well my resonator is working." She pushed me away and bent to the apparatus on its little table.

As I worried that I'd upset her, she fiddled with the control knobs. She asked me to leave the building, come back, start up the ætheric coffee-maker, stop it, pass her the glass baton which she activated and several other tests to put the resonator through its paces. At one point, she removed the dial and adjusted something behind it. I couldn't understand any of it, but she seemed pleased and I began to relax and even started to enjoy assisting her in whatever small way I could. This was easier to cope with than the feelings she caused inside me.

Finally, she instructed me to set some coffee on to boil, while she tinkered with the instrument some more. As the sound of bubbling water filled her workshop, she sat back on the sofa.

"Enough, enough," she said. "We should have coffee, eat some lunch and then we will attempt to use the resonator to find out if The Professor has been anywhere near London recently."

"You think it's working alright?" I asked, surprised that we'd been so lucky with our first guess at the foil's construction.

"I believe so. It appears that our suppositions about the ætheric foil were correct, which suggests that the maker did not have to deviate from the simple rules governing the application of ætheric science to this mechanism. This is doubly advantageous, as I now infer that his overall processes may be sufficiently simple that a novice such as myself can reuse his ideas to assist in her own work."

I started the foil again, measured coffee into the little hopper and added water. I unwrapped the sandwiches and cakes I'd bought on one of my trips out of the resonator's range, placing them on two plates and crossing to the sofa. However busy we'd been, Chrystal refused to eat food on the go, insisting that we stop our work and eat from a plate. It was a novel experience for me. As a child, I'd usually eaten in front of the telly. And once I started work, I'd never taken time out for a meal unless I was on a date or something. We ate our sandwiches in companionable silence and then she poured the coffee.

"So who is this Professor we're looking for?" I prompted her.

"He is an old friend I have not seen for a year or more. I wish to consult with him about recent trends in the natural world that have been brought to my attention and I have no means of contacting him until I have built an ætheric transmission device."

"Can't you reach him by more normal means?" I asked.

"You're welcome to use my phone, if you haven't got one of your own. Or does he have an email address?"

"No, neither of those. He travels by means of an ætheric device and it is not possible to reach him by any 21st century means. I am hoping to build an ætheric apparatus that will signal to him my desire to talk."

"Ooo-kay. You'd better explain that to me in small steps!"

She swallowed her last small bite of cake and smiled at me. "The ætheric resonator can be tuned to respond to disturbances in the æther, allowing me to see whether an ætheric craft has passed by recently. Like looking for the wake left by an ocean-going vessel. Do you understand?"

I nodded.

"If I find that he has passed this way, then I hope to send out a signal to follow his wake, telling him I wish to converse with him. Is that sufficiently clear?"

I hesitated just a second before nodding again.

"So I need to build a device capable of sending that signal. Still clear? Think of the resonator as being like a radio – which can detect signals left by someone else and I need to construct one that can send a signal back."

"I get it. You're building a phone that works over this æther of yours!"

"Mmm, a little like that. Except I will not be able to hold a conversation over it, merely send a signal to let him know that I wish to do so. He will have to visit me to hold the discussion," she replied.

"And he will understand that from your message?"

"I will send an impulse that is focused on reaching him, with an indication that it is I who sent it."

"Like caller ringback?"

She looked confused and so I became the teacher for a while, explaining stuff I didn't know I knew about the way modern phones communicated with each other and how each one was uniquely defined by its number and you could find out who'd been trying to call you by using ringback. I talked until we'd both finished eating and emptied our coffee cups. Chrystal picked up the dirty pots, stacking them in the box that cleaned them.

"And so, on with the search," she said, opening the back of the resonator.

She pulled out the foils on their little stand, checking them closely and remounting one where it had curled a little since we'd fixed it in place. Satisfied, she reassembled the resonator and opened its control panel.

"Now, I set the resonator to detect the paths of ætheric craft," she turned the knobs as she spoke. "Then reduce its sensitivity to ignore background disturbances generated by the city. And finally increase its range to maximum like so..."

As she twisted the final knob, the needle reacted sharply, leaping to point to about two o'clock on the dial. One of the blue lights pulsed slowly, with a steady rhythm. Chrystal jumped up.

"Yes!" she half-shouted. "We have a trace."

"How do you know it was him?" I asked.

"Well, strictly I do not. But there are not many ætheric travellers who would pass so close to London, so it is likely to be The Professor. I will be able to make a more positive identification when my new apparatus is complete."

I had a dozen more questions I wanted to ask, but she looked so happy that I just had to hug her. And one thing led to another, as they say.

Chapter 14

In which the British Museum is revisited

Chrystal was up with the larks again the next morning, although I wouldn't know a lark if it bit me. You never got larks in the centre of London. But I just turned over and pulled the quilt over my head. From there, I could ignore the sounds of her showering, going out and coming back again. But at the smell of *pain au chocolat* warming in the little ætheric oven-thing and freshly-made coffee, I rolled out of bed and pushed past the curtain.

"Morning, Sleepyhead," she greeted me, without looking up as I made for the shower. "Did you remember that we need to dress in the Steampunk fashion this morning?"

I paused, turning to look at her and noticing the cream, balloon-sleeved blouse and bum-enhancing brown skirt she'd chosen to wear. I really liked the way that pad emphasised her curves - a *bustle*, she'd said it was called.

"I hadn't forgotten," I replied. "But I still think it's a daft risk to take. The place will be crawling with police - and someone might recognise us."

"And mayhap The Professor will have realised the significance of the theft and left a message for me there," she said.

I smiled at her and opened the door to the herb-scented bathroom.

The Museum looked just as it had last week, apart from the large piece of plywood fixed over a missing pane of glass in one door and the half a dozen uniformed police officers in a huddle inside the main doors. Chrystal steered us straight past them, waved cheerily at the young man behind the counter and pulled me into the first gallery. She seemed determined to educate her "niece" and kept up an outlandish commentary about the various *objet d'art* we passed. I might have enjoyed listening to her if I hadn't been so worried about being there and tense with the possibility that someone would recognise us from the CCTV footage and arrest us.

I was uncomfortable in my long black skirt. It was really more of a costume than proper clothing and I wasn't sure how well it would stand up to being worn all day. Chrystal had added a piece of her ætheric foil to Kerry's pin, so now it sat on my cape with a little tail of twisted metal sticking out below the top hat with its gears. Chrystal wore a different brooch, with dull silver wings behind the gear wheels and a similar tail of foil. She'd warned me to tell her if it began to untwist, as this would indicate that someone had left an ætheric sign at the Museum. I tried to ignore it, but the thought of something fastened to my clothing that might begin to move preyed on my mind and I kept finding myself touching it, just to make sure it hadn't started to do something unexpected. It was as if it had an insect hiding inside and she'd told me it might come to life at any moment.

I was fiddling with the pin as we entered a third gallery of exhibits when my worst fears were realised. A deep voice boomed out across the little hall,

"Wait there, please, Ladies!"

I grabbed for Chrystal's arm, but she was already walking towards the figure in its familiar bowler hat. Under his jacket he wore a dark waistcoat that glistened greenish-purple like oil on a wet road.

"Major Peterson, how good to see you again," she smiled, offering her gloved hand. He took it and bowed to her as I caught up, smiling as I arrived, with a slight inclination of his head towards me.

"Ladies, what a pleasure to see you again. I presume you

have heard about the terrible events of Monday night?"

"Why, yes, Major," said Chrystal, all wide eyed and looking as if ice wouldn't melt in her mouth. "Someone broke in and stole some of the exhibits, did they not?"

"Thankfully only one," he replied, patting her hand soothingly. "But it was in the very gallery where you and I spent those happy minutes chatting!"

"Good heavens," my *Aunt* replied. "Was it terribly valuable?"

"They say not," said the Major. "The papers say the Museum staff are at a loss to explain why that one piece was taken and nothing else. They've got those valuable Chinese statues here on loan, but that gallery wasn't even touched. Maybe someone knows what happened, but if they do, they're not admitting it."

"How very exciting. Shall we go visit the scene of the crime?"

The major shook his head. "I'm sorry, my dear. But the police have closed off the whole gallery with that dratted yellow tape of theirs. No members of the public are permitted to enter. I'm afraid your visit to that particular display will have to wait for another day."

I stopped listening as they continued to chat, staring at the people milling about, so I was startled when Chrystal raised her voice.

"Oh, but we would love to – wouldn't we, Samantha?"

I glared at her for the use of my full name, but remembered in time to keep up the act.

"I'm so sorry, Auntie, I wasn't listening."

"Major Peterson was just suggesting we join him for lunch," she explained. "I told him we would be very happy to do so."

"I know an excellent little restaurant of the Italian persuasion, if that would be of interest?" he suggested, leaning a little too close to her for my comfort. He wrapped a proprietorial arm around her waist as they both watched me, waiting for me to answer. As if I had any influence over either of these strange people!

"Um, yeah. Italian sounds great."

"Excellent. Then we're decided. If I may...?" The Major offered his right arm to Chrystal, who looped her left hand through and leaned against him. They turned as one and made for the main door, me trailing along behind. I noticed that, although he was slightly taller, her hat reached higher than his bowler.

In the lobby, the police had set themselves up at the door and were stopping everyone as they entered or left, checking IDs. I gulped and hung back. Chrystal turned and beckoned to me with her free arm.

"Come along, Samantha. We must not lose each other in this crowd." She grabbed my arm in that vice-like grip and pulled me in line with the two of them.

And then we were facing a portly policeman with sergeant's stripes on his shoulders. Chrystal leaned in towards the Major and yanked my arm to keep me close on the other side.

"Good morning, officer," said the Major. "How may we assist you?"

" 'Morning, Sir, Ladies. We're just taking some details from visitors to the Museum. Nothing serious," he answered.

"Oh, how exciting, Inspector," bubbled Chrystal. "Is this because of that break-in?"

"Indeed it is, Ma'am," he answered. "But it's only 'Sergeant' I'm afraid."

"Oh, surely that is an oversight," she simpered. Really, I could have punched her, but the Sergeant seemed as smitten with her as the Major.

He held out a clipboard and Chrystal released my arm to write her name and address in the relevant boxes, and the date of last Thursday, in the box labelled, "previous visit". She then passed the clipboard to the Major, who began to fill in his own details.

"And this is my niece, Sergeant," she gestured at me, but continued to smile at the poor policeman. "She is staying with me for a few weeks. Shall I enter her home address or mine?" She actually batted her eyelashes at him. I'd never seen anyone do this before and always thought it was just a figure of speech.

"Oh, I should just add her name to your own," he answered, passing her the clipboard again. I watched her tilt it away from the Major to write *Samantha Flint* beneath where she'd written what looked like *Chrystal Phillos* before passing it back.

"Do you think you will find the thieves in the Museum, Inspector?"

He didn't correct her this time, but smiled conspiratorially and leaned closer. "It's very common for criminals to visit the scene of their misdeeds, Ma'am. It's something the criminal mind seems to find irresistible. It's quite possible that we will find them here."

"Oh, how exciting. So we are under suspicion, Inspector?"

"I hardly think a lady like you needs to worry about that," he replied. "If I had my way we wouldn't even be troubling you for your details. We have good footage of the thieves and I would prefer that we only checked out the young men with the same height and build as those images. But the powers-that-be insist that we take details from everyone who visits the Museum. Waste of time and energy, but I didn't tell you that," he said with a wink his boss would have seen across the hall.

The Major was right to recommend the little Italian

restaurant he took us to. The maitre d' who conducted us to our table told us they were a family business, with his sisters working as waitresses and their mother in the kitchen. Whatever the setup, the food was delicious and we opened a second bottle of their rich, red wine as the three of us lingered over desserts and sweet nibbly things the waitress kept bringing. Chrystal continued to flirt with the Major, although she wasn't as blatant as she'd been when she'd sweet-talked the police sergeant into letting us pass without asking for proof of identity. They both sloshed back the wine like it was fruit juice, although my head was spinning pleasantly. After the main course, I excused myself to visit the loo, but I don't think either of them was paying any attention to me and I could have Can-Canned my way across the restaurant for all that they'd have noticed. As I came back, Chrystal was speaking and I hung back for a moment, shamelessly eavesdropping.

"... I would be delighted to spend the evening there."

"I'm flattered that a beautiful young woman like yourself would consider dancing with an old duffer like myself. Doesn't the difference in our ages bother you?"

I bit my tongue to prevent myself bursting out laughing, but Chrystal heard my suppressed splutter and turned my way.

"Ah, there you are, Samantha. The Major was just inviting me to a tea-dance next week."

"Next week?" I asked. "But I thought you were in a hurry to..."

She interrupted me before I could complete my sentence. "Oh, I'm sure it'll take us more than a week to contact The Professor. And why not take part in such an enjoyable event whilst we are waiting for him to come visit us?"

"I'm afraid it's strictly invitation only as they wish to keep the numbers even," elaborated the Major. "Or I would be delighted to take both of you ladies with me. Maybe next time?"

"Um, it doesn't sound like my sort of thing," I answered, settling back into my chair. "I didn't think people did that sort of thing nowadays."

The Major smiled at me. "You'd be surprised. There are even a number of young people getting interested in such old-fashioned activities. They tell me they call themselves Neo-Victorians and many of them know all the steps to the usual dances. Most elegant to watch!"

The waitress appeared behind Chrystal's shoulder as the Major was speaking and began setting out espresso cups and saucers with the tiniest shot of black coffee in the bottom.

"Is that why you dress like that, Major? Is your title part of your costume, too?" I asked.

"Oh, heavens, no. My rank is most definitely genuine – although my postings were in very different wars to those the Victorians would have known. But yes, I suppose I do dress a little anachronistically. After so many years in uniform, it's a pleasure to attire oneself in clothing from a Gentler era."

Another person pronouncing *gentle* in that odd way.

"Gentler? Isn't that an odd choice of word for a military man?"

"Oh, not in the modern way. I mean gentle in the sense of a gentleman. There are too few people nowadays who behave as if manners are important – which is one reason I enjoy the company of the young people who attend these tea dances. They look to us elders with respect and speak with far greater courtesy than most people in this day and age."

"I believe the word is derived from *Gentile* – meaning a non-Jew. A distinction which was considered important back in Shakespeare's day," interjected Chrystal.

The Major beamed at her as if she were the most impressive person he'd ever met.

"Precisely. Although I'm sure no-one means it in that awful anti-Semitic way anymore. Mr Shakespeare was particularly harsh on Shylock, after all," he said.

On the way home, I struggled to keep up with Chrystal and her long strides again. She seemed very happy with our day's work.

"So you're going on a date with the Major?" I asked.

"Apparently so," she answered, slowing her pace to something I could match without running. "He is *such* a dear. So rare to find someone with good manners in the 21st Century."

"Um, yes. He's very polite. But you're actually going dancing with him?"

"And why not? I find his company pleasant and it will be good to attend such a dance again – it has been many years since I was invited to such a soiree."

"But, I mean – well, he's not really your type, is he?"

She stopped walking and turned to face me.

"Ah, the green-eyed monster roars. Is it that you mind my dallying with him?"

"Well, no. I mean, we're hardly married or anything. But I thought you weren't interested in men..."

"Ah, I see. My dear Samantha, men can be just as much fun as ladies. They are different, as I'm sure you are aware - but they have their attractions, none the less. And I have agreed to attend a tea-dance with him, nothing more than that."

"And he must be at least sixty!" I said.

"Fifty-six, he tells me. He retired on an army pension some three years ago. And I believe you heard me telling him I didn't mind the age difference!"

I knew she was trying to needle me, but I couldn't help laughing out loud at the memory. The Major really didn't know what he was dealing with – he was taking a real Victorian to a dance organised by people whose great-grandparents hadn't even been alive when she first went to a *tea dance*. I found myself almost wishing I could be a fly on the wall when she met these so-called Neo-Victorians.

Chapter 15

In which Chrystal spends time with Major Peterson

I watched Chrystal preparing for the dance, fascinated by the time she spent over her appearance. Despite her impractical style of clothes, she could dress and fasten up her hair in the same time it took me to pull on my jeans and slap on a little make-up. But today, she spent twice as long in the shower and brushed her hair one hundred times – counting under her breath as she did so. She opened a drawer and took a long corset from the tissue paper it'd been stored in, it covered her tits and hid the Chrystal from view, unless you knew where to look for it peeking out of the shadow of her cleavage. Then she slipped on a pair of real silk stockings, shaped like her long legs and with a seam running up the back. I was fascinated and more than a little jealous that she was going to so much trouble for a man. Then she opened a wardrobe she hadn't used before and pulled out a stunning dress – all blue taffeta and frills. It even had one of those sexy bustle-pads built-in. I was still amazed at how this style didn't make her look fat, but somehow emphasised her slim figure. I mused on how ridiculous I'd look in the same sort of get-up as she opened a huge round box and took out a spectacular hat, with blue-dyed feathers flopping over one side and a trailing length of lace at the back. She pinned it in place and struck a pose.

"Well, my dear. What do you think?"

"I think you're beautiful!" I said.

"Thank you," she curtsied to me. "Do you think this outfit will suffice for the Major's Neo-Victorians?"

"I think you're going to blow them away!"

At that moment, I heard a diesel engine pull up outside and the taxi driver honk once to let us know he'd arrived.

"Your chariot awaits, my lady," I said, only slightly tongue-in-cheek.

She picked up a bag that looked like the same material as her dress, curtsied again and let herself out of the workshop. I followed her onto the landing and watch her lift her skirt to one side to go down the stairs. I stared down the steps long after the taxi had left, thinking that the Major was a very lucky man.

I walked back to my bedsit to collect some clothes and pay Tony this week's rent. He commented that I didn't seem to be sleeping there much and made several leery comments about me looking a lot happier now I'd "finally found a good man". I evaded his questions and left as quickly as I could. On the way back to Chrystal's, I stopped at the corner shop to buy a notebook. Chrystal had shown me how to read the ætheric resonator, at least as far as I needed to be able to watch for ætheric ships and I wanted to write it all down before I forgot any of it. The machine wasn't difficult to use, but Chrystal seemed to think that she only had to explain something once. My teachers used to complain I was slow at picking things up, and I'd rather keep a record of what she'd told me than face her criticism when I forgot some little detail that had come up days earlier.

Back at Chrystal's place, I threw my bag onto the sofa, set the coffee maker to boil and looked for a pen. By the time the coffee was ready I'd found half a dozen pencils around the room and eventually discovered a freebie bank-biro in the bottom of my handbag. I poured my cuppa and opened the notebook.

On the first page I drew a picture of the front of the resonator, carefully labelled with Chrystal's names for the various parts. I followed this with a diagram of the open back and a quick sketch with a small mark to remind me how to undo it. Then I spent a few pages writing down the various bits and pieces Chrystal had already told me. I was amazed at how much there was – partly because I hadn't realised the number of different things she'd shown me, but more surprised that I could remember so much of it.

Having written everything I could remember, I opened the resonator to check I'd remembered it all correctly. I worked through the startup routine and set it to monitor the æther for signals. And got a reading. At first I thought I'd made a mistake and worked through my instructions again, but the blue lights still flickered at me in the way that meant they'd found a wake. I fiddled the knobs to tune it, guessing at the right way to do it as I'd never seen this kind of reading before.

"Where's Chrystal when I need her?" I muttered, desperately trying to get a stable reading. For a moment two lights stayed bright, the middle one just flickering slightly. Then the outer two faded to nothing. A sudden inspiration made me scribble a note of the knobs' positions before I moved them again, but I'd lost the signal for good.

Eventually I gave up searching.

I worked through the other tricks Chrystal had shown me, checking my notes were good. I broke off when it was too dark to read and turned the lights on. I checked the skeleton clock - it was well after ten o'clock. I'd expected Chrystal to be home by now and wondered whether to wait up for her. I brewed some tea and decided I might as well get myself some food. Maybe she'd had enough to eat in the afternoon. Did a tea dance include food? Or maybe she'd gone out for a meal with the Major. Ah well, we could fix something for her when she got in, if she came home hungry.

I wound the shower up while my dinner was cooking and tidied the room a little, but didn't touch anything on the workshop bench. I didn't know what half of the tools were for and I didn't want to find myself getting sucked through the æther into nowhere.

Opening a bottle of wine to have a glass with my supper, I settled on the sofa so I could watch the ætheric resonator while I ate. I'd turned the controls back to the settings where I'd seen the odd readings, just in case.

I finished the first glass of wine and poured another. Chrystal was very late!

I woke when a hand shook my shoulder. Startled, I realised it was Chrystal leaning over me. I must have dozed off on the sofa. Then I noticed the daylight streaming in through the windows.

"It's morning – I've slept on the sofa!" Then another connection. "You've been out all night!"

"Well, yes," she said. She was still wearing that amazing blue gown and her hair was fastened up under her hat.

"The Major is most," she paused. "Sociable."

"You didn't!" I exclaimed. In answer, she just smiled and took off her hat, placing it carefully in its box. I got up to help her with the fastenings of her dress.

"You've been with him all night?"

"Please, Samantha. A gentlewoman should never ask such questions," she reprimanded gently. But she was grinning as she spoke.

"But he's..." I paused. "I mean, isn't he too..."

"Old? Interestingly enough, that was his main objection, too. I had to reassure him several times that I was not worried about our respective ages."

"Did you tell him?"

Her gown hanging in the wardrobe and her discarded corset on the chair, she turned to look at me. "Did I tell him that I am more than three times his age? No, of course not."

"And he didn't ask why you had a Chrystal for a heart, either?"

She fixed me with a pretend-stern look.

"Our good Major was quite happy to turn off the lights at my request. And he seemed to positively like the fact that I kept my underwear on. If he happened to notice anything that felt odd, he was far too much the gentleman to offer comment," she said.

With a last smile, she wrapped her bath robe round herself and disappeared into the bathroom.

I was in the shower myself before I remembered the readings I'd seen on the resonator. I rinsed my hair out hurriedly and dashed into the workshop.

Chrystal was dressed in a fresh blouse and brown trousers, her usual *working garb* as she called it. Her hair hung like a wet curtain down her back as she measured coffee into the jug.

"I forgot to mention – we got a reading on the resonator. A new one. Last night!" I blurted.

"Really?" She stopped for a moment. "Did you make a record of it?"

I nodded, grabbing my notebook to show her.

"It was only there for a moment – less than a minute, I think. But that's what the lights showed and that's where the knobs were set."

She read my scribbled notes then looked at me and nodded. "Excellent. This looks like The Professor's signal, as we hoped. So he must have passed close by last night. At what time did you observe this signal?"

"Um, it was a couple of hours after you'd gone. Maybe seven o'clock..." I hesitated. "I'm sorry – I was so keen to write the readings down I forgot to check the clock."

"Not to worry," she soothed. "I believe I can make a recording device for the resonator, which will record all such incidents over a period of time. So long as we know we can observe his passing, then we can hurry on with building our new signalling device."

She looked up from the resonator. "That was quick thinking on your part. Very well done!"

I felt the blush moving up my face and quickly said, "Thank you. So when can we start work on this signalling contraption?"

"Very soon. I have already ordered a cabinet from a carpenter and I will set something up to record readings on the resonator today and you can cut out the new foils ready for the transmitting machine."

I kept my groan inside, trying to be grateful that I was involved in this weird science at all.

"Where do I start?" I asked.

"We already have the component foils, so you need to meld the three together using the baton and then produce a new set of shapes for which I will give you the templates," she said. "If you smooth out the foils, I will show you how to operate the glass-wand."

Chapter 16

In which a message is sent

I found working with Chrystal to be far more enjoyable than science lessons at school. It wasn't just that this whole technology seemed so weird – Chrystal was a really good teacher. Although she expected me to remember everything she'd told me, without reminders, she had a way of explaining that somehow made it easier for me to absorb what she'd said.

I was busy smoothing foils and cutting out shapes while she made a wood and wire stand that connected several pencils to the resonator. By the time I'd finished, Chrystal had a roll of paper feeding slowly underneath it and lines tracing along the paper. I watched, fascinated, as the lights flickered and the lines moved in step with them. She clicked one of the knobs and another pencil skipped to one side, leaving a sharp corner in the line it was tracing.

"Why not biros?" I asked, shattering the silence.

"I am sorry?"

"Why do you use pencils? You'll have to keep sharpening the pencils, so doesn't it make sense to use cheap biros?"

"Ballpoint pens? I do not like them. I have always found pencils to be more reliable. Sharpening is hardly a significant inconvenience. It is easy to see when they are close to running out and they never leave ink blots on the paper."

I shrugged. It seemed backwards to me, but I wasn't about to argue.

"So do we just leave this running?" I asked.

"For now. It is not actually essential, but it will help if I can see the trace left in the æther for myself. Hopefully it will reassure me that I am building the correct type of *sender* to reach The Professor."

We saw three of what Chrystal called "traces" in the week it took us to build the new transmitter. Much to my surprise, I could see differences between the lines on the paper, although I couldn't understand her explanation that none of them were the right one.

The foil arrangement inside the new, temporary, box looked quite different to the original. Although I knew the foil was exactly the same as we'd used before, it looked shinier. The new pieces were somewhat larger and had to be twisted to fit into their wire frame. She connected several control knobs, a switch and then a pair of metal rods inside the top of the case, where they would sit above the foils as they turned. She'd been making something out of bits of an old clock and I'd worked out that its frame would slide neatly onto the rods inside. Eventually she declared that we were ready to try out the transmitter. I gave up paying close attention when I realised there was nothing to see except Chrystal bending over the box, making tiny adjustments. When she finally assembled the whole thing, I wandered over to see if it was ready to use. She was closing one eye as she held the clockwork mechanism in front of the other, tilting it from side to side.

"Well, I think, it's all lined up," she said as I approached.

"How does it work?"

"Like this," she produced a metal key and used it to turn a rod sticking up in the centre, which tightened a coil of flat wire.

"Once the spring is fully wound, it should have sufficient energy to send the signal a few times. These chime wheels hold the pattern of pulses I wish to send," she pointed at a pair of oddly-shaped metal discs fixed on top of her apparatus by a rod through their centres. "And when I release the catch the device sends the signal. One moment."

She pulled a metal tray towards her and lifted the little

assembly onto it. I noticed a metal rod sticking out the bottom, which stopped the device from standing properly. Chrystal checked that this was touching the tray and flicked a catch which opened and the device whirred into life, tapping the rod loudly against the tray. It made a pattern of noises, some longer and the last ones a staccato burst of rattles.

"So, how does that reach The Professor?"

"Well, this rod will disturb the foil assembly inside the sender, rather than striking this tray," she gestured. "And what you hear as sound will travel along the æther – following the ripples left by his æther transport passing by."

"And how does he know it's from you?" I wondered.

"You have heard of the Morse code?" I nodded and she went on, "Well, according to Mr Morse's system, the pattern we send is the first two letters of my name – C and H. If you listen, you can hear it as long-short-long-short and then four short."

She flicked the catch again and the same pattern of rattles sounded.

"And that's enough to tell The Professor to come here and talk to you?"

"It is sufficient to communicate that it is I who is signalling him," she said. "He will then trace the signal back to this point."

"What – to this room?" I asked.

"Not quite. But it will bring him to this part of London. He knows of this building and will understand that this is where he can find me."

I stared at the little clockwork gadget with a new respect. Both it and the transmitter had been so simple to construct, but it was a whole new technology I'd never heard of before. And I didn't think anyone else had, either.

"Why aren't more people using this system? I mean, it seems so simple and it's not costing you anything like a phone would."

"Ah, but it is simple," she explained. "This little device will do no more than send my two little letters. To hold a conversation would need a much more sophisticated assembly than I can manufacture. This is less useful than a telegraph system would be and much harder to direct. In many ways, I can only make use of the æther in this way because no-one else is sending signals – if there were more it would be too, um, noisy for anyone to make sense of it."

I nodded.

"But surely there must be some way to direct your signal? Like dialling a phone number?"

"I believe it can be done, but you will need to ask The Professor how it may be achieved," she said.

"Now," she continued. "Why do you not think about moving in?"

"Sorry?" My stomach knotted up and my mouth was suddenly dry. Was she saying what I thought she was saying? Surely I'd misunderstood her again, got the wrong idea from the strange way she spoke.

"Well, it does seem a little ridiculous, you paying rental for a lodging you are not using," she elaborated. "I could open one of the other rooms, to give us more space to live in."

"Oh, er, well," I stammered. "Yes, of course I could. Um – is there a proper kitchen anywhere? It would be nice to have somewhere to cook again."

She looked taken aback.

"I'm sorry," I said. "I didn't mean to sound critical. But I'd like to prepare a proper meal occasionally. Instead of just living on take-outs and packaged food."

"Well, of course. If that would make you happy. The other room on this floor also has water piped in, although you would have to make do with ætheric heating, as there is no electricity connected here. Nor gas pipes, either," she answered.

"Um, fine. If you show me how to use it." I'd seen the

kettle-thing, of course. And the box that mysteriously washed our plates without water, but there was only the little oven-thing that warmed things like croissants - it wasn't really big enough to cook properly. And I wasn't sure how hot it could get. I wondered briefly how I'd charge my toothbrush if I moved in here, or how my friends would contact me if my phone never worked because of her ætheric devices. But Chrystal seemed to manage somehow and no-one ever called me anyway.

"We can do better than that," she beamed. "You must help me build a device – which will assist with your education about the æther as a source of power!"

Much to my surprise, I found I liked the idea of further lessons about the way Chrystal harnessed this invisible force to achieve things I would have thought impossible. My physics teacher would have been shocked.

"So what do we do now?" I asked.

"We wait for The Professor's signal again and we send my little signature into the æther in his wake. Here, this is the control," she said, indicating the switch on the outside of her transmitter.

"When the pencils trace the pattern I have drawn on here, it indicates a ship passing through the æther and we have only to send the signal after it to alert him to our desire to speak with him."

"Do we have to do it immediately?"

"No, not really. The wake will remain for at least a few hours – unless another ship cuts across it. Of course, the longer we delay, the longer it will take for him to receive our communication – and the greater the possibility that he will no longer be travelling in that direction. But all we can do is to send and hope that he hears us."

We spent the afternoon cleaning the room across from Chrystal's workshop. This had taps and worktops around the sink, so it would be simple enough to establish a kitchen in there. Next we carried the dining table from her workshop and setup a seating area on the other side of the room using the sofa and a couple of armchairs that were already in this new room. I couldn't get my head around the idea that Chrystal owned the whole building but chose to work and live in one cramped room. There were a couple of heavy old cupboards, which I cleaned thoroughly and we struggled to move into position. I'm fairly sure they didn't come from Ikea. The flowery pattern on the wallpaper had faded to just a hint of shapes, except where it had been covered by cupboards. I could see dark red roses with green swirls that might have been stems, or maybe they were meant to be ivy. I was going to have to suggest that Chrystal pay for some decorators - or did she have some magical ætheric trick for re-papering a room?

The workshop looked a lot bigger without the sofa and Chrystal was deciding what else to move when the pencils attached to the resonator started to move. We both stood and stared as they traced out the exact pattern Chrystal had told me to expect.

I broke the silence. "Is that him?"

"It is likely," she replied.

"But you don't know?"

"I do not have sufficient knowledge to identify a particular transporter from the trace it leaves on the æther."

"So how do we know?"

She grinned and flicked the switch I'd come to think of as the "SEND" key on the sender in its temporary case. "We wait for him to answer!"

I stood and stared at the paper feeding through the resonator for several more minutes, but Chrystal returned to her workbench and began sorting through a pile of stuff left over from our work, placing tools back in drawers and generally tidying. She looked busy, but she kept glancing at the resonator when she thought I wasn't looking. I was pleased to see her on edge – I had thought it was just me. But after a while I found myself trying to watch her without being obvious about it and went to continue my cleaning in the other room to ease the tension.

Chapter 17

In which a pirate is given a target

The screen in the wooden bureau was divided into four separate scans. Two showed the intermittent blips and flickers of ætheric activity, another looked like a geological scan of a meandering river's course. The fourth showed a satellite's-eye view of central London, sprawling roads interspersed with occasional green parks.

Farran leant in to get a better look and jabbed at the satellite view.

"Somewhere in this area?" he asked.

The seated figure nodded. "Yes. The scan shows only two life forms in the vicinity. Our informant says they are both women." Even seated, he was as tall as the man in pirate clothes.

"Women?" Farran looked up. "That makes things even more interesting."

"Do not be so hasty. We have crossed swords with one of them before. She proved to be quite resourceful when we had her cornered."

"Yeah," said Farran with a leer. "I know what you mean."

"I am not sure that you do, pirate. But we need to know what they are doing. And what they know. Remember that as it is more important than you getting to play with them, Farran."

The pirate's face betrayed his frustration.

"Yes, Your Eminence," he muttered.

"Kill the women if you have the chance, but it is more important to find out what they know. There may be others who would take their place if they were removed."

Farran nodded.

"And make it look like a human crime. A robbery or something. Dress in common human clothes and be careful not to arouse suspicions," hissed the hooded figure, his head moving oddly under its cowl, darting from side to side.

"So no ætherics?"

He turned his chair to face the pirate.

"You may take a personal transporter, charged for one trip. This will allow you to leave the scene without interference once you have completed your mission. And wafers for two days to allow you time to observe before you pounce."

"And armaments?"

The hooded head turned slowly from side to side.

"No ætheric armament. Use a weapon that will not be remarkable to the human constables. And be sure to leave nothing behind."

Chapter 18

In which a sailor visits

I don't know why I expected an immediate response, but I was disappointed that the next few days passed without an answer to our message. I asked Chrystal how long she thought it would take for The Professor to contact us, but she just shrugged.

"He may well be busy about his own business. If so, it could be a week or two before he is able to respond."

"But I thought you were in a hurry," I said.

"It is true that we have a deadline," she answered without looking up from her bench. "But there is nothing we can do except wait. And hope that we are not too late. Wait and hope."

And with that I had to be content.

I found myself spending more time in Chrystal's apartment than back at my bedsit. She was fascinating company, once you got used to her strangeness. And gradually, she was thawing - becoming less distant during the day as well as our intimacies at night. She asked me to give her blood for her heart again and showed me the correct way to use the brass syringe in its little box and I found it an oddly erotic feeling - to give her my blood in this way.

As the days ticked by, I stopped watching the resonator and threw myself into the job of turning Chrystal's rooms into more of a home. Although by then I knew she owned the whole building, she still referred to the few rooms we were living in as her "lodgings" and wouldn't even consider opening up any more. She also insisted on keeping the bed in its alcove off the workshop, so we slept in that room, but cooked, ate and relaxed in the second. It seemed odd to me, but it worked okay. And the little cooker she'd dug out of a cupboard worked well, although controlling its ætheric heating properties seemed more of an art than a science. I'd never been much of a homemaker, which was probably a good thing, because Chrystal wouldn't hear of doing anything in a modern way unless I could give her a very good reason. And that meant her interpretation of a good idea, not mine!

I left the house one afternoon, after Chrystal had gone to the jewellers to collect some new foils we'd ordered. I carried a shopping bag and had nothing more on my mind than fetching a few supplies and preparing something nice for our dinner. So I wasn't expecting the man who grabbed hold of my arm as I stepped onto the pavement.

"And who might you be?" he asked.

"Oh, um, I'm staying here," I answered.

He looked me up and down and looked unimpressed with what he saw. In return I gave his outfit the once-over: a half-undone, baggy-sleeved shirt under a black waistcoat with a chain hanging from its pocket. His trousers were tucked into high boots and he seemed to be wearing some sort of holster on the side away from me. There was a denim jacket tied around his neck like a schoolboy's jumper. He had a gold-coloured chain round his neck and I caught a glimpse of something shiny against his chest. I'd seen Steampunks dressed as pirates many times before, but none as convincingly *rough* as this one.

"Are you the mistress of the house?"

"Am I...?" I asked. And then the penny dropped. "Are you The Professor? Did you answer Chrystal's call?"

"Crystal? Was that who sent it? I fear her message was very brief. It has taken me several days to locate this house in search of her," he replied.

There was something funny about his voice. He had an odd way of speaking, like Chrystal, but it didn't seem as natural to him. An odd accent, too – a bit like Australian, only not quite.

Looking closer, I could see that he hadn't shaved for a few days and smelt as if he hadn't taken a shower, either. Either he was a proper absent-minded Professor or he took his costume-persona very seriously. And he'd pronounced her name wrongly, which seemed odd, if he was her friend.

"I'm afraid Chrystal is out at the moment," I said, slightly emphasising the proper pronunciation.

"That is a shame," he answered. "Perhaps I could come in and wait for her?"

"Oh, of course. I should have offered. Can I make you a cuppa in the meantime?"

I unlocked the door and held it open for him. "It's on the first floor – door on your left," I explained as I removed the key and then followed him up into the workshop.

"She'll be back soon," I told him. "Meanwhile – tea or coffee? We've got enough milk for one each - I was just on my way to buy more."

"Tea, black," he answered.

I poured water into the little metal pot Chrystal used to boil water, started the ætheric heater and turned round to see him peering at the device Chrystal had built to send for him.

"I guess that's pretty basic stuff to you, Professor?" I asked.

He didn't respond for a moment, then his head snapped up.

"Oh, yes. Very basic indeed. I can't even be sure what it does...?"

"It's what Chrystal calls her *sender*. That's what we used to contact you. After we'd spotted your wake with the ætheric resonator."

He was examining the cabinet and twisted the clasp to remove the back.

"She has been teaching you the means of operation?"

"Well, a little. I'm afraid I was never very good at science," I answered, watching him poking at the foils. "They're mounted on a little stand – here."

I reached into the cabinet and snapped the foil holder out of its clip, handing it to him. He spun it briefly, then spread out one of the foils to see its shape.

"And the signal...?"

I picked the cabinet up and slid Chrystal's clockwork device out. It was fully wound, so I pressed the lever and its familiar rattle played out.

"Most ingenious," said The Professor slowly. "You have been a clever student."

"Oh, but I didn't build it. It's all Chrystal's work, really."

"All of it? I'm sure you must have done some of the work," he said, looking at me a bit like a cat watching a mouse.

Feeling a little uncomfortable, I didn't answer him. Instead, I ducked past, heading for the water pot which was bubbling and busied myself with pouring boiling water onto the tea leaves in the little teapot whilst watching him out of the corner of my eye. He was examining Chrystal's sender closely, replacing the foils and pushing their stand to make it turn. Even though he was a friend of Chrystal's, I really didn't like him. There was something predatory about the way he looked at me. And he seemed very interested in what she'd described as a very basic ætheric device – given that he was a Professor and all. I jumped at a sudden noise, then realised it was just the familiar sound of Chrystal's signal. He must have pressed the *send* lever.

"And you wind it how...?" He held the little device out. I put our teas down on the table and took it from him, picking up the key at the same time. A few turns and it *clunked* firmly.

"That's fully wound. It's enough to send the pattern twice," I explained.

"And what did you use to manufacture the foils?"

"Um, it's in three layers, five different elements in total. But I can't remember what they were..." I hesitated, glancing toward my notebook and wondering if he expected me to look it up in my notes.

A strange expression crossed his face, but I heard Chrystal's key in the lock downstairs before he could answer.

"Here she is," I said, relieved. I didn't like being alone with this Professor friend of hers, however much he might know about ætheric science.

He surprised me by coming round the table and grabbing my pony tail in his left hand. He yanked it hard enough to hurt, pressed something sharp against my throat and hissed,

"Not a peep out of you, okay?"

I didn't answer. I was too afraid to speak and daren't nod because I didn't know what he was holding against my windpipe.

The door opened and Chrystal stepped in, carrying the artist's folder we used to transport foils. Her smile dropped as she took in the situation.

"Who?" she asked.

I tried to answer, "The Pro-," but he increased the pressure at my throat ever so slightly and I stopped.

"And you are the mistress of the house?" he said.

Chrystal put down her folder and stepped towards us, taking off her gloves.

"Stop there!" he ordered and she did so.

"I repeat – who are you, Sir? And why are you threatening my niece?"

"Who am I?" he repeated, mimicking her voice. "I'm just a shadow in the night. And I'm just about to leave and take that clever little box with me."

Chrystal looked worried and I could feel myself beginning to panic inside.

"You will have to release my niece to take the sender," said Chrystal and I realised she'd called me her niece again. Was she trying to tell me she had a plan? I couldn't think of any other reason to call me that. Unless she wanted me to think of something, like I did in the Museum gallery. Oh, hell! My brain was too busy running round in panicked circles to come up with an idea.

"I think not," he answered and began to move to the side, forcing me around the table with him.

"Pick it up," he ordered me as we reached the sender. When I hesitated, he pressed on my throat and I reached for the flimsy wooden box, trying to cradle its various attachments so nothing would break off. I thought about hitting him with it, but there was no way I could twist round and hurt him quickly enough to avoid him using his weapon. Together, he edged the two of us forward, keeping the pull on my hair strong enough to bend me backwards so we moved crabwise as he turned to keep Chrystal in his view. When we neared the end of the workbench, she lunged forward, knocking his hands away from me with a clank and pulling me past her. I felt The Professor stumble as I fell forward, then heard him yelp. I spun around and realised Chrystal had hold of his crotch, his knife was on the floor and he was trying to beat her arm away.

After a moment, he stopped struggling and just stared at her, his face purple and his eyes full of hatred.

"That is better," she said calmly. "What is your name, pirate?"

He glared at her, then blanched. Chrystal met his gaze, her dark eyes boring into him and I couldn't even imagine what her right hand was doing to him.

"F-Farran," he stuttered eventually.

"Then F-Farran, you are going to leave my home and never come back. Is that clear?"

He nodded.

"And you will not attempt any further mischief against either of us. Agreed?"

He nodded again.

She looked at me over her shoulder, as I stood clutching the sender.

"Now, I am going to let go and you will leave this building immediately."

This time he was nodding before she'd even finished speaking.

Chrystal let go and he walked gingerly towards the door. We heard him on the stairs and Chrystal came towards me, looking concerned.

"Your neck..." she began.

I noticed something was missing from the workbench.

"My notebook!"

Chrystal was out of the door and down the stairs in an instant. But I caught up with her just outside, where she'd stopped in the street.

"Can you smell that?" she asked.

I sniffed and realised there was an odd, metallic smell in the air. Kind of coppery, like blood.

"He must have some means of ætheric transportation," she said. "We will not catch him now."

She led me back into the house.

"That wasn't your Professor friend, was it?" I asked, feeling stupid.

"No," she shook her head. "I do not know who that was – some ruffian who has acquired a way to traverse the æther."

"I thought he seemed interested in what we'd done – I should have realised it wasn't how a Professor who's an expert..." I answered, feeling very stupid at being taken for a fool.

"That was your notebook of ætheric studies?" she asked as we locked the door behind us.

"Yes. It had everything in it – the foil shapes, the metals, everything."

"You can rewrite it – I will assist," she said.

"But now he knows everything you told me!"

She smiled. "You used a ballpoint to write in your book, did you not?"

"Um, yes. Of course."

"So our pirate will learn something else about the æther today."

I just stared at her.

"You see, passing through the æther affects many materials in ways that people may not expect. And he will soon learn that it distorts handwriting written with a ballpoint pen. By the time he reaches his destination, your notebook will be unreadable."

"What? But how?"

"I do not fully understand. I know the modern form of ink remains on the surface of paper and so travels differently through the æther, whereas pencil marks become one with the page and travel intact."

"But... why can't he just trace the marks in the page? Where the pen's left a dent?"

By now she was grinning. "Of course he could do that, but it would be inaccurate and require patience. I do not think he is a patient man!"

She bent to pick up the knife where it had fallen.

"Here – this is your knife now. May it bring you better fortune than its previous owner."

I took it gingerly, realising the blood on it was my own.

"I have a small collection of weapons I was nearly killed with," she continued. "I believe that you have begun to collect them for yourself."

She was pushing me gently towards the sofa, where I sat as the adrenalin of the last few minutes caught up with me.

"I will make you some tea in a moment. First of all, allow me to dress your battle-wound."

"It's nothing," I muttered, but she fetched the first aid box and I couldn't be bothered to argue as she washed the scratch and applied a dressing. By the time she'd finished bandaging my neck, I was trembling with shock.

Chapter 19

In which a dog is surprised and knowledge is lost in the rain

The young woman jogged onto the grass to overtake an elderly couple walking arm-in-arm ahead of her, the Dalmatian at the other end of the leash keeping pace easily. White wires trailing from the jogger's ears to her breast pocket may have explained why she didn't react to the odd sounds just off the path, but she stopped quickly enough when the leash pulled her arm back. Her dog was growling at a section of the undergrowth, hairs along his back standing on end. After a few unsuccessful tugs, his owner swore softly and pulled her earphones out.

"What is it, Magus?" she asked the dog.

In response, he stepped towards a particular bush, still snarling.

"Is there someone there?" she called and moved in for a closer look.

The man that stood up in front of her was dressed oddly, like someone who didn't understand how clothes worked together, but she only had the briefest moment to look at him before he ran past, knocking her over as he fled the park. Her dog barked wildly, straining at the leash she clung to desperately as she pulled herself back to her feet. She stared after the direction the man had run in, but there was no-one in sight.

Farran stumbled through the trees, wanting their cover but unable to push through. The last thing he needed was a stupid human jogger asking awkward questions. Once he was sure he'd lost her, he leant against a tree to get his breath back. He pulled Sam's notebook out from inside his jacket and opened it at random. The whole page was covered in meaningless blue squiggles. Cursing, he opened it at a different point, only to find more unreadable lines. Frantically he flicked through the entire notebook. At one point there was a pencil drawing of something that looked a little like a circuit diagram, but the rest of it was simply random inky markings. He threw the notebook on the ground and kicked it away. Somehow those women must have swapped this useless book for the real notes.

This gave him a problem. Returning to his master to admit he'd failed to either kill the women, find out what they knew or to take their ætheric technology from them wasn't an option. He knew what happened to those who failed the man in the dragon-skin cloak.

There was nothing else for it. Farran would have to go back to that house and try again. Before anyone realised he'd made a mistake.

It was starting to rain - a thin, miserable, drizzle. Farran straightened his jacket and slipped back onto the path, carefully checking that no more joggers were likely to see him there. He opened a pouch on his belt, sheltered it in his hand as he pulled out a small, pinkish wafer and ate it. He closed his eyes briefly as a shudder passed through his body, then he turned and ran for shelter in an Underground station.

The notebook lay open on the ground, its pages absorbing the London rain.

Chapter 20

In which Sam recovers and meets a Welshman

I don't actually remember much of that evening. I kind of fell apart after the shock of being in a fight. And realising that I could have died. I do remember Chrystal tending my wound and I think I was leaning on her by the time she'd finished. I don't remember going to bed, getting undressed or anything like that. But I woke to the familiar smell of coffee brewing and heard her moving about the workshop. I closed my eyes again, wondering if I could use the night's scare as an excuse to stay in bed. Then I realised Chrystal was talking to someone – and the voice answering was a man. They didn't sound like they were arguing, but I couldn't laze about while she might be in trouble. I pulled her robe over my head and peeped round the curtain.

Chrystal had her back to me and was listening to a short man stood on the other side of the workbench. He wore dark trousers and a long black jacket over a mustard-yellow waistcoat and gestured as if he was describing something, but his voice was too low for me to hear any words.

As I stepped into the room, he looked up and smiled.

"And you must be Sam-of-the-boy's-name," he said. "I'm Rhys Bevan ap Gwilim and I'm always happy to meet a friend of Chrystal's."

"Um, pleased to meet you, too," I answered.

"The Professor was just explaining how our friend with the knife was able to track us here," said Chrystal.

"I can assure you he's no friend of mine, either. And *please* call me Rhys," he said.

"You know who he is, then?" I asked.

"No, but I know the type. They call themselves pirates – but that's just their romantic view of themselves. There's nothing romantic about thieves."

I felt myself starting to flush and hurriedly asked,

"But he travelled through the æther to get here, didn't he?"

"No-oo, not through. I presume he uses a device that allows him to shortcut the usual three dimensions, but it's different to actually travelling the æther itself," he replied.

"It sounds the same to me," I said.

Chrystal interrupted him before he could reply.

"Perhaps we should reserve the explanations until after brunch? Sam – the shower is fully wound for you."

Clean, dressed and full of food Chrystal must have fetched from the deli, I sat on the sofa. The Professor - Rhys - smiled at me and I asked him something that had come to mind while I was in the shower.

"So if that pirate doesn't actually travel through the æther, how come Chrystal says my notebook won't be any use to him?"

"We refer to such travel as *through the æther* because it's the most sensible way to say it. While all you're doing is using the æther to connect two places. But that's enough to break the association between paper and ink from a biro."

I probably looked as confused as I felt. He sat next to me, opened a notebook and began to draw a diagram.

"Let's say you're a spider, Sam," he began, drawing a circle with eight legs.

"And say you want to get to a new leaf on a different plant." The spider now had a leaf under her feet and a second one just out of her reach.

"Now, you could just climb down to the ground and across to the new plant. But that would take too long," he continued.

"And there may be creatures on the ground that would enjoy a tasty spider for lunch," interrupted Chrystal, who was fiddling with something on her workbench and not watching the explanation.

"Yes, indeed," commented The Professor, unfazed. "So instead of going the long way round, you spin a length of web, throw it out and bring the other leaf closer so you can step onto it."

He folded the page, bringing the other leaf to touch the first and mimed his spider stepping from one to the other.

"Okay," I said. "I can see that, so...?"

He smiled. "So I have a machine that's like the spider's web. I can throw it through the æther to bring another place closer to this one and just step between them."

I struggled with this idea. "So you move two places together? Why doesn't anyone else notice?"

"Because they're only touching if you look at them through the æther. I'm not affecting the first three dimensions at all."

"Um," I said.

"Just imagine I'm folding three-dimensional space through a fourth dimension. Like you'd fold a two dimensional object through a third when you crease a piece of paper," he said.

"But I thought time was the fourth dimensions," I said, weakly.

"It's another dimension after the three we're used to, yes," he replied. "But there are several more dimensions that our 21st Century scientists don't acknowledge as yet."

"And æther is one of them?" I asked, feeling relieved that I'd finally managed to make sense of any of this.

"Well, strictly speaking, it's three of them. But that isn't important right now," he said.

"Three?"

"As The Professor mentioned," interrupted Chrystal. "That is unimportant at this stage. What is necessary is to understand that the æther can be used to connect two points in our day-to-day world without the necessity of travelling through all the places in between."

I was struggling to get my head around this idea.

"And you just step between them?"

"Yes," smiled The Professor.

"Without travelling through the æther?"

"You see, it's very difficult to travel through the æther – you'd have to be chopped into very small pieces. And then be reassembled at the other end of your journey."

"Ri-ight," I said.

"It's only really feasible for liquids, and not all of those survive the trip. Chrystal used to have a wand that relocated certain fluids in that way," he said, half-turning towards her where she was fiddling with something on the workbench.

"I still have," she said without looking up. "You have seen me use it, Sam. Although I do not know if you realised it."

For what felt like the first time that day, I actually understood what someone was talking about.

"The glass wand!"

Chrystal nodded. "Indeed, the tool I use to relocate glass."

"But glass isn't a liquid – it's solid!"

"Not exactly," said The Professor. "It never entirely sets, but it's a fluid that moves very slowly."

"And my little rod persuades it to move more quickly and to travel back to my workshop through the æther." She gestured at the wire cage, which held a smallish ball of shimmering – well, glass, I realised.

"So, you can see that the glass arrives in a fluid form at its destination, which is why it forms a perfect sphere. It would be far more complicated to reform it in its original shape," said The Professor.

"And even more difficult for a human being..." I was starting to get my head around the rules of this new science.

"Which is why we don't actually travel through the æther.

We just short-cut the usual three dimensions so that there's no need to travel through another," he explained.

I suddenly remembered something Chrystal had told me before about the æther.

"But, if you don't actually travel through the æther," I said slowly.

The Professor smile encouragingly.

"How do you leave a wake? I mean, that's how we found you in the first place," I finished, blushing.

"Very good question," he replied. "The simplest way to describe an ætheric wake is to say it's like a trail connecting the two points you stepped between."

"But the spider doesn't..." I began.

"Ah, beware of taking an analogy too far," he answered. "Suffice it to say that the æther doesn't obey the same physical laws that you are accustomed to. But it can be utilised for travelling."

"I still don't quite understand how you do that," I said.

"Look – why don't I give you a demonstration? Would that help?"

"Um, I'm not sure. How would you do that?"

"Well, if my translocator has recharged sufficiently," he walked over to a pole I hadn't noticed before, propped against the wall by Chrystal's voltaic pile and bent down to look closely at something fixed about a third of the way down it. He nodded.

"Yes, enough for a short hop. Shall we step outside?"

And so I found myself walking down the stairs behind a man with a Welsh accent who was carrying a four-foot pole with a bundle of wires at one end. There was a small box fixed close to the wires, with a display like the ones on Chrystal's ætheric sender. Outside, he walked to the middle of the street and halted. I stopped a few paces short and Chrystal almost knocked me over before she, too, came to a halt.

The Professor turned in a slow circle, holding his pole in one hand.

"I don't see anyone," he commented.

"There is unlikely to be another person on this street," said Chrystal. "Safe enough, I would say."

"The translocator is not fully charged, so I won't try to make a return journey," said The Professor. "So if you'd be so kind as to stand a little way down the road?"

It took me a moment to realise he was talking to me, but then I followed his pointing finger to the junction a dozen houses away. I turned to check and he gave me a thumbs-up sign. As I watched, he straddled the pole with the wires and control box in front of him. With a jolt of familiarity, I realised I'd seen pictures of people doing exactly the same when he suddenly wasn't there. I knew I'd been staring at him, standing a few feet from Chrystal and then he was just gone. I gasped and spun round as I heard someone running towards me from the other direction. It was The Professor, his pole held up in his left hand.

"What...?"

"So – do you believe it now?" he asked as he reached me.

"Er, yeah. I guess."

"So," he took my arm and steered me back towards Chrystal's house. "What did you see?"

"Well – you were standing next to Chrystal. And then you weren't, and you came from behind me."

"Exactly. I didn't have a full charge, so I just moved myself a few dozen yards down the street."

"But how?" I asked, not convinced that this could be real, even though I'd just seen him vanish into thin air.

"By wrinkling the street over the æther. I know it's not what you were taught at school, but it's science, not magic."

I stopped walking and he spun about our linked arms.

"Isn't it magic? You looked like a witch riding a broomstick – but you had it the wrong way round," I said.

"Ah, well, there may be a good reason for that." He looked amused, his eyes twinkling as if there was an in-joke here that I didn't know about. "Maybe the stories are based on someone using the æther in exactly the way that I do, and that's where the legends came from."

"But..."

"And the direction of the broomstick varies between different mythologies. My controls are arranged this way round, but they could just as easily be reversed. The translocator doesn't actually fly, so it doesn't matter which way the foils point."

We got back to the house and followed Chrystal up the stairs. I wanted to think my way through all this new information. I'd just about managed to accept some of the ideas that Chrystal had been teaching me, but this really did seem like magic. Had I actually seen someone disappear? Or was it some sleight-of-hand trick that I'd fallen for and I'd simply not noticed The Professor running past me? Surely I couldn't be fooled that easily!

Chrystal was pouring coffee and gestured for me to settle on the sofa. The Professor propped his pole – translocator – back in the corner before pulling a folding chair out from under the workbench and settling in front of me.

"Are you okay? That must have been quite a shock," he said softly.

I didn't answer for a moment and Chrystal sat down next to me.

"She is a tough little bird, our Sam," she said, putting an arm around my shoulders. "She fought off that pirate last night – I am certain that witnessing a little translocation will not cause her more than momentary confusion."

She squeezed me slightly and I smiled back at her. But I was deeply confused.

"So you're a Professor of ætherics?" I asked him. "Where did you study for that?"

"Actually, I'm a Professor of a far more mundane type of physics. But I got interested in early twentieth century work on ætheric science and have been researching it ever since. Much of what was known has been lost while the physics community focused on Einsteinian theories."

"But - " I paused while I worked out exactly how to phrase the various questions that were milling around my head. He watched me patiently. "How can you learn something that nobody knows about?"

"It was difficult at first, although there are plenty of hints in writing from the nineteenth century. And once I'd mastered the basics, I could experiment with my ideas. And I've been lucky enough to meet a few individuals who have some knowledge of how it was used - such as Chrystal, of course."

"But - she said you were an expert. I didn't realise she'd been the one who taught you," I said.

"Indeed he is an expert," said Chrystal. "He knows more than anyone else alive, but even the greatest has to start somewhere."

The Professor had been nodding at her explanation and he took up the thread.

"So Chrystal told me what she knew, I gathered a little more from a friend of hers from The Netherlands. And I've been taking machines apart when we can find them. Add in copious amounts of reading, theorising and experimenting and I guess I do know a fair bit about the subject. But there are other people studying the field, too."

"You are being far too modest, Professor. You were the one who deduced the link between the science of ætherics and the modern form of physics. That understanding was the greatest stepping stone by which you have begun to advance the science," said Chrystal. "And most of those others are not truly researching the workings of ætherics, merely making use of material researched by yourself or recorded in fanciful tales handed down through the ages."

He shrugged and looked down. "All of which is only possible because you had seen ætheric devices in operation and could relate your observations," he said.

"And Dutch telling you about those gadgets were hidden in that monastery," added Chrystal.

"Dutch?" I asked.

It was The Professor who answered. "He's an old friend of Chrystal's. Been around almost as long as her, I believe."

She pulled a face. "Friend? I guess he is, despite our differences. But his arcane knowledge has been very useful."

"He's another one like you?" I asked, my hand touching my chest as I looked at Chrystal.

She just shook her head and an awkward silence fell.

The Professor looked as if he was going to say something to me, but instead he turned to Chrystal.

"So what is it I can help you with?" he asked.

Chapter 21

In which Sam in endangered

The bell jangled as I opened the door. I wriggled slightly in my t-shirt, itching from the cuttings the hairdresser's towel hadn't kept from going down my back. After a moment, the curtain behind the counter pushed aside and the jeweller appeared.

"Yes?" he said.

"I've come to collect the foils you were preparing for us," I said. I was determined not to let this unwashed, unkempt man know how much he made my skin crawl.

"Oh, yes," he said, peering at me over his near-focus glasses. "You're Missus Crystal's little *friend*, aren't you?"

I found myself bristling at his complete disregard for the way her name was pronounced, but swallowed the angry comment before it came out of my mouth. It wasn't that hard to get it right - and it's only polite to make the effort!

"I'm here on Chrystal's behalf, yes," I said. I noticed the way his eyes tightened as I stressed the correct pronunciation slightly and kicked myself for letting his bad manners get under my skin.

"Crystal's been a customer of mine for years," he said over a slight leer. "A very *good* customer, if you know what I mean."

"I'm sure you've been paid handsomely for your work," I replied.

"Of course, I could be persuaded to offer a discount. For certain considerations," he actually winked and I suppressed a shudder.

"I don't think that will be necessary," I replied, pulling the neat roll of fifty-pound notes out of my pocket. "I believe you agreed a price with Chrystal in advance."

"You don't have to tell her you got a discount, you know,"

he said. "It would be our little secret – just between you and me."

If I hadn't already got the idea, his gesture would have left me in no doubt what he expected me to do in return for that discount. I tried not to gulp at the thought of this disgusting little man and what he was suggesting. I may have worried that Chrystal had paid more for my help because we'd slept together – but that was different. She was different! She cared for me. I was no whore and my skin cringed away at the mere thought of him touching me.

"There is no need to re-negotiate what you'd agreed with Chrystal," I said, seeing him shrink back when I stressed her name again. "I have the money here – now, are the foils ready for collection?"

He glared at me, but went behind his curtain to fetch the tray of foils. I checked they were smooth, undamaged and properly labelled before I laid them in the artist's folder I'd brought, paid him the cash and left. I could feel his eyes following me out of the door and, I suspected, down the street as well. I wasn't about to turn round, in case he was watching.

If I had, I might have seen him talking on the phone as he leered after my hurrying figure.

Chrystal and The Professor were huddled over her workbench, fiddling with lengths of wire, glass bulbs and other bits and pieces. They'd been the same since he'd arrived first thing in the morning, carrying a wooden cabinet to house the new device they were working on. It reminded me of a small, old-fashioned telly, with a largish hole on one side and a couple of long slots, where the tuning and volume knobs would have fit in. They didn't even look up as I laid the artist's folder down and I couldn't understand what they were talking about. I slipped into the bedroom to change my itchy t-shirt, admiring my new pixie cut in the mirror as I did so. I wandered around the workshop for a while, but they were still engrossed in their work, so I decided to settle in the other room, out of everyone's way.

But I couldn't get comfy. I browsed Chrystal's bookshelves half-heartedly, but the books looked so dry and boring I didn't even bother lifting one down to look inside. The chairs felt lumpy whatever position I sat in. I wondered about going back into the workroom and offering to make coffee – but I didn't want to be with people who barely seemed to know I existed, however important their work was. Instead, I just grabbed a jumper and headed out. There was a big American-style coffee shop a couple of streets away – I'd go there and get them to make me a drink in the usual way, sit and chat with normal people and forget about this strange house for an hour or so.

I decided not to bother fetching my coat or my bag from the workshop. It was only a couple of blocks and I had a few quid in my pocket to pay for a cuppa. I'd be back in no time and they'd probably never even notice I'd gone. In the back of my mind, I knew I was being childish, that Chrystal and The Professor were just wrapped-up in the machine they were building. But it felt like they were ignoring me and I wanted to be among my kind of people. Ordinary Londoners who plugged a kettle in to boil water and watched soap operas and cheap reality TV of an evening.

I slipped down the stairs quietly, automatically stepping over the fifth stair because it always creaked when you trod on it. I tapped my hip to hear the soft rattle of coins and slipped out through the front door.

After an hour's worth of what I used to think of as normality, I was ready for the quiet of Chrystal's house again. I left the cosy warmth of the coffee shop and was fitting my key into the front door when an arm came out of nowhere, wrapped itself around my throat and a voice hissed,

"Make a sound and it'll be your last."

Something hard and cold was pressing against the right side of my neck. I swallowed back the panicked shout that was about to leap out of my mouth, tried to stop myself fighting and concentrated on breathing past the forearm that crushed my airway.

He reached to unlock the door with my key and pushed it open, keeping up the pressure on my throat and the cold thing on my right.

"Now, in you go," he said, emphasising his point by jabbing the metal against the skin of my neck. I hadn't seen it, but it felt enough like a gun to dissuade me from risking anything.

My mind was racing. I was sure from his voice that it was the pirate who tried to steal the ætheric sender the other day and I was kicking myself for being caught so easily again! But what could I do? He pushed me towards the stairs, pressing close against my back and not letting up the pressure on my breathing. I looked at the bare wooden boards, wondering if I could fake falling on them, breaking free of him or making enough noise to warn Chrystal. I lifted my foot onto the first step, bending backwards slightly as he kept up his pressure.

"No funny business, now," he warned and I swallowed hard against his tightening arm.

We edged up the stairs with him one step behind, his weapon cold on the skin of my neck, while his left arm pressed on my airway so I could hardly breathe. The fifth step creaked, but there was no reaction from above.

On the landing I hesitated, wondering if I should lead him into the other room. If I could somehow surprise him enough to make a sound and alert the other two. But he practically lifted me as he turned to the door into the workshop.

Chrystal and The Professor stood together on the far side of the workbench, its wooden solidity between them and us.

"... we could route the transmission - " Chrystal's voice faded away as she looked up to see me being pushed in by my captor.

"Farran!"

He didn't respond, just jerked my head back and dragged me into the centre of the room. I noticed The Professor edging towards the end of the bench.

"That's enough," snapped the voice behind me. "Let's have your hands where I can see them."

They both lifted their empty hands into view and the pirate snapped, "Where's your transporter?"

When no-one answered, he jerked my head back, making me grunt at the sudden pain.

"I asked for your transporter!"

Professor Bevan stepped from behind the bench, keeping his hands in sight. He moved slowly, taking care not to appear threatening.

"My ætheric translocator?" he asked mildly.

I felt my captor make a gesture I couldn't see.

"It's over here," continued The Professor. He walked sideways across the room and the pirate turned me to follow him. I found myself staring at a rough scar on the back of his forearm and wondered where he'd got it. Anything rather than think about the gun-muzzle against my neck.

"Moving up in the world, are you not, Farran? You only had a knife when you threatened Sam last time," said Chrystal, bringing his eyes back to where she stood.

"Now let her go," said The Professor, picking up his ætheric translocator and holding it towards the pirate.

"Give me that first," he growled.

"Here," said The Professor, edging slightly towards the window.

In response Farran tightened his arm about my neck and I felt him moving his other hand somewhere out of view. As he did so, I saw The Professor flick something on the control box on his broomstick. The pirate turned me a little more, so he could reach out to take the translocator. The Professor handed it to him and reached towards me with his other hand.

"Now let her go," he said.

My captor snatched the pole and jerked me backwards so I almost fell.

"Oh, I think I'll hang on to her as security," he said and started fiddling with the controls.

A loud click came from behind him and Chrystal hissed, "The nice Professor told you to let her go. Now are you going to do as you were told or shall I find out if this gun still works?"

He spun around, almost choking me in his hurry to face this new threat.

"Did you believe you would catch us unprepared, again?" continued Chrystal. "I told you to bother us no more, Farran."

Chrystal was holding an antique-looking gun at arm's length, its end pointing straight at my captor - and therefore at me. I tried to shrink down, make myself as small a target as possible so she could shoot the pirate. But he realised what I was doing and pulled me back to my feet, never loosening his grip. I could hear The Professor stepping quietly behind us and then almost blacked out as I was jerked towards the wall by the arm around my throat. Quickly the pirate pulled me with him, using my body as cover while he tried to keep both of them in view. Everything was going grey and I realised his grip must be choking me slowly. How terribly ironic to die that way when people were threatening each other with guns. I would have laughed if I'd had the breath to do so.

I felt his grip on me loosen a little and tried to duck down, away from him, but my knees gave way and I fell forward onto all fours, gasping for air. Then everything happened all at once. There was a gunshot, something hard hitting the floor, a scream and a loud crackle. The coppery smell was in the air again. I crawled towards The Professor, not knowing if I was still in danger. He helped me to my feet and I turned to see Chrystal picking up the translocator, an antique gun smoking in her right hand.

There was no sign of the pirate. A jagged scorch mark was seared into the floorboards where he'd been standing. His military-looking gun lay fallen next to it.

"What...?" I asked. Then, "Where?"

"No idea," said The Professor brightly. "I set the translocator to throw him into the æther at random if he tried to use it. It has an emergency setting which catapults the user across the dimensions, leaving the device behind." He accepted the ætheric contraption from Chrystal and peered closely at the controls.

"Any damage?" she asked him.

He shook his head. "Na. It's tougher than that. Can't say the same for our abductor friend, though."

Abductor? Suddenly events caught up with me and I swayed. Chrystal was at my side in an instant, one arm supporting me as she guided me towards a chair.

"Are you injured?" she asked.

"N-no. I don't think so."

I slumped against her sturdy body, feeling slightly queasy.

"Here," The Professor's voice made me look up to where he held out a glass. "Brandy. Sip it slowly."

Chrystal fussed over me for hours, telling me she liked my new haircut, that I'd been brave and other such nonsense until she convinced herself I really wasn't hurt and wasn't going to vanish if she took her eyes off me. I realised The Professor had distracted the pirate while Chrystal got her gun from wherever she hid it. Then he'd switched his device into this emergency mode that somehow sent my captor away without going itself. He tried to explain how that worked, but I couldn't focus on his words and eventually he gave up and poured me another brandy.

Chapter 22

In which plans are made

Chrystal was especially tender that night. I was so sleepy after the shock had worn off that I thought I just wanted to sleep. But she held me, murmuring nonsenses like you would to a hurt child and smoothing my hair while I relaxed. But then the tears started and, before I knew it, I was sobbing in her arms like a child who'd fallen off the swings. This gentleness was a side to Chrystal I'd never suspected. I couldn't remember anyone being so kind to me before, and that made me cry even harder. At some point I must have cried myself to sleep, because I woke the next morning in the circle of her arms. She must have been uncomfortable with me lying on her left arm, but her sleeping face looked peaceful. I freed myself from her embrace and tiptoed into the workshop.

I walked to the bench, careful not to make any noise, and filled the coffee maker with grounds and water, setting it to boil on top of the ætheric heater. As I set out our mugs, I realised I wasn't alone. The Professor lay on the sofa, covered with the patterned blanket normally thrown over the cushions.

"Enough for three?" he asked quietly.

"Um, yeah," I said, looking around, quickly retrieving a third mug from the coffee table and putting it with the others to wash.

"How do you feel?" he asked, wrapping the blanket around his powerful figure as he stood.

"Fine," I answered, noticing a pile of his clothes on the chair and wondering whether he was wearing anything under that blanket.

"It sounded as if Chrystal was looking after you, so I figured we'd continue our conversation this morning," he said, standing with the blanket tucked into itself around his waist.

Trying not to think about his state of dress, I felt myself beginning to blush. I wasn't used to having a man around the house, especially one who might be naked under a loosely-held covering, and I did my best not to look at him while I fetched the sugar bowl from Chrystal's little pantry.

He didn't seem to notice my embarrassment, but turned away and sorted through his clothes.

"Tell you what," he said. "I'll go fetch us something to have with the coffee."

He dropped the blanket and I looked away in a hurry, but not before I'd seen that he wasn't wearing anything else, as I'd half-suspected. I adjusted the bubbling coffee pot's position slightly, fighting back the red tide that threatened to sweep up my neck and face. For a second I wished I'd had a manners teacher, as Chrystal had. Although I doubted even she'd instructed her students on the right way to respond to the sight of a man's naked arse while he dressed after spending the night on your sofa.

"You like those morning rolls, don't you?" he asked, coming to stand behind me. "The ones with a honey glaze?"

"Y-yes, we both do," I said.

I turned towards him, careful to keep my eyes level with his face, just in case. But I needn't have worried. He was pulling a jumper on over his heavy shirt and running fingers through the fringe of black hair that tried to fall in his eyes.

"I'll get some milk, too. Anything else, while I'm out?"

I shook my head and he bounded across the workshop and out the door, grabbing the front door key from its hook as he passed.

I rinsed the cups and turned back to find Chrystal standing by the workbench. Her hair was a mess because she'd slept on it without tying it in her usual plait and I felt a small pang of guilt that I'd interrupted her nighttime routine so badly.

"I presume you are feeling a little better?" she asked.

"Yes. Um, I'm fine."

"And Professor Bevan?"

"Gone for breakfast. He said he'd bring milk back, too," I said.

"Then I suggest you make first use of the shower," she said, smiling.

Chrystal fixed me with a gaze while The Professor cleared the plates into the washer-cabinet and set the coffee pot to boil again. She didn't speak, just stared with those dark eyes of hers.

"What is it?" I asked.

She smiled.

"I am wondering, Sam-of-the-boy's-name, if you were prepared to travel with me."

"Travel? Where? And why?"

"A long way, and I cannot say yet whether it will be safe for us to do so," she replied.

"Well, it isn't exactly safe for us to stay here!" I said.

"More to the point, it is proving dangerous for you. There are people who wish to stop me ensuring that order continues to rule over chaos and they seem to think that it is easier to attack you." Chrystal sat back in her chair.

"Do you think he'll try again? I mean, he's done practically the same thing twice..."

"Or attempted to, at least," she replied. "But I do not think he is working alone."

"So there are more like him?"

"I suspect he is one of many - and a mere footsoldier in that army."

"An army? But where?" I burst out.

She shrugged. "It makes little difference to our plans - I would have been travelling shortly, come what may."

"So you're really going through with this?" asked The Professor from the workbench.

"I do not believe I have a choice in the matter," she replied.

"And you're thinking of setting out before we've properly deciphered the codex?"

"As Sam has mentioned, it is hardly safe for us to remain here," she said.

"True, but it's going to take me another week to pinpoint the stone's location," he said. "Maybe two - if I can at all."

"Which is time we can spend travelling. I will contact you by telephone once we have disembarked from the ship."

"That should give me enough time," he replied, his brow furrowed in thought.

"It will take us more than three weeks to make landfall in the Americas," said Chrystal.

"Weeks?" I burst in. "But a flight'll get us there tomorrow."

Chrystal looked at me. "Alas, I cannot fly on an aeroplane nowadays. Much though I would like to."

Seeing my puzzled face, she continued.

"I have not flown from an international airport for many years. Their security people would want to see my concealed weapons when their scanning devices detected what they consider to be foreign materials."

I mentally slapped myself. "Your heart! And your arm – they'd be picked up on airport scanners."

"Indeed. So we must seek a more civilised means of transport which will permit our boarding without attempting to scan us for concealed weaponry," she said.

"So – how do we get there? If we can't fly?"

She stood and walked over to her wardrobe. "We will cruise to the Americas. On an ocean liner."

"But, that's incredibly expensive," I said.

"I have told you before, Sam. I have amassed certain

means. I will pay for our passage by selling one of the items I have stored against just such a need. There will be other expenses than just our tickets, and I do not have sufficient funds available at short notice unless I make such a sale. The money will not be a problem."

"And they don't have security scans at a seaport?" I asked.

Chrystal shared a complex glance with The Professor. "We have ways of circumventing the more intrusive of their security systems," she said.

"And what do we do when we get there?" I asked, wondering why she was going to all this trouble.

"Suffice it to say that we must fulfil an ancient prophecy or face the consequences."

"What? So it's dangerous?"

She looked so severe I didn't dare ask more questions. Instead I finished my coffee and cleared the little table.

I was tipping the grounds from the coffee pot into the little bin Chrystal kept by the sink when The Professor came up to me.

"Cut her a little slack, Sam," he said quietly. "She's worried about this trip because we haven't been able to make proper sense of the prophecy. All we know is that Chrystal has to be in America before the end of this year or there will be disastrous consequences."

"But, why? And what is this prophecy?"

"She heard about it from a Tibetan who came looking for earlier this year. He brought a message from some mystic, telling her what he'd foreseen, what their traditions say and how to find the stone she must decipher, but she won't tell me what she has to do when she finds it."

"That sounds like nonsense. Who was this mystic and why is Chrystal prepared to chase halfway around the world on his say-so?" I snorted.

"Who he is, I do not know," said The Professor. "But I do know that the Chrystal that sustains her life came from Tibet and she feels an obligation to help when they ask. I've been doing what little I can to help research the prophecy, but there isn't much known about it. Even the Tibetans couldn't tell her much. We've been trying to fill in the gaps, but it's painstaking work."

He turned back to the workbench, picking up a tool lying near the birdcage.

Chrystal was packing clothes into a huge leather trunk. I'd never seen anything so vast, but it was filling rapidly as she selected dresses from her wardrobe and folded them as neatly as any shop assistant.

"Do I need to pack now?" I asked.

She looked up at me.

"I do not think so, Sam. I am merely packing the bulky items so Professor Bevan can arrange for my trunk to be delivered to the docks in advance of our boarding. You should pack sufficient clothes and other essentials to manage for a few days while we go to collect something to sell, but the remainder will await our return here." She turned back to her packing, so I went to fetch my little rucksack from the other room.

A clean pair of jeans, three t-shirts, undies and my toiletries bag. I was packed and ready before Chrystal had even finished packing just the dresses she wanted The Professor to take.

"Isn't this a bit of an overreaction?" I asked. "I mean, that pirate is just one bloke – are we really going to let him chase us out of our home?"

"He may be one man that we have seen so far," she replied. "But we suspect that he is not working alone. It appears likely that there are others involved that we have not encountered and it is that lack of knowledge that suggests we would be well-advised to make our way to the Americas sooner rather than later."

"Others? But surely he's just an opportunist. A thief looking to steal Professor Bevan's devices," I replied.

"That is possible," she said. "But it seems unlikely that such a thief should happen upon our precise location at this exact time. I have been making our preparations for some months, which may have attracted the attention of certain other groups that may not wish for us to succeed. And his behaviour was similar to others I have met before."

"Similar? How?" I asked.

She stopped folding and turned to me.

"Did he not seem oddly driven to you? A little maniacal, perhaps?"

I thought for a moment. I hadn't really paid much attention to the pirate, except as someone who'd half-throttled me and tried to shoot me.

"And his repetition - he engineered almost identical attacks on two separate occasions. Does that not seem a little unusual?"

"I guess so. Maybe he's not very bright?" I suggested.

"Maybe not, but I suspect his problem is not so simple. I have met such individuals before, and they were in the service of someone whose desires I thwarted on a previous occasion. It is easier to observe when there are more of them. Something appears to be dulling their wits whilst driving them to perform their functions in the service of whoever sends them."

"You mean, like they're on drugs or hypnotised or something?"

She shrugged. "Those are possibilities - but if it is a pharmaceutical, it is unlike any I have ever heard of before. And a sustained hypnosis of so many men is not as easy as you might expect."

I shook my head. "I really don't understand. Who are these people? How do they know you've been making preparations and why would they want to stop you?"

"The problem, my dear Sam, is that none of us truly understand what is at stake here or who it is opposing us, although he and I have crossed swords previously. This is not the first attempt made to purloin Professor Bevan's ætheric technology and it seems likely that some specific adversary is behind all of these attacks. If someone is co-ordinating the efforts made in pursuit of ætheric devices and also trying to prevent our actions, then it may be best that we move on before they are expecting us to do so. Evade their noose before it tightens, so to speak."

"By cruising to America?"

"By retrieving a fossil first. To pay for our passage to cruise to the New World," she grinned.

She smoothed the tissue paper she'd wrapped around the last dress lying in her huge trunk, then reached for the lid and swung it closed.

"That will suffice," she said. "And if the good Professor takes that with him this afternoon, then we may have a little time to ourselves."

She looped her arms around me and pulled me in for a lingering kiss that tasted of strawberries and promises.

Chapter 23

In which pursuit is evaded

The Professor arrived first thing the following morning. I been wondering if he'd have some sort of ætheric contraption for carrying Chrystal's luggage - maybe I was going to learn flying carpets were real, too. But he turned up driving a shabby, mundane, white van. I helped him load up Chrystal's trunk and a smaller box that she'd packed with a few of her ætheric tools. I watched until he'd turned the corner and let myself back into the house.

Chrystal was folding surprisingly modern-looking jumpers and tops into a burgundy coloured holdall. It took me a moment to notice that she was wearing a pair of what looked like –

"Jeans!" I shouted.

She looked up and smiled.

"Indeed. I believe that cotton fabric woven in the style of Nimes makes for the hardest-wearing trousers available to the traveller in this century. Although I generally eschew the use of such garments, I am not foolhardy enough to ignore their sturdiness and convenience when one must travel light."

She stepped from behind the sofa on which she had been folding clothes and turned a slow circle, giving me a clear view of how well the jeans fit her slender-waisted figure.

I let out a low whistle.

"They've never looked that good on me," I exclaimed.

"Well, I did have them tailored specifically," she said. When I didn't reply, she turned back to her packing.

"I have arranged for a taxi-cab to conduct us to the railway station, as we will be carrying our own luggage. We may expect the driver to arrive at quarter after ten," she said.

I glanced at the clock and made a quick calculation.

"It'll only take me two minutes to throw my toiletries into

my rucksack. Shall I make one last coffee?"

So we came to be seated on the sofa, her right arm heavy on my shoulders and coffee cups on the little table when I heard a diesel engine outside and the double-honk of a London cabbie.

"Can you take the bags outside?" she asked, collecting up the crockery and placing it in the cabinet where it would be cleaned ætherically. "I will prime the deterrent devices prior to our vacating the premises."

I wasn't quite sure what she meant, but I shrugged into my rucksack, grabbed her holdall and ran down the stairs and out to the black cab. The driver was young, clean-shaven and dressed in the ubiquitous dirty jeans and short-sleeved shirt of his profession. He threw our bags into the boot and suddenly flinched as if someone had hit the side of his head.

"Owww," he said. "Can you 'ear that?"

I listened and could sort of hear what he was talking about. A high-pitched whine, a bit like a distant plane, only somehow very near at the same time.

Before I could comment, Chrystal stepped through the door, pulling it shut behind her and reaching up to turn the key in the second lock. The cab driver whistled.

"You don't get many of those to the pound," he muttered then caught me glaring at him.

"Sorry missus," he said. "Didn't mean to be rude about yer sister."

He reached to take the wooden box of the ætheric sender off Chrystal, but she lifted it by the leather straps into the cab, next to my feet.

"We will keep this with us, driver. It is a trifle fragile and I prefer to keep it close at hand," she said.

She smiled as she spoke to him and he almost bowed to her.

"As yer want," he said and climbed into the front seat as

she closed the door after her.

"Paddington Station, wasn't it?" he asked and we were off.

Paddington was as crowded as usual, but the crowds seemed not to bother Chrystal the way they did most people. It's not as if anyone actually made way for her, but she never needed to dodge around people walking the other way or step around their luggage. Dressed in jeans, a short, grey jacket and wearing a very 21st-Century green trilby, she somehow cut through the throng like a snowplough. I couldn't work out how she did it, but she did. I gave up trying to walk next to her and followed instead, like a small boat cadging a free ride in a ship's wake. So I blundered into her back when she stopped suddenly and it took me a moment to rearrange the bags after almost dropping one. So I missed her question to the man in a dark blue uniform, but heard him give her directions to a platform.

We reached the platform just as the station staff were hurrying the last few passengers on board. She led me into the second carriage, where she stopped just inside the door, reaching past me to close it and taking the sender off me.

"One moment, Sam. Keep a tight grip on our luggage," she said and leant out of the window, looking back the way we had come. I saw a uniformed man hold up a paddle and Chrystal reached through the window and opened the door, the ætheric sender's straps firmly in the other hand. She pulled me and the bags onto the platform with her and slammed the door behind us. At the same time, the orange lights went out, the locks *clunked* and the train began moving as we stepped back from the edge. As the final carriage passed, I saw an angry man's face leaning out of the door, shouting something I couldn't hear.

"What just happened?" I asked. "Were we on the wrong train?"

"Only momentarily. But there were two men who followed

us from the rank of taxis and I did not wish for them to know our destination," she said. "Now, let us find the proper platform for our train." And she was away again, walking in her unhurried and unobstructed way before the guard could catch us and tell us off for our dangerous manoeuvre. I'd see this sort of thing in films but never thought I'd do anything so risky!

Chrystal stood back and gestured me into the window seat and we settled in place. She charmed the train's guard when he came round, paid cash for our single tickets and got him to promise that the refreshment trolley would come to our carriage as soon as the buffet car could spare someone.

"How do you do that?" I asked after he'd moved on.

She just looked at me, one perfect eyebrow raised and her head tilted slightly to one side.

"I mean, how come you get people to help you like that? I have enough trouble getting them to serve me when I wave the cash in their faces."

"Ah, I understand," she said. "I do not behave in the manner of people who were brought up in this modern world, with their demands and their expectations. I grew up in a London where my family had servants and we all knew our places. I did not have to demand that they serve me and they would know immediately that I was a Lady."

"So you just assume everyone is someone lower than you?"

"No, not at all," she replied. "I believe that I have a right to be served by those whose role in life is to serve. I do not believe that I am somehow better than them, just that our roles in life are different. It is the nature of some people to work towards making others happy and they do so willingly. I attempt no coercion."

"But," I hesitated. This went against everything I'd been taught to believe about equal rights and fairness. "Why do modern people just do what you tell them to?"

"They do not. I merely assume that people who are employed to provide a service will provide exactly that. And so they do. I do not tell them to do anything that goes against the nature of their employment. Nor do I demand it in the aggressive-apologetic way that many modern people use when they merely have to make a polite request." Now she paused thoughtfully. "Am I so very different to you, then?"

"Well, no. But why do people like to do what you want, when they resent it from anybody else?"

"It may be that my years have gifted me with a certain gravitas that others do not have. I do not know. But why do people resent being asked to do something? When it is their job to serve others?"

"Because no-one likes to feel second class. We don't have servants any more and we're all equal. That's why no-one likes to be reminded they're meant to be serving someone else!"

"Ah, I see," she said. "I have wondered about this but never understood it fully before now. You are saying that people believe it lessens them to behave as a servant to another, is that correct?"

I nodded.

"But it is not the act that makes the servant. A person's station in life may depend on the nature of their birth and upbringing. But that does not make them Gentle. Only a knowledge and acceptance of one's station in life can give one the comfort of feeling that they belong. Many people who considered themselves to be better than others were, in fact, of much poorer character than those who served them. In my day, that is."

I could feel my forehead wrinkling as I tried to make sense of this.

"So you're saying that it wasn't just about being born a Lady, but how you dealt with the servants?" I asked.

"In some measure, yes," she answered. "A person born into a wealthy family may have the benefit of money, but that may not be as important as their behaviour towards others. Many who called themselves Gentle were as badly-mannered as some who had not the advantages of wealth and education. And there were always many of the serving classes who were more Gentle than their masters."

This was too good an opportunity for me to pass up.

"When you say 'gentle' like that – what exactly do you mean?"

She looked hard at me for so long that I was about to ask her again when she answered me.

" 'Gentle' is a term that implies a degree of manners, a rightness of character above and beyond that of many people. In my day, it was coming to be used to apply to those of the wealthiest classes, but many of us recognised that those with money but no breeding were not Gentle, however they may wish to appear so. It is a manner of speaking, a way of addressing those around you and of understanding your place. Only one reared in a family of such people could truly aspire to behave as Gentle. Do you not still use the term – when you wish to refer politely, do you not use the term gentle-man?"

"Well, yes. But it's really just a polite way of saying 'man'. It doesn't really mean anything," I said.

"And that, my dear Sam, is why your society is comprised of many unhappy people. Politeness no longer has any meaning."

"So you think people are happier if they accept their role in life, even if it's to be a servant?"

"Absolutely," she beamed. "Every man since Adam, or the monkeys if you prefer the histories of Professor Darwin, is happier to know where he stands in relation to his fellow men.

And every woman since Eve needs to understand her station if she is to lead a proper and fulfilled life. Do you not feel fulfilled to complete a task well, even a truly menial one?"

I was spared any more confusion by the refreshments trolley arriving, closely followed by about a dozen teenagers in school uniforms who swarmed over the carriage, playing loud music and talking on phones, which made further conversation impossible. I tried to sleep, as I felt like I'd barely closed my eyes the night before, but it was too noisy and eventually I gave up and just stared out the window, not seeing anything but trying to lull myself with the rhythmic flicker of the scenery as we passed.

Chapter 24

In which Chrystal and Sam meet Cerys and Abi

Cardiff Station was smaller than Paddington and less crowded, but the people bustled around with no less urgency, though they looked less stressed than commuters in London. I realised I was checking them out for an easy target as they bustled past and clocking convenient escape routes. I scolded myself, remembering I didn't need to pick any pockets in this strange city. Or ever again, I hoped.

Strange? Perhaps - it certainly felt foreign with its bilingual signs all over the place. Some of the words made a kind of sense - but why spell "lift" with two f's? Luckily, Chrystal knew where she was going. She led me out through the turnstiles and onto the paved walkway outside. I'd never been here before and found myself staring round like the tourists the office crowd used to mock back in London when we went out for sandwiches. It was more than just the signs making it feel very different. It could have been the cleaner air or the open spaces between buildings. Or maybe it was just because I didn't know my way around. Either way, I felt oddly exhilarated by Cardiff, tired as I was.

Chrystal seemed to know exactly where she wanted to go. She held the carry-straps for the ætheric sender in her left hand and waved down a taxi with the other. I hefted our bags into the boot, nodding to the driver who seemed happy to keep up a running monologue, apparently unaware that I only understood about a third of his rolling accent and of the yawns I tried to hide behind my hand.

It only took a few minutes to arrive at the address Chrystal had given him and she paid him while I fetched our luggage. We were at the end of a short parade of shops and Chrystal led me to a solid wooden door between two shop fronts.

"This is where The Professor lives?" I asked.

"No. We will go to his house next. Firstly we have other business to take care of."

She produced a chain from under her jacket. I'd noticed it earlier, fastened to the belt of her jeans and hanging in a loop between the belt and her pocket. Now she pulled out a bunch of keys. Some of them looked very old, but I didn't get a good look before she'd unlocked the door and slipped the jangly lot back into its pocket. She pushed the door open and stepped through, calling,

"Cerys? It is Chrystal. May we come up?"

I heard a voice call back unintelligibly from above and Chrystal led me up the stairs.

Much to my surprise, the stairs led to a landing which opened onto a huge room, filled with rolls of material in all the colours of the rainbow. A tall, elegant woman with bouffant hair, chocolate skin and hazel eyes swept over and hugged Chrystal. She wore a long, loose dress in cream and gold that was less formal than Chrystal's usual outfits, but just as eye-catching. The way the dress moved hinted at long legs and it shimmered in the autumn sunlight streaming through the huge windows.

"Chrystal! Why didn't you tell me you were coming?" she said in a deep, mellow voice. "And who is your friend?"

Chrystal broke free and pulled me to her side, wrapping one arm about my waist.

"This is Samantha - Sam to her friends."

The stranger - Cerys - dragged me into the same bone-crushing hug she'd used on Chrystal. And, through her heavy make-up, I felt her stubble scouring my cheek.

"Any friend of Chrystal's is welcome here," she enthused. "Are you staying in Cardiff long?"

"Just a few days, I fear. We have urgent business to attend and must travel on at the end of the week," replied Chrystal.

"But you need something from me?"

"Will you have time?"

"For you, darling, I always have time. Are you looking for something special?" The strange woman - man - whatever - looked her up and down.

"Not for myself," Chrystal said. "I was hoping for some outfits for Sam."

Now the green-shadowed, mascaraed eyes turned to me and I felt myself blushing.

"Oh, I don't need anything!" I exclaimed.

"Oh, don't be such a stick-in-the-mud! All pretty girls need a new frock. Always. It's a basic law of nature!"

"We're sailing to the Americas and we need Sam to look the part," said Chrystal.

Cerys clapped her hands.

"And you want me to dress her? Oh perfect. Togs off, dear!" This last comment was aimed at me and I hesitated, looking beseechingly at Chrystal. She either didn't notice or didn't care about my embarrassment.

"Just slip off your coat and jeans, Sam. Cerys needs to measure you.

So I found myself standing on a chair in my underwear, while the odd man/woman danced around with a tape measure, scribbling notes in a hardback notebook and chatting with Chrystal all the time. At last she - he? - had taken all the measurements possible, clicked a closeup of my face with a smartphone and swept Chrystal off to a table with huge pattern books on it. I quickly pulled my clothes back on and wandered over towards them. Cerys looked up as I approached and made a shooing gesture.

"Go pick some fabrics, now. There's a dear!"

I hesitated and Chrystal looked up. "Take a tour around the room, choose some fabrics that would suit you and place the rolls on the cutting table," she said, smiling and nodding towards a larger table in the centre of the room.

"Um, what sort of fabrics?" I asked. I hadn't done any sewing since school, but even I knew that there were different types of material for different clothes. The other two seemed so sure of themselves and I felt like an idiot child trying to join in with the grown-ups' conversation.

"You just find stuff you like," said Cerys without looking up. "As many different ones as you can. That'll tell me something about your taste and I'll choose the ones I make up."

And that was that. I wandered around, pulling out rolls of anything that caught my eye. At first I put most of them back, but then I started carrying some to the table. I'd never been one for dressing up - my clothes were either comfy-functional or smart-functional, so I didn't really know what I should be looking for. Then I saw the midnight blue.

It was a roll of the deepest blue cloth, shot with silver sparkles that made it look like moonlight on a dark ocean. It hung in soft folds when I lifted the roll for a closer look and was lighter than I thought when I took it to the growing pile and placed it on top.

I found a few more to add, but moved the midnight one to the top again, then turned to see the others watching me.

"Done?" asked Cerys.

I nodded.

"Then I know what I'm working with," she replied. "Chrystal has told me what she wants and your dresses will soon follow!"

"Dresses?" I stressed the plural.

Chrystal stepped towards me, smiling. "We have been discussing patterns and styles. Cerys will make the beginnings of a wardrobe for you and we will collect them before we leave Cardiff," she said.

"But - how much will all this cost?" I asked.

"You do not need to concern yourself about that," said

Chrystal. I will settle Cerys' bill on your behalf. You need to look the part on board ship, after all is said and done."

"But..." I couldn't think of a way to argue and shut up after that one word.

"But you'll look quite edible when I've finished with you," said Cerys.

"We do not have sufficient time to return for a fitting," warned Chrystal.

"No problemo, Sweet-o," said Cerys. "If you can finish the hemming to fit, I can easily knock a few oddments out before you have to leave Cardiff."

Outside, we climbed into another cab, with our bags and the ætheric sender's box. The driver greeted us bilingually - at least I assumed that's what he said, and Chrystal spoke back to him in the same guttural but oddly lilting language. This time we spent almost twenty minutes driving through houses, shops and the occasional green park before arriving at a street of two-storey terraced houses, built of dark grey stone, little windows and pointed gables. Chrystal walked straight up the short path to one, produced her bunch of keys again and opened the front door. She held it open for me and the luggage and then followed, closing the door firmly behind her.

The first thing I noticed was a large brass-coloured clock on a table at the far end of the airy hall. I'd never seen anything like it and quickly moved in for a closer look. It was open so I could see the cogs and other workings inside the metal framework. A pendulum swung at the back, and a loop of chain that passed around something like the gears off a pushbike, only made of brass. It stood on a white marble base, with shiny gold lions guarding the sides of the clock and eagles perched next to the dial. The whole thing was covered by a tall glass dome and I thought it might be the most beautiful thing I'd ever seen.

I heard a door open behind me and I assumed it was

Chrystal going into one of the rooms off the hall. So I jumped when a strange voice greeted us.

"Hello, who's there?"

"It is Chrystal, Abi. Sorry to surprise you."

"Chrystal! How lovely!"

I turned to see Chrystal hugging a slim woman wearing a long denim skirt and peasant-style blouse. She had short, dark hair framing a pretty, elfin face.

"And your companion?" she asked, smiling my way.

"Abi, this is Samantha. She likes to be called Sam," said Chrystal. "Sam, this is Abi – Professor Bevan's wife."

"Um, hello," I said. I stepped forward and held out a hand to shake.

"Good to meet you, Sam," said Abi, waving her own hand in my direction.

Between the way her eyes didn't focus and how she missed my hand with her own, I realised she couldn't see me. I grabbed her hand in both of mine and shook it vigorously, trying to cover my embarrassment.

I mumbled something and wondered whether there was a proper way to respond when a blind person greeted you. Maybe this was something else Chrystal's manners teacher had covered and once again I wished I'd had lessons in proper manners when I was at school.

"I apologise for not calling out as we entered, Abi," Chrystal was saying. "I did not believe you would be here. I was under the impression that you were staying with friends at the moment."

Abi laughed, a clear sound like a delighted child.

"Ah, did Rhys tell you that? He always underestimates me. I came home two days ago, but he tends to forget I can do that for myself."

She turned her unseeing eyes in my direction again.

"But I'm forgetting my manners," she said. "Sam, any

friend of Chrystal's is welcome here. Please make yourself at home."

"We would like to stay the night, if that is acceptable to you," said Chrystal. "Tomorrow we need to head north, although we would like to rest here again once I have completed my business near Rhyadar. It will take me a few days to complete my transaction with one of the dealers here in Cardiff."

"Sounds fine to me. The spare bed's ready for use, as always," said Abi. "Shall I make up the little room, too?"

"No, the spare room will be more than sufficient for us both," said Chrystal. A knowing smile appeared on Abi's face and I blushed, feeling grateful that she couldn't see me. Then I felt guilty for being grateful for her disability. Then I...

"I'll show Sam where everything is, then," Chrystal interrupted my see-sawing thoughts and led the way up the stairs.

"You might have warned me she was blind," I hissed, once we were alone in the large spare room Chrystal brought me to.

She stared at me, taken aback.

"I did not expect Abi to be at home," she said. "And I do not believe that her lack of sight is something you needed to be warned about."

I bit my tongue. She may have been right, but I felt awkward for not realising she couldn't see the hand I'd held out to her.

We unpacked the few things we'd need for a single night and made our way downstairs again, although I was tempted to crawl under the rich patchwork quilt on the huge bed. Chrystal opened the door that Abi had come through when we arrived and I found myself following her into a cosy little sitting room with tall, winged chairs and a solid tree stump fashioned into a coffee table.

"Ah, there you both are," said Abi and she reached for a

pot of bubbling coffee resting on a familiar-looking stand.

Chrystal waited until Abi had walked past with the coffee pot before swinging one of the chairs closer to the little table where our host had set out mugs and plates with slices of chocolate cake on them.

"Do help yourselves," she said with a wave at the table. "There's no need to wait on ceremony when you must be hungry from travelling."

I didn't need telling twice. I'd been trying to ignore my rumbling stomach for the last hour and the cake was as tasty as it looked.

"You're raiding the cache, then?" Abi asked.

"Yes. I have need of funds to pay for our transit to the Americas," said Chrystal.

"So you're looking for the calendar? You're actually going through with it?"

"I believe that I must. If Rhys is correct, there is little risk to me from fulfilling the prophecy."

Abi humphed. "And if anyone tries to stop you? That's a risk!"

"Crossing the street is a risk, Abi. I think this is one I have to take," replied Chrystal.

I kept quiet, trying to work out what wasn't being said but afraid of what I might hear if I tried to pry.

Abi broke the silence. "So you're selling something. More artwork?"

"No, I believe the market is better suited to a fossil at this moment in time," replied Chrystal. "I think this would be an auspicious time to sell the Maxberg one."

"Ah, that beautiful bird. One of my favourites," said Abi.

"How do you..." I blurted out before I could think.

The room fell silent for a long breath and I felt myself reddening again. Then Abi seemed to realise what I was about to say.

"How do I know it's beautiful?" she asked. "It's alright, Sam – I know how little most people understand the blind."

She smiled warmly and continued, "I cannot see an artwork, but I can appreciate fossils by touch. The Maxberg is a bird with very elegant lines, which I can feel, even though it has been crushed in the rock for millennia. I do appreciate the fossils that Chrystal showed me when she and Rhys took me to raid her cache for money to buy this house."

"You bought this house?" I asked Chrystal, but it was Abi who answered.

"Yes, the house belongs to Chrystal. She uses it for somewhere to stay when she's in Wales – but Rhys and I live here the rest of the time."

"It is an arrangement that has benefits for each of us," added Chrystal.

"And what is this cache you keep referring to?" I asked.

"I have a number of, um, collectable items stored in a cave about fifty miles north of here," she said. "I find it convenient to purchase singular objects as they become available and retain them against future needs. It can be simpler to retrieve one of these and sell it to a private collector than to keep large sums of money either in a bank or a less secure place."

"So you've got a lot of – what? Paintings and things?"

"Yes, there are some paintings stored in there. There are a number of other items, too. The one we're collecting tomorrow is a rare fossil."

"A fossil of a bird?"

"Not just any bird," said Abi. "It's known as the Maxberg Archaeopteryx."

I must have looked as confused as I felt.

Chrystal set her mug down on the tree-stump table.

"The man who owned it was interested in selling, but did not wish to pay the punitive taxes to the German government. I purchased it from him in 1979, in a cash transaction which he did not declare to the authorities. To continue the subterfuge, he replaced it with a simple plinth of the same stone which he stored under his bed. He lived alone, so such a hoax was reasonably simple for him to perpetrate."

"And it's been stored in Wales ever since?"

"Indeed. And it has achieved a degree of notoriety in the decades since its removal from public view. Any museum would pay handsomely for that specimen."

"So you're selling it to a museum?"

"No," said Chrystal. "I will sell it to a dealer who will not ask me any questions once he has verified the authenticity of the piece. Then he will sell it on to a museum or private collector, refusing to name his source as he does so. I have no doubt that potential purchasers will be so pleased to learn that the item has resurfaced that they will not enquire too closely of a business man wishing to protect the anonymity of the contact he has bought it from."

"How will they know it's what you claim it is?" I persisted.

"There were photographic records taken when it was on display in the Museum before the owner hid it away. That was the Maxberg Museum, for which this particular fossil is named."

"And it's worth enough to pay for our tickets?"

"Oh, certainly," said Chrystal. "A dealer will pay handsomely for this particular bird and still make a sizeable profit for himself when he sells it again. That is the reason for my keeping these items in storage. Many such transactions grease the wheels of finance as well as the more visible movements of the economy."

"And it's a bird?"

"It's an archaeopteryx, Sam," said Abi. "The very first bird – and a very rare fossil even today. And truly beautiful, as you'll see for yourself."

Chapter 25

In which Sam learns of treasures

I slept like a log in that huge bed. Chrystal's side was already cold by the time I woke up even though the sun was hardly up and I followed the smell of breakfast downstairs, to find her chatting with Abi in a warm kitchen at the back of the house.

"Ah, there you are, sleepyhead," Chrystal greeted me.

"Why didn't you wake me?" I asked.

"We thought you'd better have chance to catch up on your sleep," said Abi. "Coffee or tea, dear?"

By the time we'd each eaten bacon sandwiches that would have satisfied the big bad wolf, Chrystal and I made it back to the railway station just before nine. She bought our tickets and we sat on a platform bench to wait. I was amazed when our train arrived – I thought this type had gone out of service years ago. It had those heavy door handles you had to turn two-handed to get them open and the seats were covered in faded blue material that had seen better days. Probably better decades, truth be told.

I was carrying a flat wooden crate that Chrystal had produced from somewhere back at the house. It was the size of a big picture frame and had leather straps fastened around it ending in handles, it hung from. I assumed this was to carry the fossil back and hoped it wasn't going to be too heavy. We both wore anonymous fleeces, jeans and heavy boots we'd borrowed from Abi's house, and I was glad of the warm coat as we settled on the lumpy seats. Chrystal had a leather shoulder bag over one arm and wore a relatively tame grey trilby, which would almost pass unnoticed in a crowd. She waved me to the window seat and settled next to me where she could catch the trolley when it came past.

The train took an hour to reach our destination – a tiny little station with no shelter and one small notice board per platform. There was no-one in sight and we were the only passengers leaving the train. I watched it chug slowly away, feeling like I'd been abandoned in the middle of, well, nowhere. I stopped to look at the station's name and wondered how to pronounce it. There were too many consonants arranged in an unlikely order and hardly any vowels.

"Through here," said Chrystal, holding open a gate that led to a narrow gravel path.

We walked in silence for a while. The crate banged against my back, my borrowed boots were too big and I had to watch the uneven path carefully. Chrystal walked in front and I was glad there wasn't enough room for us side by side. Despite the late morning sunshine, I was fed up of uncivilised countryside and wanted to just turn around to the comfortable bed in Cardiff. So I had my head down and almost walked into Chrystal when she turned to one side and ducked.

"Wha...?" I began and then saw the big black shape turning in the air and coming back for a second attack.

"Ravens," said Chrystal. "They will not hurt us, but they are big enough to startle anyone!"

I nodded in agreement as the gigantic black bird was joined by a second, then a third.

"What do they want?" I asked, covering my head with my

free arm. I was afraid they'd break my arm if one flew into me. "Why do birds always attack you?"

"Not all birds attack me in this way," she replied. "I have already mentioned it is only the corvidae that do so. Unfortunately they will persist in harassing us until we are underground."

"And we're safe then?" I asked.

"The corvids will not follow us into the cave."

All three ravens flew close above our heads, making us both duck and ending our conversation.

Chrystal turned off the path, pushing through ferny undergrowth and ducking under branches. I flinched from touching the dank, mossy bark, but at least the trees blocked the birds from dive-bombing us. I could hear them calling and occasionally saw one flying past but unable to reach us. I carried the crate under one arm so it wouldn't catch on the trees as we passed.

After five minutes of hurrying while frustrated birds yelled abuse, we reached a massive pile of boulders. It was about twelve feet high and looked like any other heap of rocks. I nearly walked into her again when she stopped.

"And we are here," she said.

"Here? This is your cave?"

I stared at the rocky mass, trying to imagine how it could hide a cave. Let alone one big enough to hold the treasures I'd been imagining. Chrystal took a brass lantern out of her bag and pushed through the ferns, towards the right of the pile. I looked up for any birds and when I turned back, she'd vanished.

"Chrystal?" I called, uncertainly.

I saw a flash on the rocks, faint in the sunlight, and made my way towards it. I came round the boulders and noticed a triangular crack in the rocks with light glinting inside. I looked in and saw the ground sloping away sharply inside. The narrow entry was higher than it had looked and I barely had to stoop to pass through. Chrystal was winding a key in the top of her lantern as she stood inside a passage into shadows that felt like every childhood nightmare.

I swallowed hard and stepped inside.

"This is your cave?" I asked, knowing how stupid that sounded, but needing to break the silence.

"This is merely the entry-way, but yes – down here is the cave I mentioned. Are you prepared to venture under the ground?"

I nodded and she turned briskly to descend deeper in. I hesitated, dreading the dark closeness, but hurried after her when she turned a corner and the shadows began to close in.

Speaking over her shoulder, she pointed at the rock wall.

"This is a natural fissure inside what the geologists call an intrusion. You may think of that as a cork made of volcanic rock that has filled a space left where older rocks have slipped apart slightly."

"Volcanic?" I asked in a small voice.

"Yes, although it is no longer active of course. This whole area has been geologically stable for millennia, but it has certain unusual features that result from its long-ago formation."

I hurried to catch up as she stopped by a deep hole. The passage plunged into a darkness that her lantern didn't touch. There was no way forward, the lantern showed only a rough stone wall. I glanced down into the abyss and quickly looked away, gulping down my fear. *We, were, going, down, THERE?* I closed my eyes for a moment and when I opened them again, Chrystal was looking at me with a quizzical expression.

"You do not like being underground?" she asked.

I shook my head. "It's the darkness – and lack of air," I half-whispered, hearing even that low sound echo back at me.

"Would you prefer to await my return at this point?"

Realising we only had one lantern, I shook my head emphatically.

"No, I can manage."

She looked at me for a moment, then reached for the crate I had been carrying. She laid it on the ground and I noticed a narrow ledge running along the side of the chasm in front of us. The crate fitted neatly onto this, as if it had been made to fit.

"The passage is very constricted at this point, but I will help you through. There is only the slightest danger," she said, fastening the lantern to a clasp on the left of her belt.

I didn't answer but watched her crawl onto the crate over the gaping hole, trying not to think what she meant by the *slightest danger* and fighting down the image of Chrystal falling, the lantern plummeting down until it smashed on a rock wall. Then she stopped and reached up with her right hand, lifting herself through a hole I hadn't noticed. Her feet vanished along with the light. Before I could panic, she moved the lantern so I could see dimly again and her head appeared in the hole she'd just wriggled through.

"Onto the bridge, Sam and be ready to climb through. Do not concern yourself with things that will not occur," she said.

I took a deep breath, dropped to my hands and knees and

began to edge onto the crate. I fixed my eyes on Chrystal's head poking through the hole with the light behind her. This stopped me looking down and reminded me how close she was. A few more inches and I felt her hand grab my arm.

"Now stand and come through here," she said.

I half-stood, gingerly, turning towards her and realised my head and shoulders were already through the hole in the rock wall. She pulled and I tumbled through, scuffing my jeans as I landed untidily in another stretch of the endless corridor.

Chrystal helped me to my feet and I saw she'd retrieved the crate from its place over the abyss.

"Not far now," she said and set off again.

It felt like an hour walking through that dusty hole of a tunnel, trying not to imagine the weight of stone over my head, but it must have been only a minute before we turned a corner and the passage opened up into a sizable cave. I gasped and stopped as Chrystal lifted her lantern and the full scale hit me. It was as big as a house, the rough walls meeting way above my head, where the light barely touched the craggy surfaces. The floor was level, but dusty and littered with small stones. I'd imagined it heaped with glittering treasures, like some dragon's hoard in a book, but the reality was more mundane and more exciting at the same time. There must have been twenty-odd crates piled against the far wall and Chrystal was striding towards these. I hurried after her and watched her check through the pile. With a jolt I realised they were all the same size – at least they'd all fit the ledge on the way in, though some would be a lot higher than the shallow one I'd been carrying.

"Here we are," said Chrystal, easing one out of the stack. It looked like all the others apart from an odd symbol burned into the side.

She laid it on the ground and unfastened a metal catch on the side. She lifted the lid, revealing a layer of grey-brown packing material wrapped around something that took up most of the crate.

"This is the Maxberg," she said with a smile. "Now we have to merely retrace our steps and take it to a dealer in fair Cardiff."

I answered her smile with a weaker echo, thinking of the difficult scramble through the caves to the surface and wondering how we were going to carry such an obviously heavy load. While I worried, she'd closed the crate, slipped the leather straps off the one I'd been carrying and was rebuckling them onto the new box. Suddenly I realised how well she'd planned everything and bent to pass her a strap. While she continued packaging it, I wound the clockwork lantern to make sure we could see to get out.

Exiting the cave was easier than I'd feared. Chrystal reached through the hole to position the crate, climbed through and lifted me onto solid ground as I scrambled after her. We were soon back in the free air and she rearranged the straps to share the burden, leather bands surprisingly comfortable on our right shoulders as the crate swung between us. The ravens were waiting for us, but I was getting used to them and tried to ignore their attentions as Chrystal did.

I stared out of the window as the rattly train took us back to Cardiff, our precious crate on the floor between us.

"You know, I'd never realised Wales was so pretty," I commented.

"No, I was not aware of that fact," replied Chrystal. "But it is a truly beautiful country. I always believe that it is important to appreciate the areas through which one travels. Rather than merely regarding a journey as a necessary evil."

"It's hard to appreciate anything from a plane."

"So it is, but one may still appreciate the endless display of nature's clouds. Or the stars, if one travels at night," she said.

I turned back to the view out of the window, trying to see it through Chrystal's eyes rather than my own.

Chapter 26

In which Chrystal sells a bird

Back in the tall grey brick house, we laid the crate on Abi's kitchen table as she bustled about, making us a late lunch. Or an early dinner – I wasn't sure which. But the smell of frying onions was driving me half-mad with hunger.

Chrystal unbuckled the straps from the crate, unfastened the clasp and pushed back the lid. She removed the packing material, dropping it onto the lid where it lay across two chairs. Then she lifted a slab of rock, followed by another layer of padding. For the first time, I saw what we'd gone to so much trouble to fetch – and it was incredible.

A second sheet of rock lay in the fluffy packing. Inside it lay a fossil like I'd never imagined. About a foot across, its bones were folded painfully, making it hard to make out the shape of the animal. I couldn't see a head and it wasn't clear which way up it had been. Then I looked closer and saw the impressions of feathers around the skeleton. It could have been a very scrawny chicken, squashed and covered with a layer of rock. Kind of.

"The Maxberg Archaeopteryx," announced Chrystal, her eyes sparkling mischievously. "Lost to science since 1974 and now miraculously re-discovered in Wales."

"It's beautiful," I whispered.

"Isn't she?" came Abi's voice. "Your omelettes are ready, so you'd better come eat while they're hot."

I didn't need telling twice and Chrystal and I tucked into fluffy omelettes bursting with melted cheese, fried onions and mushrooms, served with thick slices of fresh bread to soak up the juices.

Abi had washed her hands and was exploring the fossil with her fingers, an ecstatic expression on her face. No-one spoke for a few minutes until Chrystal laid her cutlery on the plate.

"Abi, that was truly magnificent. If I thought it was possible, I would say your cooking improves every time I am fortunate enough to sample it!"

I agreed silently as I stuffed the last scraps into my mouth.

"It's the very least I can do, my dear. You've done so much for us," said Abi.

"Nonsense, I owe both you and The Professor far more than I could ever repay," said Chrystal, pushing her empty plate away.

"Do you really have to sell her?" Abi was caressing the fossil again.

"Unfortunately so," said Chrystal, crossing the room to stand by the shorter woman. "But there is every chance that she will be exhibited in a museum where you could visit her."

"Maybe so, but they will not let me touch her." Abi sounded so wistful and I wondered for a moment if there was another way Chrystal could raise the money, so we could leave the fossil with this remarkable blind woman.

"I am sorry, Abi," she said. "Perhaps I should have left the old bird with you all these years. If I had known how much you loved her, you could have had the pleasure of her company, instead of my storing her underground."

"Not to worry," said Abi. "I've enjoyed the chance to be with her again today and that will have to be enough."

"But it'll be here for a few days," I interrupted. "Until we can sell it."

"I'm afraid not," said Abi. "I contacted your buyer whilst you were fetching the fossil from the cave – and he wants to see her immediately. He's given me his home address and asks that you take it to show him this evening, if possible."

Chrystal stepped around the table and hugged her, wordlessly.

For a long moment no-one moved until Abi said, "So you'd better pack her away again. Before I change my mind!"

Chrystal obligingly replaced the contents of the crate and buckled the straps into their carrying position. I could hear Abi in the hallway, phoning for a taxi to collect us with our precious burden and found myself feeling guilty as if I was stealing something. While we waited, Chrystal flicked idly through the phone directory and I chatted with Abi. She was remarkably well-informed about all sorts of things, and she spoke passionately about the regional rugby team while I made agreeable noises and tried to sound as if I knew something about the sport. So I was glad when the taxi arrived and Chrystal helped me carry the crate outside.

The buyer's home was on a small estate in another part of Cardiff. The taxi had to stop at a gate while a man in a grey uniform phoned through to check we were expected. The driver stopped outside a large, detached house and settled to wait for us.

A short, balding man met us at the door and led us inside.

He squeezed my hand hard enough to hurt when we shook and I watched his face as he tried the same with Chrystal, knowing that she could more than match his grip. His eyes bulged for a moment until she released him with a smile.

"You have it with you?" he asked.

Chrystal tilted her head slightly and lifted the crate onto the table he indicated. She unfastened the straps, released the catch and lifted the lid, the dealer craning his neck to see what was inside. Chrystal removed the first layer of wadding and lifted the upper stone, revealing the impression of the fossil. He cooed over that as if it was an infant, so he wasn't watching as Chrystal lifted the wadding that protected the bird itself.

I've never seen anyone look so surprised – and so greedy. Within seconds he was caressing the piece, trying to cover it with his arms as if he needed to protect it from us.

"I can assure you of its authenticity," said Chrystal, interrupting his blissful inspection.

"Oh, I'm sure, I'm sure," he warbled.

"And the price...?"

He straightened and looked up at her.

"I can have it by Thursday," he said.

"Then we will return on Thursday," said Chrystal. She replaced the wadding and reached for the stone cover.

"What? No!" he started.

"Yes, I will return with the item on Thursday, once you have the money ready to transfer."

"But..."

"And in the meantime I have one last thing to do with the archaeopteryx before I part with it," said Chrystal.

"What are you doing with it?" he asked, sounding both

defensive and aggressive at the same time.

"Nothing that need concern you," said Chrystal. "Neither is it anything that will detract from the item's value. We will return on Thursday."

"Wait! I'll need to take a photo," he said, pulling her away from the fossil.

"Quickly then," she replied and uncovered the crushed chicken-form again.

The dealer took several photos from different angles before Chrystal recovered it and swept out to the taxi before he could argue further.

I didn't understand half the words in the address she gave the taxi driver, but he seemed to know what those throaty, musical syllables meant.

"Do we really have time for this?" I asked. "I thought we were in a hurry."

"There is sufficient time for us to make a friend happy. Even if that necessitates our hurrying a little more," she replied.

The taxi stopped outside a small unit on an industrial estate of similarly anonymous boxes, somewhere on the edge of the city. Once again, Chrystal asked the driver to wait for us and led me to a human-sized door set into the massive metal shutters at one end of the building. Before she could knock, the door opened and a head appeared.

"Yes?" asked the head and I realised it was a woman.

"Hello, my name is Chrystal. I am looking for the sculptor."

"Whatever it is, I gave already," replied, the stranger,

pulling her head back and beginning to close the door. Chrystal blocked it with her foot.

"I am not collecting for a charitable venture. In fact I was hoping to pay you for your services."

The door opened a few inches and the head appeared again.

"Go on," it said.

"I believe that you work in plaster of Paris?" said Chrystal.

"I don't plaster walls," she replied. "And I'm not a nurse, either."

"Thank heavens for that. I was looking for someone skilled in more artistic uses of fine plaster. I believe you make works of art from such materials?"

For the first time, the woman stepped out of the building. She was quite short, a bit stocky and her short, blond hair was messy with fine, white dust.

"You wanted to see the work I have for sale? There's only a few in stock at the moment..." she said.

"I was planning to commission a new work from you, actually."

"You'd better come in, then," said the woman, stepping back to hold the door open for us.

Chrystal led the way into an echo-ey room. A stack of metal shelves held paper sacks, plastic bottles and a few stark, white things I assumed were the sculptures the sculptor'd mentioned. I moved closer for a better look. The lower shelf held models of curiously-shaped hands with webbed, elongated fingers that looked as if they'd been thrust through a wall. There were several of each and I found them oddly beautiful. On the shelf above were larger pieces, one of a naked breast and the curve of a waist – again breaking through a wall. On these, the wall part had been painted with the kind of almost-white colours that used to be fashionable for dining rooms, the skin in a delicate sky-blue. There were other body parts represented on that shelf, all in the same style. The more I looked at them, the more I liked them. The sculptor obviously had an eye for taking everyday shapes and turning them into a work of beauty.

Chrystal was talking to our host.

"... as faithful a representation as possible."

"And it's a fossil?"

In response, Chrystal took the crate from me and laid it flat on the hastily-cleared workbench. She unfastened it, lifting the lid and removed the wadding. The blond woman whistled.

"That's certainly pretty. And you just want a single copy?"

I realised what we were doing here and tried not to grin at Chrystal.

"Yes, I require just the one copy in plaster. I will collect it from you on Thursday morning."

"Thursday? I won't have time to paint it for you," she said.

"There is no need to paint it. I wish for it to be left plain, but sealed against the environment."

"The sealant doesn't make it rainproof, you know. You can't leave it outdoors."

"You need not concern yourself with that. The piece will be, er, exhibited indoors, but I require it to be able to be handled. Also, it is important that the sealant preserve as much detail as possible."

"And you're sure you don't want it painting?"

Chrystal shook her head and I moved away as they started

discussing the price for the work. I was fascinated by the sculptures. I found what I realised was the mould for the bust and waist one. It was a dark green, rubbery shape, with the smooth curves of the sculpture on the inside and a rougher surface on the outside. I picked it up, fascinated to see how it would peel away from the finished piece once the plaster had set inside.

It had gone quiet and I looked up to see the other two watching me. Chrystal's face was blank but the sculptress was smiling.

"Yes, that's how I make so many of the same shape, if you were wondering," she said.

I put the mould down hurriedly and walked back towards them.

"Oh, don't worry. I don't claim the casts are unique. My buyers know they're getting one of a limited run. See?" She picked up one of the stretched hand sculptures and showed me the base. Some numbers were written in a black felt-tip.

"This is number two-three-five out of five hundred. Once I've made the full five hundred, I destroy the mould and that's the end of that line."

Feeling awkward at being caught poking around, I tried to sound interested.

"Are they solid plaster?"

"These small ones are, it'd be too fiddly to do it any other way. But the larger ones are hollow." She tapped one which rang like a big plant pot.

"Only I use a wire framework to support the plaster. So they're not too heavy to carry and hang on a wall," she smiled.

"You are confident that you can complete the work before

Thursday morning?" interrupted Chrystal.

"Yes, absolutely, because it's fairly shallow. I'll mix up the rubber immediately and leave that to set on the original overnight. That'll leave the plaster a day and a half to dry out."

"Excellent," Chrystal smiled and inclined her head before leaving the studio, with me hurrying after her.

Chapter 27

In which Chrystal and Sam travel to a port

Thursday morning passed chaotically in a tangle of taxi rides and hurried visits. First we dashed out to the industrial unit to collect the fossil and check the copy, leaving it with the sculptress while we visited the art dealer's shop in the city centre. Chrystal carried the small briefcase of cash he gave her as our cab driver took us back to pay for the duplicate and we were back on the road, this time with the crated plaster replica at our feet. The incredibly patient driver said he'd wait as we delivered the cast to Abi. If I'd had any doubts about the time we'd wasted on getting it, they vanished the moment I saw her face. Her smile lit up the room as if we'd uncovered a hundred of Chrystal's clockwork lanterns. But there was only time for us to make a quick farewell and run out again with our overnight bags, the briefcase of cash and the ætheric sender.

Chrystal spent the journey dividing the cash wrapping most in two cotton bags and pushing them to the bottom of our luggage. She kept a little back - a couple of notes to pay the driver and a few others she folded into her wallet.

Our final visit was to Cerys, who presented us with a huge suit carrier that strained at its seams. Chrystal paid him (her?), they exchanged kisses and we were back in the waiting taxi in record time.

The driver got us to the station in time for our train, thanked Chrystal enthusiastically for his tip and pressed business cards into our hands, "In case you good ladies ever come back to Cardiff and need a driver again." Chrystal handed the empty briefcase to a man with an armful of *The Big Issue* outside the station, instructing him to sell it and buy a hot meal. Then she bought tickets and we dashed down the stairs to our platform as the train pulled in.

Chrystal chose a nearly empty carriage and placed her bag and the sender's box on the window seat before sitting next to them and crossing her legs. I sat opposite, breathless, hugging my rucksack and trying not to think about the money it contained. I couldn't believe Chrystal had trusted me with so much cash - especially since we'd met when I tried to pick her pocket in the tube station.

But then again, she had that uncanny knack of tracking me down when I didn't think she knew enough to find me. So maybe she wasn't trusting me at all, just the uncanny ability way her Chrystal could locate me if I tried to steal her money. Uncertain, I clutched the bag even tighter and looked up to see her green eyes staring at me. For the first time in a while, I felt that she'd been following my unspoken thoughts.

"Perhaps you could fetch us each a coffee?" she suggested. "I believe the buffet car is that way." She gestured forward along the train and I stood to go, then paused and looked at my rucksack.

"Um," I began. She looked up but didn't reply, so I swung it onto my back and smiled.

"Did you want anything to go with it?" I asked, trying to sound casual and not as if I had more money on my back than I'd ever seen before in my life.

"Do look to see if they have any cakes that look edible," she replied and I set off, tightening the shoulder straps as I did so.

Walking back, with two coffees and a paper bag with fresh Danish pastries balanced in front of me, I couldn't worry about the money in my bag and wondered if that had been the idea. I'd never make much of a secret agent, if I couldn't even carry a bundle of cash without behaving as if I expected everyone to grab it.

Chrystal was writing in a notepad balanced on her leg, but looked up as I handed her one of the coffees and sat down opposite.

"Cinnamon or apple?" I asked, tearing open the bag of Danish.

She took the cinnamon swirl and we ate in companionable silence. Surprisingly, the cake was fresh and quite tasty, the apple filling moist with real fruit chunks and not too much sugar.

"We need to work out our next moves," said Chrystal as we finished and wiped our hands on the paper napkins. I couldn't remember the last time I'd been on a train cross-country before Chrystal started steering me around. I'm sure they didn't used to be this comfortable. Even the coffee was worth drinking!

"Firstly, the train will convey us to Southampton. We will stay in The Royal Hotel for one night before boarding our ship on the morrow."

"Wow - no wonder you were in such a hurry. What about our luggage? The stuff we sent from your flat?" I asked.

"That will be awaiting us in our cabin. Everything has been booked, deposits have been paid and it only remains for me to make the substantive payment."

"Don't they expect payment months in advance?" I asked.

She smiled that in infuriating way. "They are always very accommodating for their established customer," she replied.

I stared out of the window for a moment, watching fields and cows flash by. I wondered how much all this was costing Chrystal. She'd got so much for the fossil, but even that would run out sometime. But then my I pictured the stack of crates in Chrystal's cave in the Welsh countryside and realised she must be even richer than I'd thought. I looked up to see her looking at the notebook in her hands, flicking through pages as if searching for something. I saw her neat writing and lots of strange characters I didn't recognise. There were even a couple of sketches that looked like parts of a church.

"Um," I started. She looked up, smiled gently, then closed her book and rested her hands on it.

"I was wondering. About those crates we saw. Are they all yours?"

She glanced past me and turned to check the carriage behind her seat. Seeing no-one in earshot, she leaned towards me to answer.

"Indeed, they are my personal safety fund."

"Are they all fossils? Like the archaeopteryx?" I asked.

"No, not at all. I have purchased items of all sorts over the years. I selected the Maxberg on this occasion because I felt that this is an auspicious time to sell it as there is increased interest in fossils in recent years. There are other fossilised items in the crates, but also paintings, small sculptures, jewellery and other pieces."

"But why? I mean, why not just keep your money in a bank?"

"Banks may be worthy institutions, but they are not entirely safe." She paused and then went on, "I lost considerable savings in the bank collapses of the *soi disant* Great Depression of 1929. Since then, I have endeavoured to keep readily-saleable items in storage, rather than cash in bank vaults."

"So you buy things that will go up in value, rather than storing actual money, which will go down in real terms?" I commented.

She smiled at me and I decided to make the most of her good mood.

"So what else is in there? Are there any great treasures I'll have heard of?"

She thought for a moment, then, "It is possible that you

may have heard news of some of my collection. Are you aware of a fossil referred to as 'Peking Man'?"

"Yes, I have!" I was excited to think I knew something about Chrystal's treasures. "Is that in there?"

"There are a few bones stored in one of the crates. I purchased them from an American sailor who claimed they were the spoils of war. I believe he may have stolen them from the cargo ship he worked on. But it was war time again and many things went missing, never to be seen again."

"But wouldn't they be important to museums and scientists? I'm sure they'd want to examine the bones now they've got better technology. Aren't you being really selfish?"

Chrystal laughed lightly. "The bones are half a million years old. I am certain your modern scientists can wait a few more years to examine them."

I stared out of the window for a moment. The green scenery rolled past like a film set, black and white cows in a few fields, cotton wool sheep in many more. The occasional little town whizzed past in a clatter of tracks, a few people waiting at level crossings. I remembered something and said,

"You know, I don't think I've been to Wales since I was seven years old."

Chrystal turned to look at me. "I am sorry?"

"I was just thinking about Wales, and I realised we came here for a family holiday. I must have been seven because it was the last holiday when we were all together. I didn't want to go, but my parents couldn't leave me on my own."

"You would have preferred to be alone in your house? Rather than travelling with your parents?"

"Well, no. But I didn't want to go away for a fortnight and leave all my friends behind. I think I sulked for the whole holiday," I said with a smile. "I was a real brat at that age."

"Seven years of age?" replied Chrystal, slowly. A thoughtful expression came over her face and it was a moment before she continued. "It was very different when I was a girl. Children were expected to behave as miniature adults for much of the time. That was about the age when my brothers began to wear trousers instead of dresses."

"Your brothers wore dresses? That's weird," I said.

"Not for us," she smiled. "So many children did not reach maturity, we were treated as a group for many years. We only began to distinguish ourselves as we grew older."

I struggled with this whole idea, that children somehow didn't have individual personalities.

"And you started dressing differently at about the age of seven?"

"My brothers did. Girls wore childish clothes until about twice that age. I was given my first boned corset when I became a woman, which is when a young lady starts to think about looking for a good husband and thus understanding the need for a womanly figure," she said.

"And that meant starting to wear a corset? Really?"

"An adult one. We had all worn light ones since we could walk, but the boys cease to wear them and the girls go on to the ones with bones. Or metal, if that was preferred. I remember being very pleased that I was grown-up enough for Mother to buy it for me."

"And you were what - thirteen, fourteen?" Chrystal nodded. "At that age I had my ears pierced again and got my hair bleached. Mum threw a fit, but what could she do?"

Chrystal looked wistful but didn't comment.

After a moment I went on, "And you've been wearing corsets ever since?" I knew how tiny her waist was and I'd seen her lace herself into a boned undergarment more than once. But it'd never occurred to me she'd been wearing them all these years.

"Well, yes. In Victoria's day, a lady would not be properly

dressed without one. I would feel undressed were I to appear in company without a corset."

"But aren't they terribly uncomfortable?"

"Only a little. One does get used to that small discomfort. And I have allowed myself to ease the lacing, over the years. I do not believe that a woman is judged by her waist measurement as we were in those days."

I snorted. "Oh, yes we are!"

"Surely not in the same way. I have not seen anyone attempting to reduce their waist below twenty inches for more than a century."

"Twenty inches?" I couldn't believe my ears.

"Oh yes. A woman was considered fat it she were more than that. I held mine at nineteen for many years. And many went even smaller!"

"But, isn't that too small? I mean, that couldn't possibly be healthy."

"Healthy?"

"Wearing something that deformed your body. What if a woman was ill? Or pregnant?" I blurted.

"There were different corsets for ladies who were with child, of course. But many women lost their children, which may have been a consequence of their corsetry, in part. It is true that they brought their own problems. But I still would not feel right were I not to wear one."

I was saved from having to answer by the train slowing down as we reached our station. Chrystal stood to lift the ætheric sender down and I grabbed Cerys' suit carrier and our bags.

Chapter 28

In which a great ship is boarded

I'd been to Southampton before, but never paid much attention. I guess we'd just driven from the motorway to the port, so I must've seen bits of the city but couldn't remember anything about it. I used to think of myself as fairly well-travelled, but today I was thinking how little I'd seen. Just airports, hotels and beaches with occasional trips to see the guide book's idea of scenery or cultural buildings. I realised I'd only been a tourist and now I wanted to travel instead. Chrystal was muscling in on my thoughts all sorts of ways!

And I wasn't sure I liked it.

I might find her fascinating and enjoy sharing a bed with her. But I wasn't sure I wanted to become like her, even in a small way. There was something more than unsettling about Chrystal's company. It wasn't just that she was much older than anyone I'd ever met, or even that lump of stone in her chest. She could find me when I thought I'd given her the slip and she seemed to know what I was thinking a little too often and that made me uncomfortable.

I stared out of the window, trying not to appreciate the sights Chrystal pointed out as the taxi drove us from the station. Eventually she took the hint and stopped trying to get me to chat.

Our taxi reached the front of the queue. This driver seemed as surly as the Cardiff one had been friendly and barely said a word as he unloaded our bags onto the concrete. I left Chrystal to pay him and went in search of a trolley. I may not have been on a cruise before, but everything was pretty much the same as any airport I'd ever flown from. I got back to where Chrystal was waiting and helped her load the bags, suit carrier and ætheric sender in its wooden case.

"Sam? Are you alright?" she asked, touching my hand as I strapped the box on top of the pile.

I kept my face down, unsure of my own feelings and unwilling to talk to her. I stepped round the trolley, getting into position to push it through the glass doors and onto the concourse, but Chrystal grabbed my arm and swung me gently to stand against a concrete pillar. I tried to ignore her, knowing I couldn't escape her grip. But instead of talking she caught my other shoulder and pulled me in for a kiss. However unsociable I felt, I couldn't resist and, after a moment, returned the kiss passionately. I became aware of someone wolf-whistling and broke contact, meeting Chrystal's mischievous eye.

"That is better," she said softly. "I know things have been rather fraught these last few days, but we are mere yards away from our accommodation. If you can bear with me until we reach that, then we will be able to talk in private. Or just settle down and unwind for a while, if that is what you need."

She still had her arms around me and I relaxed into her embrace, taking deep breaths until I trusted myself to speak.

" 'M sorry," I muttered into her neck. She hugged me briefly and we both straightened up.

A group of young men stood in the doorway, evidently enjoying the spectacle we'd been making of ourselves. They were whistling and offering suggestions that sounded anatomically unlikely, and I braced myself to push the trolley round the side of their little huddle. I hadn't banked on Chrystal, though. As I got the trolley moving, she stepped ahead and walked straight through the middle as if they weren't there. I couldn't see her face, but they could and the gang parted like water off the proverbial duck's back. And then we were inside.

The airport flavour continued, with roped-off queues

waiting for check-in desks. I looked for the shortest queue, although none of them looked as long as I was used to; but Chrystal ignored them all and marched over to a man wearing a uniform with four stripes of gold braid on each shoulder of his dark jacket. She waited for him to notice her and inclined her head to him just as I drew level with our luggage.

"Ma'am?" he asked, smiling pleasantly.

"Good morning, I was wondering if there may be an expedited route for passengers travelling in the Queen's Grill Suites on board the good Queen Victoria?" She gave him one of her wide-eyed looks, smiling in that innocent fashion I was learning to understand.

"And you are one of our Queen's Grill passengers, Ma'am?" He looked her up and down appraisingly and I could see him taking in her wasp-waisted figure in tailored jeans and blouse, with her short jacket over the top. Then he turned to look at me, standing at her side, and his face hardened a little. I took a deep breath and tried to look as if I were the sort of person who travelled in exorbitantly expensive suites on ocean liners whenever I wanted to. He didn't look convinced.

"Why, yes. We're in the Berengaria Suite, Captain," Chrystal's tone caught his attention and his gaze flew back to her. I breathed out again.

"The Berengaria, Ma'am? I'm sure we can assist you." He nodded to his companions who stood aside as he held his right arm out to Chrystal. She made a move that would have been a curtsy if she was wearing one of her dresses, smiled sweetly and slipped her hand through his elbow. The two of them made their way towards the far end of the check-in desks and I followed after with the trolley, until a young man with an official-looking lanyard-tag took over. Then I had nothing to do except try to keep up as the crowds parted ahead of Chrystal and closed back together after she passed.

At the end of the check-in desks was a separate channel labelled "Cunard Staff Only", with two large men in dark uniforms leaning on the counter. The smartly-uniformed young woman on the other side of the desk looked up and beamed at Chrystal's escort.

"Good morning, Captain Himes," she said.

"Kazumi, this is Lady Carstairs. She and her companion will be cruising with us. In the Berengaria. Would you do what you can to expedite her check-in, please?"

"Of course, Captain." She swept her full-beam smile over me and onto Chrystal. "Your passports?"

Chrystal produced her document and passed it over while I rummaged in my handbag. I always meant to have it to hand, but I never remembered and it always slid into the bottom of whatever bag I was carrying. So I was used to the look from the member of staff who had to wait while I fumbled. At last my fingers closed on its green leather case and I passed it to her. I was grateful she only glanced once between the picture in there and my face and rattled quickly through the usual questions, although I was beginning to wonder if her face smiled like that even when she was asleep. She handed us back our passports together with boarding cards and a small handful of papers I hoped weren't important as I didn't have chance to look through them.

We left our luggage to make its own way, and I tried not to stare after the trolley as I remembered how much money was sitting in the bottom of my little rucksack. Chrystal had paid a lot of her share over the counter for our tickets, but my bag was untouched. I swallowed hard, keeping my eyes forward as we stepped into the Departures area. The Captain stood waiting and once again offered his arm to Chrystal. Much to my surprise, he then offered his left arm to me.

"Now, let's see if we can get you two ladies on board the *Queen Vee*, shall we?" he said.

I'm not sure how much he managed to trim off what should have been the full process, but we seemed to walk straight through with only a couple of brief stops for people to check our boarding cards and passports. We went through a channel labelled *Crew Only* instead of queuing for the metal detectors. Chrystal kept up a steady flow of chatter, alternately flattering the Captain and enthusing about the cruise. They didn't seem to need me to speak, so I just hung onto his arm and kept up. Chrystal was so infuriating - loving and tender when we were alone, but treating me like a servant the minute someone more interesting came along. I guess I should have been grateful to get on the fast-track in this way, but I didn't have to like being the hanger-on. We stopped in a couple of the duty-free stores where Chrystal bought a couple of overpriced souvenirs, some perfume and several pairs of lacy knickers. Then she changed her remaining cash for dollars.

Eventually we came to a pair of huge glass doors, with the ship immediately outside. I gasped at the sight of it - I knew it was going to be big, but I hadn't realised...

"Beautiful, isn't she?" the Captain squeezed my arm. He waited for me to answer and then went on, "Second-best day of my life, being given the Old Girl as a command. I'd say the best day, but my wife always complained."

"You are married, Captain?" enquired Chrystal. "You did not mention your lady wife."

He shook his head. "I'm afraid the Memsahib passed away a few years ago. Cancer. Terrible business, but at least it was quick."

"Oh, I am so sorry to hear that, Captain. What a terrible shame," said Chrystal.

"Not for you to worry yourself about, my dear," he said. "Ancient history, ancient history."

"And you have not found yourself a new lady?"

He stopped at the double doors, released our arms and turned to face us both. "Never found the right one to replace her. Guess I'm married to the ship now, unless I meet someone who'll put up with all my little habits," he said, winking.

"Now," he went on. "I have to leave you two ladies while I make a last few checks with the land-crew. But if you'd take a seat in here, I'll send one of my staff officers to collect you as soon as the ship's ready to board. The Ladies' room is over there."

Chrystal smiled at me, then followed the Captain's gesture and disappeared into the toilet. I dumped my handbag on a seat near the wall and had a quick rummage for my hairbrush. Chrystal reappeared after a few minutes, looking as fresh as if she'd just showered and dressed. I left my bag and slipped into the loo.

When I came out, Chrystal had moved to one of the furthest seats, her back towards the desk by the doors and she gestured me into the seat opposite, next to my bag.

"Is she listening?" she asked under her breath.

"I'm sorry?" I said.

"The staff member on the desk, is her attention on our conversation?"

I looked over her shoulder. The uniformed woman had a phone clamped to her ear and was tapping on a keyboard or something behind the counter. There was no-one else in sight. I relayed all this to Chrystal.

"That is well," she said. "You must continue to watch her and warn me if she appears to be interested in what we are discussing. Or if another person should come into the waiting room."

"Okay, but why?" I asked.

"Because we need to be certain that we both tell the same story to anyone who enquires. As the crossing will take a number of days, it is important that we are prepared to deal with curiosity from crew members and our fellow passengers. So there is need of a more in-depth explanation than we have used to date."

"Right. So who are we now?"

"Much as we have been previously," she smiled. "You may still call me your Aunt, but should anyone enquire further, you may mention that we merely distant relations. I am bringing you on this cruise as a matter of some charity, as your own family could not afford to offer such costly diversions. This will afford us a simple explanation for your not having been brought up in Gentle surroundings and yet being present on this ship."

She paused and I said, "Okay, that all fits. So you're the one with the money and I'm a poor niece along for the ride?"

She smiled. "Indeed, although I do not wish you to view yourself in that light. It will merely make for an easier life than explaining our true relationship to others."

"How are we related, then?"

"You may work out whatever details you feel appropriate. I am travelling under the name of Olivia Carstairs, but my preferred use-name is Chrystal and I will encourage people to use that name."

"So why Olivia Carstairs? Why not use your own name..." I petered out as I realised it was a dumb question.

"I cannot register using my original details, of course," she answered. "I have papers which give my identity as Olivia, who was born in 1981. This is the name on my passport."

"So who is Olivia Carstairs? Doesn't she mind you using her identity?"

She smiled sadly. "Olivia Carstairs passed away when she was a babe in arms. Tragic, but it enables me to obtain copies of her documentation and use her name. Carstairs was my family name and I prefer to use that when I can. But I require a new name and documents every ten years or so, in this paper-obsessed century. I have learned much about such subterfuges over the years and now ensure that I have another name ready to use before the current one becomes too *old* for my purposes."

"So you have another identity ready?"

"Three, actually. I obtain details of an infant mortality when it happens, being sure to choose one that has few relations. Then I apply for a copy of the birth certificate a few years later and store them until they would be close to the age that I appear. This enables me to apply for a passport in that name, which serves for ten years and then I move on to the next in line."

"Wow. That must get really complicated! Don't you get confused?"

"It is not so difficult as you may expect. More often than not, I have been able to use the name Carstairs - and I always quote Chrystal as my use-name. Many people do not like to be called by their given name, so it is not seen as unusual to offer an alternative. But I am sure you can understand that - Samantha!"

She said my full name with such a mischievous smile that I could not take offence. I hadn't considered the difficulties she'd had to work around, not being able to use her real identity for anything and this seemed like a good system. But I'm sure I couldn't do it half as well.

"But what about these new passports?" I asked. "When they'll have biometric data and fingerprints and stuff?"

"As yet, I have not had to face these problems," she replied. "Neither do I know how I will work around them. I will concern myself with such details when I need to do so."

Before I could quiz her further, the big doors opened to admit a young man in a uniform similar to the Captain's, but with only two stripes on his shoulder-tabs.

"Uh-oh, company," I hissed as he strode across the room towards us.

Chrystal stood and turned as he approached.

"Lady Carstairs," he asked, holding out his hand to shake.

Chrystal just smiled and he continued, "I'm Ryuu, the Third Officer. Captain Himes asked me to escort you ladies to your suite. If we hurry, we can get you aboard before the gangway is opened for the remaining passengers. It's always a little chaotic and I'm sure you'd both rather be getting yourselves comfortable while the ship loads." As he spoke, he picked up our shopping and led us both to the doors. He waved at the girl behind the counter and walked us straight through. Whenever he paused for breath, Chrystal prompted him with a question and we were on board before anyone could interrupt and ask for our papers. A knot of uniformed people stood chatting at the end of the gangway and they untangled into a line as we approached. The first was Captain Himes and he bowed to us.

"Ladies," he said and smiled as we passed along the line. A thin man gave us bottles of hand gel and I heard voices and footsteps on the gangway just as we passed the end of the smiling line.

The Third Officer led us into the ship proper and through a maze of corridors. I gave up trying to keep track and stared around me rather than listen to Chrystal flirting with the officer. He looked oriental and his age could have been anything from twenty to fifty. His dark eyes missed nothing as we walked and he'd barely given me a second glance. I found myself trailing along behind the pair - as usual.

He took us to a lift and then along a corridor to a door labelled, Berengaria Suite. He opened the door with his key-card and held it open for us both to enter.

It was amazing! Although Chrystal and various crew members had called it a Suite, I was expecting nothing more than a bedroom with a little sitting area. But this was larger than my old flat had been! You could have dropped my bedsit into the comfy lounge we were standing in - and it would have rattled around.

Ryuu placed our bags carefully on the sofa.

"Ladies, may I introduce you to your butler," he said. A stocky man in dark suit and bow tie stepped forward and bowed to us. I'd guess he was late twenty-something, blond hair gelled and a neatly-trimmed moustache and small beard.

"Good afternoon, Ladies. My name is Storm and I'm very happy to serve you for the cruise," he said.

I choked back an exclamation - a butler! Fortunately, Chrystal wasn't fazed.

"Good afternoon, Storm. A pleasure to make your acquaintance," she said with a slight tilt of her head.

"Now if you'll excuse me, ladies," said the young Third Officer. "I'm afraid I must dash off - other duties to attend to while we board the ship fully. I'd suggest you stay in here for the duration, although you'll want to be on deck as we set sail. I'm sure we'll bump into each other again during the voyage."

Chrystal thanked him for his assistance and he hurried off, leaving us in the opulent surroundings. Storm held a stiff white envelope out to her.

"I believe this will be an invitation to the Senior Officers' Party for this evening, m'lady," he said.

Chrystal accepted the envelope, opened it and pulled out an embossed ivory-coloured card. I moved closer to see, it read

Dear Lady Carstairs and Ms Fletcher,
You are cordially invited to
meet with the ship's company at
The Senior Officer's Party
in The Queen's Grill.
7-30pm for 8pm
Dress code: formal, black tie.

"Excellent," said Chrystal. "That will give us sufficient time to unpack and dress for the evening's entertainment with the Officers."

"There will of course be a lifeboat drill after we sail, Lady Carstairs. And I will be most happy to assist with your unpacking," said Storm. "As well, of course, with any other questions you may have...?"

He left the question hanging and Chrystal gestured through a doorway, then followed him through, grabbing my hand to make sure I wasn't left behind.

The bed looked huge, already made up with a duvet in an embroidered cream-and-coffee coloured cover, with a few of those little throw-pillows and a dark brown mini-quilt at the foot end. A dressing table sat against one wall and tall cabinets on either side of the bed. Storm had carried on through another door and we followed him - into a walk-in wardrobe. Or dressing room. I wasn't even sure what to call it! He turned on his heel and stood next to a pile of trunks, cases and the luggage we'd checked in earlier.

"I believe this should be all of your luggage?" he asked.

"That appears to be everything," said Chrystal.

"Shall I begin to unpack, m'lady?"

She looked at me for a moment, then answered him, "No, thank you, Storm. If you would please arrange for some coffee and light refreshments, we would like a little time to freshen ourselves ready for the necessary lifeboat drill. Perhaps you could return with them in about two hours?"

"Of course, Lady Carstairs," he said stiffly.

"And please bring back a supply of little envelopes," she added. I didn't understand, but the smile on Storm's face suggested that he not only knew what she was talking about, but very much liked whatever it meant.

"Thank you, m'lady," he said with a bow. "I believe the drill is scheduled for Twenty-Hundred hours." When neither of us said anything further, he left the dressing room and we heard the door to the corridor pulled shut behind him.

Chrystal didn't waste even a second. As soon as the door closed, she turned, strode back through the door and I hurried after, to find her sprawled on the massive bed. She rolled over as I entered, grinning hugely.

"Welcome aboard, Sam-of-the-boy's-name. Do you find the accommodation sufficient?"

"Sufficient?" I landed on the bed next to her. "It's incredible! Why didn't you warn me? I think it's bigger than your whole apartment!"

"So it is, and it even comes with staff to fetch and clean for us."

"And this is all yours?"

She rolled over and lifted herself on one elbow to meet my eyes. "All *ours.* It is your home as much as it is mine for the next two weeks," she answered.

"Can we explore?" I asked, feeling like a little child.

Chrystal stood smoothly and held out her right arm. I locked hands with her and she pulled me up effortlessly. Then she looped our arms together and led me through a door with two satiny bathrobes hanging on it, into the adjacent bathroom.

"There's a bath!" I said, realising what a stupid comment it was even as I did so.

"And a separate shower cubicle, if you prefer," she replied. I had chance to register a shiny little metal rack with bottles of toiletries in it and the heavy-looking towels draped over a rack on the wall. Then she pulled on my arm again, past the pair of basins and the built-in make-up bench with its lights and mirrors and we were back at the sofa and comfy chairs we'd seen first.

"Wow! It's amazing."

Chrystal grinned again.

"Not finished yet," she said and led me into yet another room, furnished with a dining table and *six* chairs! While I was still reeling from that surprise, she pulled me through another door and I found myself standing on,

"A balcony!"

"Our balcony," she corrected me. "It is private to our suite and cannot be reached from anywhere else on the ship."

I leaned on the metal railing and took a moment to get my bearings. We were at the back - aft - of the ship, on one of the highest decks. I looked down and to the side, watching people bustling on the quayside and two men loading boxes onto a smaller boat tied-up behind ours.

When I went back inside, I found Chrystal with the suit carrier I'd been carrying since Cardiff until we handed it to the staff at the port.

"Would you like to see what Cerys made for you?"

I didn't need telling twice. I'd been longing to open this more than anything since I was a child and still believed in Santa.

The suit carrier was hanging on a wardrobe pole, so all I had to do was unzip it all the way round and push the cover back so it fell away from the contents.

I gasped.

Chapter 29

In which a trail is seen to go cold

The screen showed very few lights, only one of which lasted for more than three seconds, many flashed just once. A fingernail tapped impatiently on the display and long fingers twisted brass knobs. But nothing could change the increasingly obvious fact that there was no significant display of ætheric activity on the screen.

"She has vanished, Your Eminence," drawled the portly figure standing beside his master. "She must have realised something was wrong. All she had to do was stop using her ætheric technolo-"

He stopped abruptly as the long hand slashed round and grabbed hold of the back of his head.

"I know how she has vanished from our monitors, you fool," he hissed. "What I want to know is how our people let her get away so easily when they had her in their sights."

After a moment's spluttering, the grip was released and the shorter man fell to the floor where he gasped in several large breaths and hacked. He looked up, caught the black, reptilian eyes staring at him and ducked his head back down.

"They were following her until the railway station, Your Eminence," he said once he'd got his breathing under control. He didn't look up at his master, but spoke to the centre of the cloaked chest. "And then she contrived to evade their pursuit. We don't know where she went after that and there has been no trace of ætheric activity."

"But we know that she was packed for travelling?"

"Yes, Sir. Both women were carrying bags when they evaded our pursuers..."

"Carrying *bags? As if they were away for a weekend stay? They would need considerably more luggage to travel any great distance," hissed the taller figure. "Human women do not undertake a journey lightly-laden."*

"Maybe they sent their luggage ahead. You know how she likes to travel," his voice faltered and he bowed his head.

"Maybe? *So the watchers did not see cases being sent? Has anyone checked her apartment since she left?"*

The short man swallowed hard and kept his face down.

"No, Sir. She's left an ætheric disrupter in the flat. It's really uncomfortable for our men to, um, check the flat out."

"An ætheric disrupter, eh? What a surprise," a finger tapped at the one constant light on its screen. "How did we not notice that being set up? Did it not make someone suspicious that she might be planning an extended absence?"

"I'll, um, send someone immediately, Your Eminence," the stocky man backed away, bowing.

"Send those bumbling fools who lost her at the railway station. Maybe a little discomfort *will teach them to do their jobs properly next time," he hissed as he spun on his heels and stalked towards the door behind the throne, certain his orders would be carried out this time.*

Chapter 30

In which the ship sails West

"Cerys has excelled herself," commented Chrystal from the doorway.

A small part of my brain agreed with her silently, whilst my eyes soaked up the rich colours and fantastic shapes unfolding in front of me. It was a dress made of a rich, dark red material, the kind of red my hair dreamed it could be. Gold ribbon followed every curve of the bodice and traced along the panels of the skirt. It was shaped a bit like the ones Chrystal wore, although it didn't curve in as much for my waist. Not as fancy as some of hers, but the most dramatic dress I'd ever owned. It was simply stunning.

"And it's for me?"

"That one and whatever else Cerys has made for you," smiled Chrystal. She lifted the red dress to one side and hung it on the pole. Behind was a dove-grey dress, with an emerald green waistcoat over its bodice. The skirt hung in swathes, showing darker grey hints of its underside with little bows of the emerald velvet holding everything in place. I brushed my hand over the skirt, watching its soft folds falling like water. There was a fabric bag hanging from the coat hanger and Chrystal lifted this off.

"This will be underwear - I asked Cerys to include corsets for you," she said.

"Do I need one?"

"We will see."

Chrystal lifted down the grey dress and I saw something made of the twilight blue fabric I'd fallen in love with in Cerys's loft. This skirt had swags of material cut sideways so the silver shimmer glittered in the loops. Cerys had used spangly silver ribbons to emphasise the shape of the low-cut bodice. I'd never seen anything so beautiful in my life. It was hard to believe anyone would make such a beautiful object from commonplace material and ribbons.

Chrystal snapped me out of my trance by waving a corset at me. It was a bit like the ones she wore, although it was meant to sit below a bra, rather than replace it and I realised it was meant for me.

"Um, I've never worn one," I said.

"Then I will assist you to dress. I have considerable experience in wearing such undergarments," she said, handing me the corset.

I took it in both hands, surprised at how heavy it was. I'd once worn a cinch under a bridesmaid dress and that hardly weighed anything. I turned it over and looked at it from all sides. I could see the wires that held it in shape, the little lilac flower at the point that would sit below my cleavage and ribbons that laced up the back. Whenever I'd seen Chrystal getting dressed, she seemed to just pull her corset on and tighten it very easily and I hoped she didn't expect me to be able to do it that quickly.

"First things first," she continued. "We should cleanse ourselves after our exertions before you try on your new outfits."

"Um, of course. I'll have a look at how the shower works," I said.

"Or you could run a bath."

"Oh, yes! But I thought you preferred to shower," I said.

"Ah, because there is no bath in my apartment. The ætheric heating system would take a long time to heat sufficient water for a bath. But there is a large tub in the bathroom here, with unlimited hot water," she said and took my hand.

The tub was indeed large and well-stocked with luxurious toiletries - a far cry from the little bottles of green gloop I was used to seeing in business hotels. *Gilchrist and Soames*, it said on the label - I'd never even heard of them. Chrystal picked a bottle from the chromium rack and tipped a little of its contents under the water steaming from the tap. Then she left me there, returning a couple of minutes later, wrapped in a silky grey robe with large flowers printed on it. I took the hint and dashed into the bedroom, shed my travelling clothes quickly and slipped on the matching red robe she'd left lying on the bed.

Chrystal sat at one end of the bath, the bubbles covering her legs but leaving her tits exposed and her Chrystal heart clearly visible in its frame of ornate brasswork. She'd looped her hair up and pinned it in place with some sort of off-white ornament. I hung my robe on the hook next to hers and lowered myself into the opposite end. The taps sat midway on the longer side and the tub was large enough for us both to be comfortable. The warm water felt silky against my skin and I relaxed, aware that this was the first time in several days when I hadn't felt the need to hurry.

Chrystal reached for a natural-looking sponge that hung on the wall and beckoned with it.

"Turn around and let me wash your back," she ordered and I was happy to slide around in the water and allow her to sponge my back. Then she pulled me back against her body, my head relaxing onto her shoulder. She lifted the sponge and squeezed it so I could feel the water cascading over my tits. I closed my eyes and gave in to the sensations of her washing me. Then I turned my head slightly to kiss the underside of her jaw, just where her face joined her neck.

"Not now," she said. "We want to be on deck when we sail, do we not?" Her words were stern, although her voice was husky.

She let go the sponge and hugged me from behind. After a brief moment I sat back up and slid to my end of the bath. Chrystal turned as I had done and it was my turn to wash her, being careful of the brass and stone of her heart, until I realised it was as well protected as any natural part of her body.

Chrystal got out first, leaving me to wash my hair with shampoo that smelled of fresh grass and some flower I couldn't name. I found Chrystal in the bedroom, sitting in a chair, brushing out her dark blond hair.

"I wish my hair looked as good as yours, but it goes terribly frizzy when I try to grow it," I said.

"And I always hated my hair, when I was younger," she replied. "My mother had the most beautiful curls and we tried everything to make mine do the same. But it would insist on staying straight, no matter how much we bound it in bandages."

I was used to Chrystal's habit of brushing her hair one hundred times every day - sometimes twice. But this was the first time she'd mentioned trying to do anything with it other than brush it straight and fasten it up in one of her elaborate hairstyles. I tried to imagine what she meant by saying they'd *bound it in bandages*, but she interrupted my train of thought.

"Now, if you'd care to put on your usual underwear, I will assist you in fitting your new corset."

She didn't have to tell me twice. I quickly towelled my own hair dry, ran a comb through it and dug out a clean bra and panties from my overnight bag. Chrystal meanwhile brushed out her hair, stood and picked up the cream-and-lilac corset.

"You begin by loosening the laces," she said, her fingers deftly doing just that. "Not too far, or they will tangle when you tighten them. I think that will be sufficient." She guided me to stand sideways-on to the full length mirror on the wall, stepping in front of me and positioning the corset below my bra.

"Now, these fasten the *busk* at the front like so," she said, pulling the two sides together and hooking a series of fasteners from just under my tits to where the corset sat on my hip bones. She checked that everything was lying flat and then stepped behind me.

"You should watch this in the mirror," she said and I watched her smoothing a panel of fabric against the skin of my back. Then she took hold of two loops of lace somewhere near the small of my back.

"These are called the pull laces and these are what will tighten the corset to give you the correct wasp-waisted appearance," she said. "But first I need to begin at the top."

And so I watched her pulling the laces tight, working from the top to the pull laces and then beginning at the bottom and working up. She repeated the whole pattern again and I felt the garment growing firmer around my middle. Much to my surprise, it didn't feel particularly tight, but I could see in the mirror that my little pot belly had vanished.

"And you now need to take a deep breath and stand as tall as you can," said Chrystal. I did as instructed and felt the corset tighten about my waist. I watched her in the mirror as she tied the long laces in a neat bow and stepped around to the front to check that it was still seated correctly.

"You may breathe out now," she reminded me as she turned me to face the mirror.

"Wow!"

"Dramatic, is it not?" she asked.

"Well, yes. But I didn't think I was all that fat!"

She chuckled. "You are not fat - at least not by the standards of this century. But a little assistance from the correct underwear will bring out the proper curves of your body."

I stared at myself in the mirror, running hands over my body's newly-acquired contours. I'd expected my waist to look a bit smaller, but I was amazed at the way it curved in. I'd always thought I had a boyish shape and knew I'd never have Chrystal's hourglass figure, but neither had I thought I'd look so, well, womanly! I was more surprised by how much bigger my boobs looked. That must be because she'd squeezed my middle in so tightly. And yet I didn't feel uncomfortable. This was far less restricting than the modern cinch I'd had to wear! I stared at my reflection, my hands still running over this miraculous garment. I'd expected it to pinch, weigh me down and cause all kinds of discomforts. But instead it felt almost like a second skin, only firmer than my own. And sexy, too. I ran my hands down my sides, wiggling slightly to watch my body react to the constriction. My reflection in the mirror looked *hot* and I felt my face flushing as I thought about Chrystal fastening herself into her corset, too.

"When you are ready..." said Chrystal from behind me.

I turned away from the mirror reluctantly, Chrystal fastened a belt around me, adjusted the way it sat over my bottom and I could feel a pad sitting there. Then she held up the grey dress, its front panel hanging open, helped me into it and fastened the little hooks along the sloping panel, concealing the join carefully with the decorative edge. I only glimpsed the simple elegance of its construction before it was hidden from my eyes as well as anyone else's. She slipped the green waistcoat over the dress, fastening its single button at my waist and straightening its long tail over my arse. Then she took my arm and led me back to the mirror.

This time I was speechless. I knew it was me. Apart from anything else, my face framed with almost-dry hair sat on top of the vision in front of me. But the rest was a picture of elegance. The dove-grey dress settled perfectly onto my newly-discovered curves. The bright green waistcoat made my tits look bigger than they ever had and the gentle curve of the skirt flowed as if I had no legs. I turned to view one side and then the other, noticing the bustle pad making my backside look pert beneath the dramatic inward curve of my middle. I couldn't believe how damned sexy I suddenly looked. The skirt swirled around me as I changed position, posing at my own reflection. I could have stood there for hours, amazed at the transformation, but then I heard three blasts of a huge horn outside.

"That is the signal for the ship to cast off," said Chrystal and I turned to find her fastening her own dress. It was the same brilliant green as Cerys had used for my waistcoat and I realised we were going to match.

"If you have quite finished admiring your reflection," she continued, "then we should go outside and wave as we set sail."

I blushed as I realised she'd dressed in the time I'd been staring at myself in the mirror. Then she passed me a narrow-brimmed grey hat from a trunk she'd just opened. I tried to position it and she came up behind me and adjusted it. There was a band that passed around the back of my head and she neatened my hair over this.

"That should hold it reasonably well in place. But please be aware that there may be a more substantial breeze outside and use your hand should it threaten to blow away," she said. "I would hate to lose my hat to a coastal gust."

As she spoke she'd lifted another hat, with green feathers, onto her own head and secured it with a pin to her rolled-up hair. Then she held out her arm and led me to the doors onto our balcony.

It wasn't exactly the throngs I'd seen in black-and-white footage of similar launches, but there was a small crowd waving from the concrete quayside as the ship edged slowly away from them. Chrystal stood, smiling and waving, looking so beautiful that my breath caught in my throat. And much though I loved the way these new clothes made me feel, I realised I wanted to get myself out of them. And Chrystal out of hers, too.

Chapter 31

In which the atmosphere is strained

We were still in bed when I heard someone knock once on the door and open it.

"Lady Carstairs? Ms Fletcher?" called Storm.

I sat up, pulling the duvet up over my tits and simultaneously trying to cover Chrystal where she dozed face-down next to me. Since I didn't have four hands, I failed to hide much of anything and looked up as the butler walked straight in.

"Oh, I'm so sorry, ladies," he said, raising his eyes to stare at a fixed point on the wall well over our heads.

With hardly a pause, he went on, "Perhaps I should lay out the refreshments in the dining area? It will take me a few minutes to check that the cupboard is correctly provisioned." He turned, keeping his eyeline at the same, discreet height and left the room.

"Thank you, Storm," said Chrystal as he left. She yawned and stretched herself into a seated position, the duvet falling unceremoniously from her legs as she stood and started to dress. I sat for a moment, pathetically clutching the duvet to my front.

"But, Storm's there," I hissed.

"Yes," said Chrystal. "And he is laying out our refreshments. I, for one, would dearly like some good coffee and a few canapés before the lifeboat drill. Would you not?" She continued to dress in the comfortable clothes she'd left neatly on a chair before we dressed up to see the ship out of port. I stood up and followed her lead, though with frequent uncomfortable glances towards the door.

"But he *saw* us," I hissed.

"And he is a butler," replied Chrystal in a normal tone. "A good butler notices everything, sees nothing and repeats even less outside of the privacy of his employers' home. I'm sure one as experienced as Storm will have seen much worse during his employ on the ship."

"And he'll know you're not really my...".

"What does it matter what Storm knows?" she asked. "So long as he does not gossip to others? I am certain we can trust in his tact and diplomacy."

She had started walking as soon as we were both respectably covered and arrived in the dining area just after she finished speaking. Storm was pouring thick, dark coffee into two tiny cups set out on a silver-coloured tray. A plate of delicious-looking mouthfuls already sat on the table.

"If you'd care to be seated, Lady Carstairs, Ms Fletcher," he said.

"Oh, this looks wonderful," I said, wondering if there were any etiquette rules I should know about eating in front of a butler who'd just seen the two of us naked in bed together.

"The galley always has canapés available," he said with a slight bow in my direction. "I merely had to ask them to fill *your aunt's* request." There was the slightest emphasis on the way he said *aunt*. I glanced over at Chrystal.

"We are quite distantly related," she said. "Although we would prefer for other details to remain in this suite."

He bowed to her, deeper than he had to me.

"Of course, Lady Carstairs. I would not dream of mentioning anything."

They both smiled.

"Indeed, I was about to offer to have the bed made up as two singles, but I presume that service will not be required?" Chrystal held his eye and he went on. "And there will be no problem with the chambermaids, m'lady. They are the very souls of discretion."

There was a folder of information, describing life on this incredible ship. Take the grandest hotel you've ever stayed in and imagine it's afloat. And it's huge. So many floors - decks, I should call them - and a different cuisine to be served in the restaurant for every day of the week. And luxurious! Those up-market toiletries weren't the only little detail they'd included. And if something wasn't sitting there waiting for us, it seemed that a quick phone call to Room Service would bring someone running. I was almost tempted to call them and ask for a bottle of fresh mountain air, just to see what they'd do.

"So what's this about?" I asked her, walking into the dressing room with the invitation to the Senior Officers' party waving in my hand. She glanced over.

"That will be our invitation to join the Captain and his officers for dinner this evening. It is traditional on cruise liners to invite all passengers to a welcome meal on the first evening of the cruise," she said.

"All the passengers? Isn't that an awful lot?"

"It would be, but there will be various events happening over the course of the evening. The Purser will have made arrangements to ensure that everyone is invited to one of the events and the ship's officers will circulate as appropriate. I presume that our invitation is one of the few for the Senior Officers' Party. We are, after all, in their most expensive suite."

"So it's kind of like a class thing? The more money you've got, the better the do you get invited to?"

She stopped what she was doing and looked at me. "If by 'do' you mean event, then yes. This is one of the privileges afforded by paying for a first class berth. But I can assure you, no-one will feel that they are getting poor treatment this evening. The Captain wishes for a happy ship and that can only be achieved by making everyone feel that they are served well by the staff aboard."

Somewhere in the back of my mind, a little voice was telling me that I should be offended. I'd been brought up to believe that everyone's equal, no-one should be treated any better or worse than anyone else. Yet here was Chrystal telling me that we were getting treated to the very best that the ship could offer, whilst other passengers were kind of second class citizens. But that small voice was drowned out by a very excited little-girl feeling, that this was an exclusive party and I'd been invited to sit at the top table.

"We should select our outfits and begin to get ready," said Chrystal. "There are some of my dresses that could be altered to fit you and I have brought them along with us. Or would you prefer to wear something that Cerys made especially for you?"

"Oh, definitely one of Cerys's!" I said. The little-girl voice was getting more and more excited.

"Many of my dresses were made by Cerys, too," Chrystal explained. "But I had assumed that you would wish to wear one of your new ones. I can assure you that there will be more such invitations during the voyage and that you will have ample opportunity to wear each outfit at least once."

"I suppose I should save the best one, then," I said, fondling the midnight blue and silver one. "So, perhaps the red?"

In response, Chrystal opened the lid on the brass-bound trunk in the bottom of the wardrobe. Inside, it was divided into compartments and Chrystal opened one of these, extracting three hats nested together, with layers of tissue paper separating them. One of these was a dark gold, narrow-brimmed one with a gold flower on one side. She held it up, checking it against the dress and nodding. Then she laid the hat on the dressing table and lifted the red and gold dress off its hanger.

"This will need hemming," she said with a smile. "Cerys left all of your new dresses unfinished, so we could be sure they hung correctly on you. It is one thing to wear an unhemmed dress briefly on one's own balcony, but one could not possibly appear at the Senior Officers' Party in such a state. So..."

I didn't need any more of a prompt. I peeled off my jeans and t-shirt so Chrystal could help me into the corset and then the red dress. She got me to stand on a chair and worked her way around the hem with pins from a little sewing kit Cerys had included for us, fixing it carefully to the right height.

"You've done this before," I observed, impressed by the efficient way she worked.

She looked surprised. "I was never too grand a lady to assist another with hemming her skirts," she said. "And it has been necessary for me to do the same once someone had pinned up for me, for many years now. Cerys is a dear, but even she cannot always do all the work one would like her to."

That reminded me of something I'd been meaning to ask.

"Why do you call Cerys a 'she'?"

She pushed one last pin into my skirt and looked at me. "What other word would you expect me to use?"

"Well, 'he' of course. I mean, he's really camp and all, but surely Cerys is a man?" I said, my voice getting fainter as I spoke.

"Mayhap your scientists would say that Cerys is a man, but Cerys prefers to dress and live as a woman. I merely do her the courtesy of respecting that choice. Is that not more important than mere biology?"

"I suppose so," I muttered. Chrystal had sounded genuinely surprised at my question, rather than annoyed. But she had a way of saying things that made me feel guilty for taking things for granted. I wasn't sure if it was the way she said it or my own conscience, but I sometimes felt like a child who didn't know how to behave in front of guests.

"Were there people like Cerys in Victorian society?" I asked, hoping to deflect the conversation onto the slightly safer ground of Chrystal's earlier life. She stood and helped me down off the chair.

"Yes, we used to call them macaronis," she replied.

"What? Like the pasta?"

"Indeed, it is the same word, from the Italian. I believe there was a child's rhyme about a man who *stuck a feather in his hat and called it macaroni*," she replied.

"Yankee Doodle," I said, unfastening the front of the gorgeous red dress on its hanger. "So that's what it means?"

She nodded and went on, "Macaroni was the name of a type of wig - I believe the rhyme was meant sardonically. Applying the term to a person could be seen as insulting, although I know that some used it to describe themselves. As is often the case, it is not the words that matter, so much as the intent behind them."

"And do you know how Cerys would describe him-, um, herself?"

"Again, it is not a matter we have discussed. Cerys is Cerys. I believe there have always been people who felt they were born into the wrong body, perhaps by reason of gender. But it was harder during Victoria's reign for a man to dress in a manner different to his peers. This is one way in which matters have improved under the new queen."

It took me a moment to work out she was referring to Queen Elizabeth. We'd been celebrating her Diamond Jubilee and Chrystal called her *new.*

"So did your manners teacher ever teach you how to refer to a man who wanted to be treated like a woman?" I asked, discomforted by the reminder of my companion's age.

Chrystal's eyes sparkled. "No, I do not believe Miss Featherstonehaugh ever addressed that particular thorny issue. I suspect that would have been rather more confusion than she could have borne."

As Chrystal lifted the gown over my head, I found myself irrationally pleased there was a situation the long-dead manners teacher hadn't coached Chrystal about. Then I felt a little guilty for thinking so uncharitably about a woman who I'd never met and who had probably died more than a century before I was even born. Damn, it got confusing, talking with someone who'd been around for as long as Chrystal.

"Do you ever think about people you used to know when you were young?" I prompted. "I mean, you don't talk about your family or anyone. Do you miss them?"

"Sometimes. They never knew what had happened to me, of course. I could not return to my life with a lump of rock beating in my chest where my heart used to be. I knew from the newspapers when they decided that I must have perished, even though they never found my body and I suspect they may have held out hope that I was still alive. It seemed kinder to make our parting as swift as possible, so that they could begin to grieve and then move on with their lives."

This was more detail than I'd ever got out of her before, and I hesitated to push her further, worried she might clam up if I reminded her I was here.

"And men? Was there a man in your life? Or did you always prefer women?"

She shook her head. "No man that I was serious about, no. My father and mother had never pressured me towards marriage and I did not seek out the company of any man in particular. There have been lovers in my life, of course. But fleetingly, so fleetingly." I noticed she didn't reply to my question about preferring women.

"You've never been tempted to settle down with someone?"

"And watch them grow old while I continued to live, hale and hearty for no reason I could share? That would be a cruel thing."

"So you've never told anyone about the Chrystal before?"

I was shocked. It'd never occurred to me how *alone* she must have been all these years.

"A few, over the years," she paused, so wrapped up in her memories I hesitated to intrude. "But people do not respond kindly to those who are different. Once I began to understand how very different I had become, I learnt to conceal my more evident variations from the normal."

"But surely people have seen your arm? And even..." I gestured to my own chest.

She sat down at the dressing table and cut herself a length of thread.

"I mean, people like Cerys. And you must have been to bed with someone else!" I continued.

"Cerys has seen both of my modifications," she looked up as she explained. "And she remains as silent about my differences as I do about hers. And yes, there have been lovers before you, my dear Sam."

"So they must have seen?"

"No, I have generally remained clothed. I was brought up in a society where it was usual for people to retain their undergarments at all times. Even a man and his wife may live their married lives together and never see each other fully unclothed."

"But nowadays? I mean, everyone's so casual about nudity now."

"And for that reason, many people are pleasantly surprised at my apparent, ah, reticence to be seen. Or to remove my rather old-fashioned underwear. I have rarely been asked to explain, but I can always say that I am scarred and prefer to keep my scars concealed. It is not, after all, an untruth."

"And nobody's ever thought to ask about them?"

"A few. But if I tell you that it is a scar and it feels like a scar in the dark of the bedroom, why should you question the fact?"

Why indeed?

That first evening on board was amazing. We arrived at the Queen's Grill, dressed up to the nines and sweeping into the suddenly-quiet room. I'd never been one to enjoy the limelight, always hiding my face when anyone took photos and trying to stay in the background at parties. But Chrystal didn't have a single wallflower gene in her body. She walked in as if the whole shindig had been arranged for her benefit and stood just inside the door, soaking up the admiring looks. Not to mention the jealous glances from some of the other passengers. Everyone was obviously wearing a party outfit, but they looked positively dowdy or chavvy next to us in Cerys's creations.

The Captain greeted us warmly from his position at the head of the welcoming line, but had to speak to the self-conscious man in the ill-fitting dinner suit who followed us in and so we passed along the rank of officers. When we reached Ryuu, he took Chrystal's hand but, instead of shaking it, he lifted it to his lips and planted a lingering kiss on the back. He kept hold of her hand for a long moment before dropping it and reaching to shake mine briefly. Then we were past the line, offered glasses of Cava and into the Queen's Grill.

Several faces were fixed on us as Chrystal took my arm and led me straight across the open space. I realised she had taken my left arm in her right and wondered briefly if this was to ensure no-one touched the heavy pistons in her forearm by mistake. She stopped close to the wall and gestured to a stocky young man in a waiter's uniform, carrying a tray with more glasses of wine on it. He came over, glancing at our nearly-full glasses and looking puzzled.

"Good evening, er, Topher," said Chrystal after checking his name badge. "Perhaps you would be so kind as to indicate at which table we will be seated?"

"Um, er," he was staring up at her eyes and looked completely confused. I doubted he'd ever met someone wearing full Victorian dress before and guessed that his training hadn't covered this possibility. "Um, it's based on which Suite you're in, Ma'am."

She smiled down at him. "Why, we're in the Berengaria, Topher," she said.

"Oh, that's simple, you'll be at the Captain's table." He sounded relieved that she'd asked him something he could answer.

"Perhaps you could do me a small, favour, Topher," she went on. He just stared at her while a redness crept up his throat towards his face.

"You see, our dresses are a little larger than is usually allowed for at these functions," Chrystal continued when it became obvious he wasn't going to reply. "I wonder if it would be possible for us to gain a little extra room at the table?"

She tilted her head slightly to one side and gave him her most disarming smile. The blush had reached his cheeks and he looked as if he'd never been so embarrassed in his life.

"Of course, Ma'am, I'll see to it straight away," he said. He laid his tray carefully on a table and practically bolted across the room. I watched his progress and then as he shuffled chairs and table placings, enlisting the help of a waitress who came over as he worked.

"Do we really need that much more room?" I asked Chrystal.

She smiled coyly. "Not entirely, but they do tend to crush everybody into as small a space as possible nowadays. And I do dislike having too little room at table!"

"And you're going to do this every meal?" I asked.

"There will not be the need. The staff will understand that we have a right to a little more table space - after all, they are here to keep their passengers happy."

I was learning to read Chrystal's moods a little better and I realised she was enjoying herself.

"But isn't that a little unfair? I mean, won't everyone else get crammed into less space just for us?"

"Not at all," she gestured towards the table where our young waiter had roped-in several more staff to help him. "They always allow additional space at the ends of the table, in case it is necessary to accommodate an additional person. I have merely persuaded him to make that additional space available for our use, instead."

After a moment, she continued, "Unusual name, 'Topher'. I do not believe I have come across that one previously."

"It's short for 'Christopher,'" I told her. "I guess it's better for someone who doesn't want to be just 'Chris'."

"So what is wrong with a simple 'Christopher'?" she asked, rolling her eyes at me.

Before I could answer, two women stepped up and the grey-haired one held her hand out to Chrystal. "Imelda Slatcher, platinum pin. And this is my daughter, Jessica." Imelda was short, dressed in a tired-looking blue evening dress with a fur collar and leaning on a walking stick. Jessica looked about thirty, with short blond hair, a bored expression and green eyes which matched her cocktail dress .

Chrystal took her hand and smiled. "Chrystal Carstairs, with my niece Samantha. It is a pleasure to make your acquaintance," she said.

"Crystal?" asked the younger woman.

"Chrystal," I corrected her. "And I'm Sam." I returned her smile and reached out to shake hands. Jessica had a firm, dry grip while her mother's hand felt like a week-old piece of fish.

Introductions over, Imelda asked, "Your first voyage?"

"It is for Sam," said Chrystal. "I have travelled on this ship a few times previously. And others of the fleet, too."

"I don't see your pin," said the matriarch.

"I rarely wear it - they can be so bothersome and I do not like to risk damage to my attire. The crew soon learn who I am."

Imelda looked as if she was annoyed about not knowing something but couldn't see how to push for the answer she obviously wanted. After a little more inconsequential chat, she grabbed hold of her daughter's elbow and the two of them made off to speak to more new arrivals. Jessica looked back over her shoulder as they left, pulling a face and winking at me.

"What's all this about pins?" I asked.

"Ah, there is an award system based on how many times you have travelled on this fleet before. Many passengers find a level of security in attaining the higher levels and are therefore proud to tell you that they have done so."

"And she was 'Platinum' - is that the top level?"

"Not quite, there is 'Diamond' above that," she explained but I was stopped from pursuing it any further by the appearance of Ryuu at my side. He bowed to Chrystal and she smiled back at him.

"Lady Carstairs, I wonder if I could...?"

He took her arm and led her away across the room, leaving me alone.

Chapter 32

In which Chrystal is friendly with the crew

Back in our suite after the party, I slipped off the red dress and hung it carefully in my wardrobe. Storm seemed to sense my mood and left me well alone after greeting me at the door and running the bath I asked for. Chrystal still hadn't returned by the end of my soak, so I slipped into bed on my own, determined to stay awake until she arrived.

I woke at the sound of Storm laying out our breakfast on the dining table. I could smell the fresh coffee and opened my eyes to see morning light creeping round the curtains covering the doors to our balcony. I could feel more than hear the ship's engines chugging away several decks below, pushing us steadily westwards. I turned my head to the side and looked at Chrystal's un-slept-in side of the bed.

I washed my hands and face, pulled on my bath robe and followed the smell of the coffee to where Storm stood almost at attention, his white gloved hands at his sides.

"Toast?" he asked as I entered and placed the little toast rack in front of me when I sat down, with equal-sized triangles of mixed toast. He poured me a coffee and retreated to his usual corner, where he stood until I'd emptied my coffee cup and begun buttering my toast. He picked up the pot and moved to refill my cup.

"Will Lady Carstairs be joining us for breakfast?" he asked.

"How would I know? I don't even know where she's spent the night!" I bit viciously into a piece of granary and Storm actually splashed a spot of hot, black liquid onto the table.

"She's not here? But, I thought you two were..." he tailed off, looking flustered for the first time I'd ever seen.

"Yes, I thought we were too," I snapped. Suddenly the toast tasted like cardboard in my mouth and my stomach rebelled at the thought of eating any more. I stood up, knocking the table so that Storm had to jump and catch it before anything could spill.

"I'll be in the bathroom," I said as I hurried out and away, feeling the heaving in my belly.

I still didn't have a firm idea of how to cope with this situation, so I showered and dressed quickly, grabbed my handbag and left Storm in the suite while I dashed off into the ship's corridors.

I wandered aimlessly for a while, then decided to spend some of my free internet allocation in checking my social networking sites. I'd been neglecting my online friends for months and this seemed like a good time to catch up.

My emails were mostly spam and people trying to sell me stuff. On the social side, Rose was mooning over some film star I hadn't heard of. Chelle was still bitching about everyone and accusing them of being at fault. There was some sort of love triangle involving two sisters I knew from Uni and some boy I vaguely remembered meeting at a wedding last year. I logged off in disgust - had everyone been so shallow all along and I'd never noticed? Did *I* used to be that bad?

I tried to think of something to do. I used to spend hours online at weekends. So much to view, so much to laugh at. But now I couldn't think of a single thing I wanted to do. Glancing up, I happened to meet Ryuu's eyes as he entered the computer room. He blushed and turned away, looking somehow furtive. Or guilty! So that was where Chrystal had spent the night, I was suddenly sure of it. I stood, pushing my chair back so hard it bounced off the man sitting behind me. I didn't even bother to apologise on my way out of the computer centre. Ryuu hurried across the room behind me, heading for the PC I'd vacated.

I slammed the door behind me, not caring who might be listening. I was even prepared to ignore Storm if he was in the suite. I bulldozed into the bedroom, where I could hear noises. I was unsurprised to find Chrystal there, watching herself in the mirror as she tightened the ribbons of her corset.

"Sam. Are you all right?" she asked as she saw my reflected expression.

"Where the fuck have you been all night?" I exploded.

She turned to face me and held out her hands. "Sam, are you upset? What is wrong?"

"What's wrong?" I saw her flinch at my anger. "You stay out all night and then have the, the audacity to..."

She took a step forwards and reached for my shoulders, but I struck her away, bruising my arm on those bloody rods of hers.

"Sam," she said. I could hardly bear to see her looking so hurt, but I steeled myself.

"How could you?" I said, trying to stop my voice from cracking with the emotion that washed over me. I'd been upset, sure it was all her fault but now that she was in front of me, I wasn't so certain.

"I spent the night with Third Officer Ryuu," she answered slowly, watching my face as she spoke. "He was most attentive at the Captain's party and I did not realise you expected me to be here every night."

"Well, that's what normal people do. When they're in a relationship. They spend the night together. They don't go swanning off with some *man!*"

"It was only for one night, Sam," she said. "I had not an idea that you thought..."

"Thought what? That we were exclusive?" I spat.

She didn't even look embarrassed. "Sam, you know that I enjoy the company of men. Did it not occur to you that I may wish to indulge myself? Even for one occasion?" Satisfied with the fit of her corset, she tied the ribbons behind her and shook out her half-dried hair.

"No, it didn't!" The anger was coming back to me now. She'd used me again and walked away when she fancied a bit of a change. And she came back here as if nothing had happened. I glared at her.

"Samantha, my dear. Sam-of-the-boy's name," she said, softly. I found I was even more annoyed at her stupid nickname for me than at the use of my full name and took a step backwards to keep the distance between us.

"There is no need for you to be angry. I am sorry if I have caused..."

"I don't want to hear it. I'll get Storm to have the beds separated and you won't have to put up with me sharing your bed any more. Or I'll sleep on the sofa!"

She sighed. "No, Sam. It is I who have offended. I will be the one to sleep elsewhere. You may consider the Belengaria Suite to be yours for the duration - I will find accommodation elsewhere on the ship."

"What?" I couldn't believe my ears.

"I will arrange to sleep elsewhere if that is what you would prefer. I will come back here for my clothes, if you are content for me to do so. But I will not trouble you beyond that," she said.

"Elsewhere?"

"The Suite is yours, Samantha. Use it as you see fit. Bring young Jessica here if you can separate her from her mother. I think you'll find her a willing companion," she went on. She lifted a pale blue dress off its hanger in front of the wardrobe and slipped it on.

I didn't answer. I'd been spoiling for a fight and she'd sidestepped the issue. I watched her leave the bedroom and heard the door open onto the corridor and close again behind her. I knew she didn't mean it - this was just her way of avoiding an argument because she knew she was the one in the wrong. Give her a few hours and she'd be back.

I was wrong.

She didn't even try to talk to me again. I saw her about on the ship, often with Ryuu or one of the other crew members. And I knew she'd been in the suite because the clothes hanging in her wardrobe would change and sometimes she'd leave little gifts on my pillow - a single rose, a small box of expensive chocolates. I always threw them straight in the bin. It took me a couple of days to realise that Storm must be telling her when I left the Suite and I toyed with the idea of coming back unexpectedly, to see if I could catch her there. *But what good would that do me?*

Antigua came and went. I didn't even bother going ashore, but stood at the rail, watching Chrystal leaning on the Captain's arm as he helped her into the motorboat that powered them to shore. She met my eye as the last passengers boarded and I got the impression she was trying to tell me something. But then the motor started and the boat swung away. And I wasn't sure if I'd imagined it. Ryuu followed me into the dining room when I went for lunch, but he avoided meeting my eye although I caught him watching me as I ate. I was starting to feel uncomfortable around him and wondered if he somehow blamed me for Chrystal's behaviour.

I lingered over my food, pushing it around the plate. Then I walked slowly back to a Suite that had always been too large for two people and was full of shadows and echoes now there was only me staying there.

Chapter 33

In which the ship travels in American waters

Tortola, St Kitts, Grenada. Magical place-names for countries I'd always wanted to see. But not on my own. Jessica seemed to welcome my advances, but her mother had cottoned on and did everything to keep us apart. And I really wasn't that interested anyway. There was only one face that crept into my dreams at night, only one voice I strained to hear across a crowded deck. But she obviously had more interesting diversions around her on this ship. I was just some girl she'd picked up for a bit of fun and now she'd moved on to the next one. Or more than one - I saw her with several different people over those bleak days when I always felt cold. Maybe she was working her way through the ship's officers - though I envied her that cute blond who looked as if her uniform jacket was in permanent danger of exploding down the front. If Chrystal didn't need me, I wanted her to know I could live without her!

But I couldn't find the enthusiasm for anything and hung around the Suite most of the day, wanting nothing more than to see Chrystal, however fleetingly, but hating to see her happy without me. Storm still did everything I could want, though he kept very much in the background. I knew he must be telling Chrystal when I was out and I wondered what would happen if I didn't leave the suite at all. Would she come anyway - or could she outdo me on waiting, too? I couldn't decide whether I really wanted to test her patience.

Although I didn't see enough of Chrystal, I kept spotting Ryuu. Whenever I went out, he seemed to crop up; he never spoke to me, just hung around at the corner of my sight. I thought he might be stalking me, but that didn't seem likely. Maybe he hoped to use me to get back with *her*.

Then I came back after lunch to find her sitting elegantly on the sofa in the lounge area of our suite. I paused, just inside the door, uncertain of myself. I couldn't see Storm, either, so I was on my own.

"Sam," she said with a smile. "It is good to see you."

I swallowed hard and let the door close behind me. I walked over, perched on the edge of the easy chair opposite her and took a deep breath.

"Chrystal."

"I have missed your company," she went on.

"You knew where to find me!"

"But you did not wish to see me. I attempted to make it simple for you to continue living in the suite without my presence. I trust I succeeded in that?"

"Mm, yeah. I guess. But why didn't you just come back? And why are you here now?"

She fixed my eye and leaned forward a little, conspiratorially.

"I will answer the last question first," she said. "I am here because we need to leave the ship at the next port of call. And to facilitate our actions, we will need to pack certain of our belongings."

"You mean go ashore? On, um," I paused.

"On Barbados. Yes, to go ashore, but we will not be rejoining the Queen Victoria. Instead we will travel on to mainland America."

"But..." There were so many objections turning over in my head that I couldn't decide which one to mention first.

"You should pack what you need for a week's hard travelling. Leave behind your dresses and finery, I will arrange for those to be repatriated," she said.

"My dresses?"

She smiled again.

"Yes, the beautiful dresses Cerys made for you. I assure

you, they will be treated with the proper respect and returned to my accommodations in London."

I thought wistfully of the wonderful clothes that I'd only worn a few times and hadn't even looked at for the last week. Lost in the pictures in my head, I didn't realise that Chrystal had stood up until she pulled me to my feet.

"I have missed you, my Sam-of-the-boy's name," she said and kissed me before I could answer. A deep, gentle kiss that reminded me how tender this strange woman could be. Then I stopped thinking about anything else. For a while.

We were seated together on the sofa when Storm arrived with food Chrystal must have ordered earlier. I had no idea where he'd been all afternoon, but she'd obviously arranged for him to leave us alone in the suite for a few hours. And it had been a busy afternoon. Our overnight bags were packed with shirts, undies and toiletries while our dresses hung neatly in the walk-in wardrobe. We'd spent a wonderful hour in bed, making up for the last week and now I was ready for some good food. I heard Storm cough loudly before came out through the door from the entry hall.

"Ah, Storm. Excellent timing," said Chrystal. "Would you be so kind as to lay our meal in the dining room? And then bring the champagne through here."

We sat silently, as Storm dealt with the contents of the trolley he'd brought and then he returned, carrying an ice bucket and three glasses. He hesitated.

"Will your guest be joining you later, Lady Carstairs?" he asked, placing the three glasses on the coffee table and the ice bucket in its stand.

"I certainly hope so, Storm. Please be seated," she said.

For only the second time I'd ever seen, confusion crossed

the butler's face. Then he recovered his usual unflappable expression and did as she'd instructed. Chrystal meanwhile had removed the foil and the wire cage from the bottle's neck. Once Storm had seated himself, she passed him the bottle. He popped it expertly and poured three foaming glasses. Chrystal handed one to me and raised her own between the three of us.

"To kinship and loyalty," she toasted.

We all drank and Storm and I waited for Chrystal to speak.

"Storm, we will be leaving the ship tomorrow," she began after a moment's pause.

"Visiting Barbados, M'lady?" he asked.

"Visiting, yes. But we will not be returning to this estimable vessel afterwards," she said.

He looked puzzled and I couldn't blame him.

"Not returning, Ma'am? But - are you staying on the island?"

"Briefly. We have urgent business on the mainland and will be flying there in a few days," she explained.

"I see. And shall I make arrangements for this flight?" asked the butler.

"No, there is no need for you to do so, but there is something further we do require of you," she said.

"Of course, whatever I can do to help," he said.

"You will be suitably rewarded, naturally," she said with a smile.

He made a dismissing gesture. "It has been my pleasure to serve you, Lady Carstairs. And you have been most generous throughout the voyage."

I'd seen Chrystal passing him the little envelopes and had a fair idea of how much she had been tipping him over the course of our trip. On top of the daily gratuity automatically added to her bill, of course. I'd been a little shocked to realise how much it was costing for all of this, but then - it went some way to explaining why people were so keen to serve her.

"Nonetheless, there will be a small additional consideration for you."

He bowed his head. After a moment she went on.

"We will leave the ship with everyone else, but I would like you to come ashore, too," she told him. "Bringing luggage that we cannot reasonably be expected to carry for a day's excursion to the island."

He nodded and I realised that here was the solution to the problem I'd been worrying about since we'd packed our travelling bags and she'd told me how we were leaving.

"We would like to slip away without the ship's company knowing that we have done so," said Chrystal.

"That can be arranged," said Storm. "I'm sure I can keep it to myself until we've sailed again."

"But - what about the register? And the key-cards?" I asked.

"If you could leave your cards with me," he said, waiting until Chrystal had nodded before continuing. "Then I can swipe them on my return, so the register will balance and you'll be able to get away from the island before anyone knows that you are missing."

"Perfect," said Chrystal. "If you can wait a few days before mentioning our absence to anyone, that would be most helpful."

He bowed again. "Simple enough. May I enquire...?"

"Allow me to say that we need to be certain that no-one, erm, unsavoury is aware of our having left the good ship Queen Victoria," said Chrystal. I turned to stare at her.

"You think they followed us here?" I asked.

"No, I do not believe that anyone specifically followed us onto the ship, but one can never be too careful," she replied. "I have learnt over the years that not everyone is to be trusted."

"Are you in danger, Ma'am?" asked Storm.

"I do not believe we are at this precise moment," she said. "But there are those who would prefer us not to succeed in the venture we are undertaking. And it may be that there are people on board the ship who watch and report to those who would pay well for such intelligences."

I continued to stare, struggling with this information and thinking of Third Officer Ryuu. Was Chrystal saying she knew he was spying on us? *Then how and who for? Was he reporting to the people who'd sent that pirate?*

"I am sorry I had to deceive you, Sam. But it was advantageous for any watching eyes to think that we had a lovers' spat, in the hope that they would relax their vigilance."

I swallowed back a brusque reply and wondered if this was really the reason she'd been keeping away.

I didn't get much sleep that night, between spending the night with Chrystal for the first time in a week and worrying about our leaving the ship. She'd been so visible all the time, surely someone would notice she was missing? What about those officers she'd been flirting with?

Officers, plural. Of course, they'd each assume she was with someone else. Everyone knew her, but no-one thought they had a special claim on her. People might comment they hadn't seen her but nobody was going to notice she was missing because they had no claim on her. Except me.

And I was going with her.

Had it all been part of her plan?

Had I been duped along with the rest of the ship? Was I that easily manipulated?

I must have dozed off eventually because I woke to the

familiar sounds of Storm laying out our breakfast and the smell of fresh coffee drifting through the suite. For a moment I just lay there, feeling comfortably *at home*, but the smell of the coffee wasn't going away. And we had a lot to do.

Chrystal was already seated at the table, wearing the bath robe we'd be leaving on the ship, her wet hair down her back. I would never understand how she could get out of bed without waking me. For that matter, didn't she need to sleep?

Storm was holding my chair out for me and I slipped into it, then watched him lift the cover from a full cooked breakfast.

"I took the liberty of collecting a larger meal than usual, Ms Fletcher," he said.

"Very thoughtful, Storm. We do not know how long it will be before we will be able to eat another meal, as we are travelling," said Chrystal.

"I also secured a number of additional breakfast rolls and pieces of fruit, M'Lady. You will find them in your travelling bags when I return them to you on the island."

"Oh, thank you Storm. That is most considerate."

I didn't speak, having found I was ravenously hungry.

We left the ship separately, trying not to draw attention to the fact that we were together again. I was invisible in the crowd, wearing a light dress suitable for sight-seeing on this Caribbean island and carried my largest handbag. Chrystal wore a light brown skirt and matching top. She was accompanied by Storm, who helped her onto the quay but didn't seem to have any luggage. I tried not to panic, but then I saw him retrieve a large kit bag and a familiar-looking wooden box from the trolley that had been wheeled down the gangway earlier. He handed one of Chrystal's little envelopes to the officer who'd been guarding the pile from the local children who were always on the lookout for unattended bags. Then I lost sight of both of them as the crowd swept me away into the town.

I managed to lose myself in the market, when everyone was occupied with the colourful stalls. It took me ten minutes to find the cafe Chrystal had described and I found them both sitting at a table outside. Chrystal posed comfortably as she drank her espresso and spoke to Storm while he listened attentively, sipping at a cappuccino. They looked up as I approached and both smiled.

"Well done, Sam," she said. "I trust no-one noticed you leave the group?"

"No chance! They were all too busy boosting the local economy in the market. I could have can-canned my way out of there and no-one would have seen a thing."

I'd barely seated myself when a waiter brought me an espresso and bowed himself back into the doorway behind. It was scalding hot but tasted wonderful.

"So, what next?" I asked Chrystal.

"Storm has arranged for a taxi to take us to the airport," she said. "Whilst he goes back to the ship and conceals the fact of our absence for a day or two."

"Via the cotton quarter, of course," said Storm. "I will purchase the fabrics you requested which will be sent to your friend in Cardiff." He patted the breast pocket of his lightweight jacket and I realised Chrystal must have given him Cerys's address.

"Which will disguise the fact that he is carrying an empty kit bag back onto the ship," she added. "And,"

She leaned forward and pressed another of those envelopes into his hand. It looked a little fatter than usual. He looked her in the eye and nodded.

We finished our coffees and the waiter approached us again.

"Miss, your taxi is here," he said and Chrystal unfolded

herself from her chair. She left a green bill under her saucer and swept over to the waiting cab.

Storm was unpacking our bags and loading them into the back, the now-empty kit bag folded over his arm as he came to wish us goodbye. He lifted the ætheric sender into the cab and passed me the jacket I'd left on the back of my chair. I felt oddly emotional - this man had seen us in the most intimate situations and provided for our every need for the last two weeks and we were leaving him, never to meet again. As usual, I found myself wishing I'd had a manners teacher to tell me the correct way to deal with the situation, so I just kept quiet while he and Chrystal made their farewells. I muttered something and he turned away, disappearing into the tiny streets.

I unfolded my jacket to slip it on, knowing I'd have my hands full when we got out of the cab. A small brown envelope fell out of the pocket and I bent to pick it up, realising what it was.

"It's Storm's!" I said.

Chrystal smiled. "Indeed. He is a good man."

"But, why? I mean, he's been great, but that's what he's paid for." A sudden thought occurred to me. "And I never even knew his first name!"

"Of course not. He's a butler," she said.

Chapter 34

In which reports of ætheric activity are discussed

"Geb?"

The squat, hooded figure stood in front of the throne where his tall colleague lounged, showing no sign of having heard. He could have been asleep where he sat.

"We've had a report, Geb. Ætheric activity in the Americas." Behind him the screen flickered in its wooden bureau and a low-pitched beep sounded every few seconds.

"A report?" The sibilant voice was soft, but unmissable.

"The humans in the Americas have detected what appears to be purposeful ætheric activity. It is possible that the fingerprint they report is the same as the resonator-transmitter that was operating in London."

"Possible?"

"They suspect it is the same, First-Named. But it was very brief and they did not have time to triangulate the signal properly. It is possible the activity was something else. A coincidence. Perhaps."

"Is there, perhaps, a possibility that the device was in the hands of someone travelling towards a particular location ? A significant place?"

"Yes, Great Geb. We believe that to be the case."

"Is the area around the Cave properly protected?"

"The humans assure me they are watching all the approaches with both human technology and ætheric monitors. They have already intercepted two suspicious vehicles and dealt with their occupants."

"Did they find the one with the Great Heart?"

"No, Lord Geb. The vehicles were occupied by ephemerals only. But our men are confident they will apprehend her if she attempts to reach the cave."

"So convenient of the humans to use ætherically-noisy transportation systems. One might almost believe they were taught to do so," said the snake-headed man.

A guttural chuckle came from the other. "Indeed, one might," he said.

Chapter 35

In which they meet a red-headed rancher

The plane bounced about like a cork on the ocean. A very small cork on a very large ocean. In a storm. The wings wobbled up and down like a sheet of plywood and the whole plane felt like it was about the flip over and ditch in the water below.

"I do find small planes exhilarating," said Chrystal, leaning close to speak to me. I swallowed hard but still didn't trust myself to open my mouth to reply. So I just nodded and stared out of the window, looking for a level horizon I could focus on. It wasn't anything like flying in a proper plane, there certainly wasn't going to be a trolley service coming round!

We'd spent four days on Barbados. Chrystal stayed in our hotel room, making phone calls, poring over maps and scribbling notes on hotel-provided paper. Several times a day she checked the ætheric sender and seemed almost frantic to move on, but apparently we had time for her to arrange every last little detail and she was sure no-one was going to find us hiding behind assumed names and paying cash for everything. Once I started up the sender, thinking it would be more fun than staring out the window, but she closed it down quickly, without explaining why. I must have been annoying her, because she suggested I could go look round the market, even giving me a roll of dollars as she shooed me out. I should have been offended, but I was too bored with kicking my heels to object. So I enjoyed being a tourist with cash in my pocket and no-one else to please, returning to the hotel to spend my nights with Chrystal. For a few short days, I could enjoy being on holiday and life was good.

Until I found out that Chrystal's travel arrangements started with a flight in this ramshackle little plane!

Luckily the trip was short and we were soon taxiing along a pot-holed runway and slowing to stop outside a rusty hanger that looked as if it had been there since the war. The plane halted next to its corrugated green wall, curving away from us and shielding our plane from the view of anyone in the main buildings of the small airport. A battered brown car was parked ahead of us, a man leaning against the driver's door, cigarette in his mouth. The pilot helped carry our bags and loaded them into the boot while Chrystal spoke to the swarthy-skinned driver, who spread a map on the bonnet for her to point to. I barely had time to feel like a piece of lost luggage before we were travelling again, in a more civilised fashion this time.

Chrystal wore a loose beige-coloured shirt, gathered into those sexy tailored jeans and complimented by a brown suede waistcoat. She carried a short leather coat that matched her large handbag and knee-high boots. Her hat today was a soft brown thing that didn't seem to have a shape of its own but somehow looked good on her. My T-shirt, faded black jeans and trainers felt positively dowdy by comparison and I tried to keep my battered old fleece out of sight. She'd said to pack for comfort on the trip, but she could have walked along a catwalk in her idea of comfortable clothes and not looked out of place.

I hadn't made much effort to drag details of our travel plans out of Chrystal and she hadn't volunteered anything but the basics, so I was surprised when the driver seemed to be heading away from town and into an area that looked like a backdrop for a cowboy film. I half-expected John Wayne to gallop over one of the low hills, followed by a load of bad guys shooting as they rode. There were even herds of big-horned cattle in the distance and that tumbling weed blowing across the road ahead of us. I'd always thought that was made up by Hollywood, but apparently it was real. Or maybe these were props left over from all the films they'd made around here.

I should have expected it, but I was drowsing and startled awake when we turned onto a gravelled track that led through tall iron gates. I caught a glimpse of writing over our heads and then we were past. The track led towards a sprawling white-painted building that looked too large to be a house and had a wooden roof over the deck that ran the whole length of the side facing us. Our driver pulled up outside and a door opened to reveal a tall, good-looking man with a red beard, wearing jeans, checked shirt and - yes - a Stetson! We both got out, Chrystal stepping forward to meet him as he reached for her hand.

"Mizz Crystal?" he asked, shaking her hand vigorously and revealing pure-white teeth in a broad smile.

"I am Chrystal," she said. "I presume you are Henry Doyle?"

"That I am. But please, call me Hank," he said with another flash of his brilliant teeth.

"And this is my friend, Sam," said Chrystal, half-turning to gesture me forward to meet this man who seemed to have stepped straight out of the generic western I'd been imagining during the drive from town.

Meanwhile the driver had unloaded our bags and the ætheric sender we'd carefully packed in its box. He accepted the money Chrystal gave him and drove off. Hank and I stood awkwardly while this transaction was completed, not looking at each other or speaking until Chrystal walked back to us.

"Right, formalities over," he said. "Perhaps you ladies would care for a beer to wash the trail-dust out of your throats?"

He reached for our luggage and I grabbed the box before he could, leaving him to pick up the bags and lead us over to the shaded veranda. He gestured at a group of wooden chairs and disappeared through the door. We'd barely settled when he came back carrying three bottles beaded with water and I realised he was right - my throat was as dry as the desert land we'd driven through. He popped the top off one and handed it to Chrystal, then one for me and finally raised his own bottle.

"*May the road rise to meet you,*" he said.

"*May the wind be always at your back,*" replied Chrystal, raising her own bottle to chink against his. I hastily followed suit, but couldn't think of anything to add to their toast, so I just drank.

"I thought you came from England - but that toast's from the old country," said Hank, settling back in his chair.

"I am British, indeed," said Chrystal. "But I have travelled in Ireland many times. It is a hospitable country and one hears the friendly toast often enough to recognise it, even halfway across the globe."

"So I believe, though I've never visited there myself. Too busy with school and then my Daddy died and left me the ranch just after I graduated."

"I am certain he would be happy to know he left it in such reliable hands," said Chrystal.

A comfortable silence descended, so we all heard the whinny of a horse somewhere out of sight.

"So you've been running all this since then?" I asked, gesturing at the open fields.

"More or less," he said. "We hire labour when we need 'em but generally it's just us and the boys."

For the first time in my life, I found myself thinking of a man as attractive. I couldn't say why, but I found Hank seriously sexy. I could have listened to his soft accent for hours.

We chatted for a while, enjoying our beers and watching the tumbleweed blow across the open ground. I slipped into the house to use their loo - bathroom as Hank called it - and found the interior neat and spacious. He may come across as a cowboy, but it was obvious Hank was no slob.

"And so we'd better find horses for you two ladies," said Hank when I came out again. He stood and gathered up our empty beer bottles. I turned to Chrystal as he headed back into the house.

"Horses? You didn't say we'd be riding," I said.

"Would that present a difficulty?" she asked. "You did mention that you had ridden before."

"Yes, but it's been a very long time," I said.

She grinned, then leaned closer to whisper, "I haven't been on a horse since before you were born."

Hank led us to a wooden fence, which he vaulted over easily. We followed rather more carefully, with his help. He rattled the bucket he carried and a horse appeared around a ruined stone building, standing some distance from the fence. Another horse followed and then a small group appeared in the distance, trotting our way.

Within five minutes, there were a dozen or more horses jostling around us. Hank greeted each one by name and scattered enough horse nuts on the ground to keep them interested.

"Well, that's all the saddle-horses we've got for sale at the moment," he said. "Any take your fancy, ladies?"

I joined Chrystal in walking around the group, trying to remember what little I knew about horses. I'd worked at some stables during my summer holidays from Uni and done quite a lot of riding for those few months. But I was far from an expert. An image flashed through my head, of the Manager who'd kept me busy after hours as well.

Chrystal was inspecting a mare with a brown-and white patched coat. Skewbald, we'd have called her, but a pretty face and one white sock. I kept walking around the group, undecided. Then I noticed a grey standing off to one side, eyeing the rest of the herd suspiciously. Hank must have seen me looking.

"That's Steely," he said. "He's a young 'un, doesn't get on with the stallion so he keeps his distance."

"He's saddle-broken?" I asked.

"Yup, and he's well enough behaved for a rider. Just winds the stallion up."

I grabbed a handful of horse nuts from Hank's bucket and walked towards the grey horse, aiming as if to walk past, just in front of him. He watched me approach, both ears up. He didn't seem unfriendly and accepted the treats with good grace, letting me scratch his neck as he munched. I took hold of his loose halter and led him towards the gate where Chrystal stood with her mare.

"We-ell that was simple enough," said Hank, falling in on the other side of my horse. "Always good to deal with people who make their minds up quick. You've both got a good eye for horseflesh."

"I have to admit, it's been a long time since I rode a horse," I said. He just shook his head.

"Let's get them saddled up and we'll see how you get on," he said. "They say you never forget how."

I found he was right, your body never forgets how to ride. But it does forget how painful it can be. After only half an hour in the saddle, I was sore, stiff and very pleased to take a break for the excellent meal Hank's wife served up on their veranda. I was so busy eating and trying to find a comfortable sitting position, that I must have phased out of the conversation. My attention snapped back when I heard Hank mention my name.

"Sam? You're okay with that?" he asked.

"Um, I'm sorry - I was miles away," I said.

"Chrystal was just explaining you're staying in a motel tonight, ready for an early start on your trek tomorrow. I offered you beds here, if you'd prefer?" he said.

I looked over at Chrystal, unsure. She met my eyes with a

slight smile but didn't prompt my reply.

"Chrystal's made all our travel plans," I said slowly. "I'm happy to go along with her."

Hank looked disappointed. "So long as you're sure," he said.

He helped us pack our luggage into saddle-bags for each horse and swung himself onto the bare back of another mare to see us across the horses' paddock. At first the small herd followed, hoping the bag over Hank's shoulder might contain horse nuts, but they soon lost interest and wandered off again.

Stopping by another gate, he slid off to unhook the metal catch.

"Straight for those trees and you'll see the track. That'll take you down into the town. Motel's on yer right and there's stabling at the back. They'll most likely give you rooms next to the stable block - ask 'em if they forget to offer."

I looked to see where he had indicated and when I turned back, he'd opened the bag he was carrying and offered us each a Stetson hat.

"I thought these might come in useful," he said with a shy smile.

We thanked him and set off as he'd indicated. Chrystal was quiet for a few minutes, then turned in the saddle to look back at Hank. I checked too and saw him trotting his horse away from us.

"A charming young man," she said as she turned back.

"Yes," I agreed. "How do you find these people? I mean, is there some sort of directory of useful people you can look up when you're travelling? Is Hank listed there under *nice men to buy horses from*?"

"Not exactly," her face was unreadable. "I knew his great-great-great-grandfather."

"You what?" My horse laid his ears flat in reproach at my raised voice. I reached down to pat his neck in apology.

"I knew the first Henry Doyle who came here to breed horses. He had just bought his first three mares, was paying rent on the land and working to pay for the services of a neighbouring rancher's stallion. But he still found the wherewithal to offer hospitality to two strangers."

"And he lived in the same place?"

"He was just starting out. Fresh over from Ireland with his wife and sons, their life-savings and an instinct for horses. It was the younger of his sons who bought the lease on their land and Henry's family has been breeding horses over here ever since. And red-headed ranchers."

"Did you tell him?"

"Tell who? Henry?"

"No, Hank. I mean did you tell him you..." I tailed off. Of course she hadn't told him she'd met his ancestor. Chrystal was smiling quietly as I tumbled over my words.

"Okay, that was a stupid question," I said. "So how did you contact him?"

"I telephoned him from the Caribbean and said that my family had bought horses from his family before. He was more than happy to oblige. And I know that I can trust in his horses to be healthy and sturdy."

"So are these horses descended from the mares he'd bought back in - when was it you were over here?"

She thought for a moment. "It would have been 1882, I think. There were many Irish coming to America in those days. There had been bitterly cold winters for a few years and that prompted many to take their chances in travelling to the New World. The ship we sailed on carried a few - but they were the wealthier ones. Many crossed the Atlantic Ocean in boats that should never have left a sheltered harbour."

"And Hank's great-great was on the ship with you?"

"No, we sailed into New York and travelled down South

from there. Henry Doyle had made the same journey the year before. We met him at a horse auction and he made us welcome as guests. A true gentleman."

"You said, *we,*" I said. "Who were you travelling with?"

"That was Caulfield. He was my manservant," she replied.

"You were travelling alone with a man? Wasn't that a bit, um, risqué?"

"It was not commonly done in those days, it is true. But it was not completely unheard of, either." She turned to catch my eye.

I shook my head, then thought of something else that had been troubling me.

"Why didn't we stay with Hank?" I asked. "If you'd stayed with his ancestor, surely you knew it would have been alright."

"I am certain his invitation was sincere," she replied. "But it is possible that someone is tracking our movements. And I do not wish to endanger him or his family any more than I have to."

"Tracking us? But how? Even if there was someone on the ship, surely they couldn't have followed...?" I paused.

"Not from the ship, no. But ætheric technology is unusual in this century and it would be a simple enough matter to locate the sender when it is activated."

"So that's why we're staying in a motel?"

She nodded. "And we will continue to use rural accommodations as we travel towards our destination. We cannot prevent ætheric monitoring devices from pinpointing us when we check for signals, but we can reduce the number of eyes that may see us and report to unfriendly ears."

I thought about that for a moment. It kind of made sense, but it still seemed an odd way to travel.

"Why not use a car, though? Surely the sooner we get there, the better?"

"But automobiles need fuel and fuel means people. It is safer to use transport that can feed itself and travel cross country where we can. And animals are sensitive to certain types of ætheric signals. Horses may be better able to locate the calendar than we are."

"And what about stabling? Surely you don't get Wild-West style saloon bars with stabling for horses?"

"Not exactly," she said. "But there are motels which offer stable facilities for the traveller. Especially in this area where there was little to attract settlers unless they wanted land to breed their livestock."

"Did you travel by horse when you were here before?" I asked.

"Only for leisure. We were visiting the New World to avoid certain unpleasantnesses back home. For a few months we were free to stay with hospitable people and not hurry to move on."

"And it wasn't a scandal that you were travelling with a man? The 19th century was more tolerant than I thought."

She nodded, grinning wickedly.

"However, you and I are doing something entirely unacceptable to Victorian mores," she said. "We are riding astride!"

"As opposed to side-saddle? Was it really so rare?" I asked.

"No lady would ever sit on a horse in this fashion. Only a slattern would risk such a position - and no lady would risk taking pleasure from such a sensation!"

It took me a moment to understand what she was hinting at and then I tried to think of a sensible question. Before I could, she rose in her stirrups.

"Speaking of which, shall we give our horses a chance to stretch their legs a little before we take them to stable for the night?"

Chapter 36

In which horses are ridden in a shameless style

The Victorians may have been right about the dangers of a woman riding a horse in the modern style. Whatever the reasons, both of us had far more interest in each other that night than I would have expected. We'd had a long day, with physical exercise we weren't used to, so we should have been knackered and ready to collapse into bed for a good night's sleep. Instead we fell into bed in each other's arms and didn't hurry to get to sleep. Maybe it was because we'd been riding horses in that shameless way, maybe it was the effect Hank had on us - *what sort of relationship had Chrystal had with his great-great-ancestor?* Or maybe it was the joy of being back on solid ground.

I woke the next morning with sun streaming through the thin curtains. Chrystal was sprawled next to me, her hair spreading around her head like a puddle of warm gold. It always fascinated me to see how wavy it went after she'd had it fastened back all day. She lay on her back, one arm over the duvet, one shoulder half-covered with her hair. I sat there for several minutes, loving the way the sun played with her face, highlighting her cheek bones and the unlined skin around her eyes. However much I knew it to be true, I still found it hard to believe her age. I could see the fine hairs and even little freckles that weren't visible except in this strange sunlight, angled and filtered by the curtain. Wondering if she'd caught the sun a bit yesterday, I touched my own forehead and it felt warm against the cool morning air, so maybe I had too. I looked at the shadows her eyelashes cast on her cheek, tracing a brief map leading away from her eye and down her face. There was the tiniest speck of dust dancing in the sunbeam, moving slightly in her breath.

A crash from downstairs was quickly followed by a few

choice swear-words and Chrystal's eyes opened. For a second she looked confused, then a tender smile touched her lips.

"Good morning, Sam. I take it that was not an alarm clock?"

I grinned. "No, I think someone dropped something in the kitchen. Judging by the swearing, it was important. Or valuable."

"Just so long as it was not our breakfast," she said, throwing off the duvet and heading for the shower.

We never did find out what had been dropped, but breakfast was ready when we went down. Hot, tasty and plentiful, with copious cups of coffee. I'd never had proper American pancakes and syrup before and I couldn't get enough of them. Chrystal watched me without comment, but my third plateful came with a comment of,

"I feel sorry for that horse of yours!" I looked up into the hazel eyes of the motel's owner and grinned back at her before tucking into the latest heap of steaming calories. I justified it to myself by thinking about all the energy I'd burn up riding - and I'd used last night with Chrystal. But I didn't order another helping.

Our travelling quickly fell into a rhythm. We'd spend each day on horseback, heading roughly northwest and spend the night in a motel or camping out. The nights outside were cold, but bearable and we were together. We skirted around any larger settlements, sticking to the smaller towns and even avoiding roads where we could follow the right direction across open country.

Chrystal was distant, not wanting to talk about our destination or much of anything else and I spent a lot of my riding time thinking about home, what the weather would be doing back in London, whether anyone missed me and just what I had been doing with my life. The more I thought about, the more I realised I hadn't really been doing anything. I used to go into the office each day, watch mindless telly in the evening and go out with my colleagues at a weekend. Sometimes there would be someone in my life, more often there wasn't. Nothing had really changed for years until I'd been made redundant. Then I didn't have a job to go to, didn't have money to throw away and also found out I hadn't got any real friends either. For those last few months, my life had consisted of whatever I had to do to get money and struggling to keep a roof over my head. But was it any worse a life than I'd had before? Even those snatched hours with Rosalind had been more for her pleasure than mine. And when she got bored, she'd gone back to her husband without a second thought.

It seemed as if I'd been more alive these last few months with Chrystal in my life than I'd ever been before.

And I still didn't know how she felt about me. Was I just some passing diversion for her? Would she drop me when she'd had everything she wanted from me? Just as everyone else had?

I decided it didn't matter. I was enjoying my time with her and might even be doing something worthwhile for the first time in my life. And those two things mattered more than worries about the future.

I'd even lost count of the days, enjoying the mindless rhythm of riding, check the æther for signals and camping at night. I knew Chrystal was worried about pursuit or someone locating us, but I found it hard to take that seriously.

"Would you be prepared to ride on today?" asked Chrystal, breaking into my introspection. I looked up, startled.

"Um, yeah. How much longer?"

"I believe it will take us approximately three hours, maybe a little more, to reach the destination I have in mind," she replied.

"And where is that?"

"It is a small town, probably the last such civilisation that we will encounter, and the place in which I expect to locate the map which accurately describes the position of the calendar," she explained.

"And it's about three hours away? So let's get there."

She kicked Cinnamon to a canter and didn't illuminate any more of her plans.

Chapter 37

In which a map is sought and a stone examined

The first stars were appearing as we arrived at the town Chrystal was aiming for, and checked in to the first motel we saw, a tiny little place right on the edge of the town. The owner's son took charge of our horses, stabling them with their own animals. He was obviously very competent and admired both Steely and Cinnamon before Chrystal and I left to take our bags to our room.

I was too tired to appreciate the meal we were served and we went upstairs as soon as we could reasonably. Chrystal was just as tired and we were both asleep in record time.

The following morning, Chrystal suggested we walk into town. She hadn't shared her plans in detail, except that we were looking for a map. I'd given up pressing her for details and I was just pleased to be out on a chill December morning, arm-in-arm with her in a dusty little town I'd never heard of before.

So I was a little surprised when she steered me into a tall, wood-fronted building. The sign outside said, "Museum of Local History" in an ornate script, with a faded image that might have been a line of covered wagons - or a well-behaved flock of sheep.

The front door opened at a push, jangling a bell hanging overhead. The hall would have been spacious but for the shelves along both walls, stacked untidily with all sorts of stuff. I could see an old pair of bellows, bits of horse harness, several woodworker's tools and something that looked like a rusty metal whisk. The floor had a light sprinkling of dust that kicked up as we walked in, adding our footprints to the few already there. A young man's head appeared in an open hatch in one wall.

"Howdy," he said. "We don't see many tourists at this time of year." His head disappeared back through the hatch and then he walked through a nearby door, carrying a kettle that steamed.

"I was just fixing coffee," he said, waving the kettle in emphasis. "Would you like some? I'm afraid I'm clean out of cream until Ma gets back with some."

"Black coffee would be fine, thank you," said Chrystal and his eyes widened.

"Hey - you're English. I might have some tea, if you'd prefer...?" He left the question hanging, looking from Chrystal to me expectantly.

"Coffee is fine," I said. "Shall I give you a hand?"

"No, no. I'll only take a moment." He vanished back into the kitchen, but his voice continued. "Feel free to look around. I'm afraid it's none too neat, but the oldest stuff is through the arch, more recent history upstairs."

Chrystal beckoned with her head and led me through the arched doorway he'd mentioned. She seemed to know where she was going and walked straight into a large room with display cabinets along the walls. I helped her lift a few boxes away from a large stone wheel and then to dust it off. It was deeply carved with geometric shapes that I could almost persuade myself could be letters from some old, forgotten language. She moved round until she was facing the wheel from one particular side, turning her head from side to side as if trying to read it in the dim light from the single overhead fluorescent tube.

"Oh, you're interested in the old mill stone?" asked the young man, coming in with a tray of steaming coffees. "Don't ask me what it says - no-one's ever deciphered the writing. It's meant to be Olmec, but some of the letters are different to everything else we've got."

He paused for breath and passed our coffees.

"We've got some smaller stones and translations for 'em," he went on, gesturing to a display cabinet.

"No, I was keen to see this one," said Chrystal, giving him one of her best little-girl smiles. "You are indeed correct about the characters - the script is unlike anything else I have ever seen."

"Um - how did you know where to find it?" he asked. "I mean, it tends to get buried under everything else in here."

Still smiling, Chrystal gestured at the carvings on what he called the millstone.

"I had been told you had it here, and it was not difficult to locate, given its size."

"Oh. Who told you it was here? I didn't think it was special or anything," he said.

"A relative of my mother's. She knows that I am interested in Olmec writings and she remembered seeing this stone some years ago. We are lucky indeed that it is still in the same museum."

"That explains it! I don't think I've ever seen it uncovered like that. And I've been working here almost five years," he said.

Chrystal looked at him, her brow crinkled.

"But you were aware that the letters were unusual," she said.

"Ah yes, that's because of the posters. We've got one pinned up in the office," he said.

"A picture of the, ah, millstone?"

"Yes, we sell them. Posters, bookmarks, postcards - it's one of our most popular images," he said.

"Perhaps I could purchase one?" asked Chrystal, shepherding him out of the room and towards the office.

Which is how I came to be carrying a brown paper bag with a rolled-up picture of the stone wheel in it. Chrystal had settled on a laminated A3 print, claiming it was just what she needed for her studies. I struggled to keep my face straight as she paid him twice what he'd asked and then left, saying we had to call a friend and promising we'd be back later.

"That's your map?" I asked, as soon as I was certain he couldn't hear us.

She nodded. "I had seen it on a previous visit to this area, although I did not fully understand the significance of its carvings until recently."

"You can read it?" I asked. "Surely it's hundreds of years old. Well before your time, even!"

"That map is older even than Christianity, as the Olmec civilisation died out almost three thousand years ago." she said. "I can only read parts of it, and that knowledge comes from studies done by scholars with wiser heads than mine. But I have the advantage of having been able to collect papers on the subject for several decades."

"So what does it say?"

"The inscription gives directions to find a cave system, in which we may find a calendar-stone. There is a legend associated with this stone, that it needs to be fed and then *turn* to enable a new cycle to begin."

"How on earth do you feed a stone? And surely that's just a story," I said.

She stopped walking and turned to face me. "A few months ago, you would have said that someone living more than a hundred years could only be a *story*," she said. "A few months ago, you would have dismissed the æther as a Victorian fallacy, disproven by your modern science."

"Well, yes. But..." It was no use. Chrystal obviously believed this legend and I wasn't going to talk her out of it.

"So we're going to find the calendar?" I asked.

"That is indeed my aim," she said. "I will study the map this afternoon and we ride out tomorrow morning. I know that it cannot be far from here, and we have a few days left to locate the calendar."

In the back of my mind, I had a vague memory of

something I'd seen on telly. Someone was claiming that the Mayan calendar ended in 2012 - was that anything to do with Chrystal's calendar? Wasn't the world meant to come to an end on whatever-day-it-was?

"So this calendar is three thousand years old? And it's just coming to an end?" I prompted her.

"According to the researchers, the Olmecs first drew up their calendar more than five millennia ago and each cycle takes almost four hundred years to complete. This will be the end of the fourteenth cycle," she replied, staring into the distance.

"And the world is about to end?"

"No, of course not," she said. "The cycle will end and a new one will begin - but there is a need for the calendar to be turned to ensure that order continues to have the upper hand over chaos."

I struggled with my memory of that half-remembered programme all the way back to the hotel, where I went to check the horses were being looked after before returning to our room. I was quite enjoying the chance to look after horses - they had always been my favourite animals and these two were excellent animals, each with their own character.

In our room, Chrystal pored over her map, making pencil notes on a pad of paper on the desk. A modern map lay on the floor, folded to show the area we'd been crossing. She'd set up the ætheric sender and I could hear its foil whispering round inside, charging itself up in the wasted energy of a small, dusty town. She obviously didn't need my company, so I went out to see whatever sights I could find. I'd never been to this part of Central America before and there must be something worth seeing.

There wasn't very much to the town and I returned to the motel within a couple of hours. Chrystal looked up as I walked into our room. She sighed and pushed a hand through her hair.

"Problem?" I asked.

"Perhaps. I can find the general area from this inscription. And there cannot be many mesas that answer the description. But locating one specific cave may be a little more complicated," she said.

"Doesn't sound like it's much of a map," I pointed out.

"It is not a map in the modern sense, but more a description of a location and a set of instructions to identify the particular cave. I believe it was intended for use by people who really only needed a reminder of the location, rather than someone finding it for the first time."

"And we have a deadline?"

She looked at me quizzically, so I elaborated, "A date by which we have to find this cave?"

"Yes, indeed. We need to locate it before the 21st."

"But that's Friday!"

She nodded.

"And what do we have to do when we are there?" I asked.

"The legend states that a blood sacrifice must be made by *One with no heart and the greatest heart*. I believe that I fit that description," she said.

"Well, yes - but what is this sacrifice?" A sudden, terrible thought crossed my mind. "Is that what I'm meant to be?"

She looked startled, stood and stepped across the room quickly, taking me in her arms.

"Oh, my dear Sam. It is not that kind of a sacrifice. An offering, a means to turn the stone is all that is needed. Rest assured, I will not harm you to achieve this thing."

"But why do have to do anything at all? I mean, what happens if we just stay here in the motel instead of trekking across the desert?"

"The scrubland is hardly desert, Sam. And I do not know exactly what will happen if I fail to meet my destiny - only that it is hinted at in the darkest terms and that scholars of ancient texts are unanimous in their concern that the turning of the calendar must come to pass."

"But why you - and why now?"

"The scholars talk of an ancient cycle - this is merely the latest occurrence of the calendar's ending. And I do not know of anyone else who fits the description, do you?" She rested a hand on her chest and looked almost forlorn. I turned away, embarrassed to see her looking vulnerable and determined not to show it as I was still a little mad at her silences and refusal to explain herself. I was used to her being the strong one, whether I agreed with her or not. I picked up a t-shirt and folded it into my bag.

"Is it dangerous?" I asked over my shoulder, pretending to look through a drawer.

"It may be, I do not know," she replied and my heart heaved at the emotion in her voice.

"But if this sacrifice has been made before, don't your scholars know what happened?"

"The previous cycle ended in the Seventeenth Century. The records of that time and legends of previous cycles seem to say that the Meso-Americans thought the description meant their ruler or a priest. These men conducted many blood sacrifices and this appears to have sufficed in turning the calendar. The scholars now believe that the Great Heart of the legend is none other than my Chrystal and that it is I who must make this sacrifice." As she spoke, I looked back at her, trying to read her expression.

"But the Aztecs killed their victims - are *you* going to die? How will it happen?"

"Sam, I do not know what will happen, only that I have to

be there with the calendar. On Friday. And we do not yet know where it is."

"And what if you aren't there?"

"Then maybe the followers of chaos will be able to tip the balance back in their favour. Perhaps other people will attempt to make the sacrifice as it was made in centuries gone by, when much blood was shed. I do not know. But I do know that it would not be healthy for our ordered world."

"And maybe nothing at all will happen," I snapped.

She looked at me steadily. "The scholars believe that there have been periods when the calendar did not turn and chaos had power over order for almost four centuries. Perhaps I have a responsibility to those who gave me the Chrystal all those years ago."

"You think they knew you would have to do this? Do they use the Chrystal to create someone for this sacrifice?"

She didn't answer and I turned my back again, fighting back tears.

"We will be leaving first thing in the morning, so you are right to begin packing," she said.

I didn't answer, not trusting my voice to keep level and unsure of my own feelings. After a long moment I heard her open the door and then close it. I turned to check.

I was alone in the room.

Chapter 38

In which the trail is picked up again

The throne room was empty, nothing moved in the vast hall and no-one disturbed the shadows that fell between the great pillars. A rough wind sighed outside but couldn't penetrate to lift the dust in the dark corners. The dry air smelt of woodrot and fear, hanging heavily in the ancient hall.

A sharp note sounded, followed by a strident, mechanical wail. It rose slowly for almost a minute until a door crashed open and a squat, cloaked figure scurried through. Reaching the wooden bureau, he flung open both of its doors, revealing the glowing screen showing four images as it had before. But this time, one of the quarters showed a single, bright pinprick of light, standing out from the dimmer flickers all around. The hooded figure flicked a brass switch and the siren ceased. Working quickly, his taloned, stubby fingers turned knobs and pulled on levers until the screen showing the bright light shifted, centring the display. More adjustments and a second screen flickered, settling with a new picture displayed, this time showing that single point, larger and brighter. He was working on the third display when the door behind the throne creaked open. The squat figure threw back his hood to reveal a green, scaly head, with triangular teeth projecting outside the lips of his snout. He glanced over his shoulder, but didn't turn. Instead he pushed buttons and joggled levers, but the map he was working with stubbornly refused to show a light.

"Well, where is it, Sobek?" asked the tall, stooped shape that came up behind him.

"I cannot be certain, Geb."

"But roughly where?"

"Somewhere in the Americas. In the centre," he answered, still furiously working the controls.

"Save your efforts," said the tall figure, reaching for the control panel. "They are heading for the calendar. They have found a map."

The fatter man's hands dropped to his sides and he turned, slowly.

"The calendar? But it's almost the twenty-first..."

"Farran," shouted the taller figure.

"Yes, Your Eminence?" said the pirate, dashing into the hall. His shirt was even more creased than before, his flies bulging oddly where the buttons were out of step with the buttonholes.

"Take two of your pirates and use a trans-æther pod."

"A pod? Where to, Your Excellency?"

"America, it seems our foe has found the calendar."

"Found it? But our men have been unable to locate it..." Farran dried up as the cowled head turned his way and bent slightly to hiss in his face.

"SHE *has found it. That is all you need to know. Take the pod and stop her before the sacrifice can be made!" he hissed. "But she must not die too near to the calendar."*

The pirate swallowed, pulled himself erect and backed away slowly. The backs of his legs touched the front row of seats and he turned towards the door he'd come in through.

"And Farran," hissed the dark voice.

The pirate hesitated.

"Don't make any mistakes this time. If you fail me again, you will suffer my wrath," came the dark, sonorous words.

Farran bowed, then turned and fled.

Turning to the screen, the snake-headed man thumbed a switch with his long, bony hand.

"Prepare a pod for immediate travel to the Americas. Three men, single journey. And equip them with an æther-tracker."

A distant voice acknowledged his command and he

released the switch. As he turned away, he paused and flicked it again.

"Send it to arrive within the ring of humans monitoring approaches to the cave. And set it to implode one hour after landing. We don't want any evidence for the humans," he said.

"But Geb," the squat crocodile-man interrupted. "How will Farran and the others return to the stronghold?" He cowered as the dark hood turned his way.

"If they succeed," he hissed to his associate. "There will be no need for them to return."

He paused, considering. "And if they fail, they will not wish to return."

Chapter 39

In which a young horse is satisfied

When Chrystal said, *first thing in the morning*, she meant it. She'd arranged for our breakfast to be served before dawn and we arrived at the stables to find our horses saddled and huddling together in the grey drizzle. They looked as miserable as I felt at being rousted from my warm bed. Chrystal, of course, looked immaculate in her jeans, riding boots and waterproof coat. She wore the Stetson from Hank and didn't seem at all bothered by the change in the weather.

I swung my saddlebags onto Steely's back and fastened them in place. There'd been a small pile of supplies waiting in the kitchen for us after breakfast and Chrystal was fixing its leather case to her saddle, opposite the ætheric sender in its box. Her water bottle already hung from the pommel. I carried a solid loaf of dark bread to add to my luggage.

We set off before the sun was over the horizon, the horses walking at a steady pace along deserted roads. The rain kept the dust down, so we had to deal with being cold and wet, instead of cold and dusty. Chrystal, sitting comfortably on Cinnamon, led and Steely seemed content to follow them, rather than walk alongside. My thoughts bounced between resentment of Chrystal's dismissiveness and an urge to get little-girl excited about where we were and what we were doing. I'd met a real cowboy, I was riding a horse into the wilderness, we were seeking a lost artefact and trying to save - whatever. It all felt like a dream in the grey morning light.

Chrystal finally called a halt beside a mesa, where a small stream trickled through a tight copse of gnarled trees growing in the shelter of the rock wall. We'd stopped for an hour to eat our lunch and rest the horses, but had spent the rest of the day in the saddle. I had no idea how far we'd come or where we were. Chrystal seemed to be navigating by the sun or something even more esoteric - I hadn't seen her consult a proper map all day, just an old brass compass and the copy of the ancient carving we'd bought from the museum. She started to lay out a fire and I automatically tended to the horses. Both appeared fine after the long day and I had to agree with Chrystal's opinion of Hank's horse-breeding skills. Nonetheless, I checked all their hooves and gave them a good rub-down once their saddles were off. Steely seemed oddly jealous of Cinnamon, trying to get in my way as I combed her, but he stopped hassling me once I returned to the fire. *Maybe it wasn't me he was interested in,* I thought, watching him nuzzling the mare over their feed, breathing into her nostrils.

The small fire in its circle of stones was a lot warmer than I'd expected. I unrolled my bedding on the opposite side from Chrystal's and went to see what she was doing. She'd made a little platform for the ætheric sender and was closing the back of its case as I approached.

"This will monitor for signals, in case The Professor has any information for us," she said without looking up.

"But he can't speak to us over that," I said, surprised.

"There is no need," she replied. "If he has gleaned anything further from his researches, the only knowledge he may need to communicate would be in the manner of directions. He knows the limitations of my equipment and will begin by requesting that I acknowledge his signal. Once he has done so, he would send directions in the form of polar co-ordinates, using the museum where we saw the calendar stone as a start point. Or perhaps some small detail that may identify our destination."

"Okaaaay, and that means what, exactly?"

"Ah, these schools!" said Chrystal. "If he can offer assistance, he will tell me how far our destination is from the museum and in which direction. I will then correct our course to reach that point as quickly as possible."

"So we could be heading in completely the wrong direction?"

"That is not possible. I am confident that my reading of the ancient map will take us to approximately the correct location. Any amendment to our course should only be minor. If he has found anything to help, of course."

And with that I had to be content.

Dinner was simply a case of heating some stew we'd brought from the motel and eating it together with chunks of the heavy bread packed in the top of my saddle bag. After we'd rinsed our plates and filled our water bottles, I sat cross-legged on my bedding, staring into the flames. Chrystal stacked more wood carefully onto the fire, nudging the already-burning branches so they were covered. The dancing flames died down to a quieter glow and I lifted my blanket around my shoulders.

"Are you sufficiently warm?" asked Chrystal, sitting down next to me. She settled into place on my sleeping bag and draped one arm around me. I pulled the coarse blanket round to cover us both and nodded, still hypnotised by the glowing fire.

"The horses will be fine for the night," she went on. "They have had a good feed and will not stray far from our camp."

Sure enough, I could hear the animals nearby, chomping on tough grass, nickering softly and blowing at each other. Chrystal pulled my head onto her shoulder and stroked my hair. She felt warm and I nuzzled into her embrace. It'd been a long day and I knew I should be tired, but I felt oddly awake, alert to everything around me and the slim, solid presence at my side as we sat together beneath a rough blanket beside the fire. The blue sky darkened as the sun disappeared and the first stars twinkled on the opposite horizon, the cool air as clear and somehow solid as glass. The grass smelt more like hay under my sleeping bag and I heard Steely whinny quietly, saying something in his own language. Cinnamon huffed through her nostrils in reply and I, too, sighed, feeling the heat from Chrystal's body. I lifted my head from her shoulder and turned towards her, lifting my face to meet hers.

Her kiss was gentle, slow and deep. Despite my misgivings about Chrystal's behaviour, I couldn't resist her up close like this. I kissed her back, soft and lingering. Something stirred in the centre of my chest, something that hadn't been quashed by the arguments, days of silence and hard hours of riding. I gave myself up to the moment and Chrystal pulled me closer.

Steely whinnied again and I could hear him crashing about. Vaguely I pictured him rearing up as he trumpeted his challenge. Again I thought I should check there was nothing threatening the animals, but I was too warm, sitting by the fire, with Chrystal's caresses growing more intimate. She slipped a hand inside my blouse and I reached up to unfasten buttons without being sure whose they were. My breath was coming faster as Chrystal's tongue darted in and out of my mouth, warm and demanding. Our hands peeled clothes off each other, exposing burning skin to caresses and the cool evening air.

The horses were moving around nearby, making more noise, whickering at each other and I recognised Steely's occasional soft whinnies. I wondered again if I should check they were alright. But Chrystal's kisses were getting urgent while her hands on my naked shoulders pushed me back onto my thin sleeping bag and the rough ground underneath. Her slender body lay on top and I held her close as we kicked off our jeans. A bird called somewhere overhead and I heard its wings rustle as Chrystal's hair fell about my face. Every inch of my skin came alive under her touch and I responded eagerly, my aches forgotten. She always knew what my body wanted better than I did myself and I caressed her back, knowing my hands were rough from hard work and leather reins but needing to feel that resilient flesh under my touch. She smelt faintly of leather and horse sweat, her tiny waist firm but velvety-soft under my fingers. Despite the cold of the evening, we were both naked by now, caring only that we threw our shed clothes away from the still-glowing fire.

Dimly I heard Cinnamon squeal and Steely snort softly in response. Their movements were noisy, as they trampled the long grass and snapped odd bits of wood with their shuffling hooves. Chrystal nibbled at my lower lip, and I yelped as she bit lightly. I wondered fleetingly if Steely had nipped Cinnamon to make her squeal, too. But then I opened my mouth to my lover and twined my fingers into her hair, pulling her down on top of me. A warm glow filled my belly, despite the cold of the night air. Chrystal's hands seemed to be everywhere on my body at once, gentle but insistent. I felt her lips on my throat, moving down and bit back a moan. My back arched and I felt her leg pushing between mine while she nibbled and teased me. We moved together, sweating despite the evening's chill as our bodies curved and twined around each other. I stroked and kissed, feeling Chrystal's response and my own excitement building to the familiar rhythm, as ancient as the land around us. I felt the familiar tightening in my stomach. Through the blood pounding in my ears, I could hear Steely's triumphant scream as Cinnamon surrendered to his advances.

I woke the next morning to daylight shining through my eyelids and the smell of woodsmoke. My eyes fluttered open in the grey light of a December morning. I was lying on my side, facing a firepit full of ashes and the blackened remains of wood. I realised I was naked and wondered briefly if I'd pulled myself into my sleeping bag or if Chrystal had covered me when I'd dozed off. For a long moment I luxuriated in the slight warmth of my bedding, before pulling my blanket round me and starting to gather my clothes from the ground where we'd scattered them last night.

I dressed and flung my bedding over a branch next to Chrystal's, checked on the horses and then went in search of my lover. I found her sitting cross-legged against a rock, the ætheric sender in her lap. She'd partly disassembled it and was peering closely at some small components in her hand. She looked pale and I tried to remember when I had last given her blood to feed her heart.

"I wondered where you were," I began.

She didn't look up from what she was doing.

"The sender requires more attention than usual, given that we are operating it whilst in transit. It is not designed to be used in this way and I must ensure that all is working correctly."

That stung. I was all set for a reconciliation after our passion last night, expecting her to be tender and caring again. Instead she was more concerned with that bloody gadget of hers. Nothing had changed.

"I'll just make us some breakfast then, shall I?"

"That would be good, Sam. Thank you." Again, she didn't bother to look up. If she had, she'd have seen my face red with fury at her offhand manner. As if I was a servant to be dismissed - or a whore to be used and ignored. I stomped back to the firepit, brushed the ashes away and began to stack fresh wood to cook some bacon. Chrystal came back as the rashers were cooking and we ate the bread and thick rashers in silence. The coffee pot bubbled over the flames and I poured it into the metal mugs, sipping at the hot liquid as I took down our bedding and rolled both sets neatly for slinging behind us on our saddles. Chrystal examined the ætheric sender again before she packed it in its case and fixed it on Cinnamon's saddle. By the time I'd rinsed our mugs in the stream, she was mounted and looking northwest along the track, her hand shading her eyes from the still-low sun to the right of our path.

Without preamble, she said, "If we make good time today we will be in the area, with plenty of time to search for the correct mesa and the cave."

I bit back a terse comment.

"And The Professor hasn't been in touch?"

"No, he has not. I believe that is a good sign, that his researches have confirmed our initial suppositions about the direction and distance we should be travelling. The responder is detecting some unusual activity, though, and I suspect that may be echoes of our own activity reflecting from the stone that we seek."

"Does that mean you can find it?"

"Perhaps, if the echoes are focused in a way I can detect. Or if the horses recognise its presence."

"What if other animals home in on it? Will that lead us closer?"

She looked at me properly for the first time that morning. "What sort of animals?" she asked.

I didn't answer - it was only a guess.

One last check around the campsite and I flung myself onto Steely's back. He harrumphed in annoyance at the violence of my mounting and I spent a few seconds apologising and scratching his neck. When I looked up, Cinnamon and Chrystal were already a hundred yards away. I clicked to Steely and he willingly set off in his mate's hoofprints.

Chrystal reined Cinnamon back a little as I approached, but I let Steely fall into his favourite position, with his nose set to follow the mare's backside. I could feel Chrystal's eyes on me but

I didn't try to meet her gaze. After a moment, she turned to face forward, clicked to Cinnamon to start walking and Steely and I brought up the rear. Literally, in his case.

We continued in single file for a couple of hours, both keeping our thoughts to ourselves. Chrystal sat very upright in her saddle, rising easily in time with Cinnamon's gait. She kicked the mare's flanks and moved up to a canter without a word to me. I was sure I would look more like a sack of spuds thrown onto Steely's back, sore from both the riding yesterday and our rough passion beside the fire. Steely, by contrast, practically pranced along. His ears were up and every step was as bouncy as if he was walking on air. He probably felt like he was. It must be difficult for a young horse, pushed out to the edge of the herd while the mature stallion had his run of the mares. In the wild, he'd have gone in search of his own willing females and started a harem of his own, but that wasn't exactly possible when they were fenced into a paddock. No wonder he'd been sniffing after Cinnamon so eagerly. I felt that I understood Steely better than I did Chrystal and wondered if my steed felt the same towards his rider.

I shook my head. What a stupid idea. The young horse's attention was focused on the mare in front of him, leaving little brain-power to keep his legs moving and to watch where he put his hooves. Abstract emotional ideas would be alien to his mind at the best of times and even more so as he came into his adulthood. For him, this trip was only an adventure in the sexual sense, nothing more.

And it was while I was pondering what occupied a randy horse's brain that they attacked.

Chapter 40

In which an implosion is not the only strange sound

The men covered their egg-shaped craft with a coarse brown net before walking away across the open ground. All three were dressed in dark trousers, collarless shirts and waistcoats, their outfits looking worn and even shabby, even though the men looked uncomfortable in them. Gold hoops glittered in their ears and curious objects hung from their belts. They wore black boots which quickly became beige with the light dust kicked up by their footsteps. They divided a small pile of objects between their packs and set off. Each had a bandanna tied around his neck and all three adjusted their hats to shield against the bright sun overhead. The man in the lead looked down at the display mounted on the side of the metal cylinder held in a harness that enclosed his left forearm. He swept the device slowly in a circle and turned towards the South. The other two followed behind. One of them lifted the bandanna from his neck, tying it over his face against the dust kicked up by the man in front. His companion glanced over, then did the same.

A loud whump *from behind stopped them in their tracks. A curious sucking noise sounded, loud and unnatural in the desert air.*

"Run," shouted their leader, and did as he'd said without waiting for his companions. The three stumbled as they ran, away from the unearthly sounds behind them. Struggling back to their feet and heading away from their craft, they pushed through a small line of trees and a new sound echoed across the dry land. Something between a snarl and a scream, it came from a light brown shape that dashed out of the trees and landed on the back of one of the men, pulling him down. The man screamed as he fell, another sound that should never have come from a natural

source. Then suddenly all noises stopped. The two remaining men ran on until they reached the dubious cover of a scattering of rocks. They stopped, panting in the dry air, sweat running down their faces.

"What was that?"

"A lion," replied Farran, between gasped breaths. "A bloody lion!"

"Can't be, not in America," said his companion, leaning forwards, hands on his knees.

"A puma, then. Or an escaped pet. You want to go back and ask it?" Farran was staring back the way they'd come, but nothing appeared out of the heat haze.

"D'ya think it killed Leigh?"

"He stopped screaming. They've hardly made friends," hissed Farran as he adjusted the cylinder fixed to his left arm. Its glass was broken and pressing on the metal needle in the centre of its dial. The pirate hooked a dirty thumbnail under the broken glass, lifting it away and dropping it to the floor. He turned slowly, tapped the edge of the dial and scowling. The needle juddered as it turned, sticking and moving until it settled back towards the South. He started walking. The other man grabbed his arm.

"We should go back to Leigh," he said, pointing back the way they'd just run.

"He's dead. We can't help him," said Farran.

"Yeah - but his wafers..."

"You want to fight the lion for 'em?"

Both men fell silent and Farran led the way across the open ground.

"But we could get 'em on the way back. To the craft," said Donne, looking scared.

Farran snorted. "The craft? Didn't you hear it? They'd set it to self-destruct."

"What?"

"We're stranded. Abandoned. No way back to the Stronghold!"

"So we'll need his wafers..."

"You don't get it, do you?" Farran rounded on his companion, red with anger. "We won't be allowed back, not if we fail. Old Snake-head doesn't want people who let him down in his army!"

"So we're dead. Without his drug..."

"You believe their crap? That you die if you stop taking it? That's just to keep us in line."

"So why are you going on? We could find a human town, people we could use. Make our way back to Africa..."

"Because," Farran's face was scarlet, the veins in his neck pulsing visibly. "She is the reason we can't go back and that Leigh is dead. Now it's personal."

"Not for me. I say we get Leigh's wafers and..."

The shorter man stopped talking as Farran's hand closed around the hilt of his knife. They glared at each other for a moment, then Farran turned away and started walking, certain he would be followed.

Chapter 41

In which Sam and Chrystal are parted

We didn't see it coming. One moment we were cantering along past a group of trees, Steely sniffing at Cinnamon's tail and Chrystal sitting tall in her saddle. The next moment, a stone-weighted net flew out of the trees over the pinto and her rider. Cinnamon screamed and Steely spooked. He pulled to the right, getting hold of the bit so I couldn't rein him in. For a moment he pranced and I thought he was going to throw me. Then he dipped his chin, spun around and hared off, away from the trees and the men running towards us. I didn't even think, just clung to his neck for dear life and we fled.

Leaving Chrystal and Cinnamon in the hands of whoever threw that net.

For several minutes, my world was just a sweaty horse neck, pounding hooves and the dry smells of wild lands around me. I had no idea which way we were going and cared even less. Steely was terrified and I wasn't any better. Eventually he slowed to a trot, then a walk and finally stood, his head bowed and I could feel him trembling under me. I slipped off his back and grabbed hold of the saddle for support as I realised my legs were shaking as much as his. We stood like that, both breathing heavily, until the shock wore off. I straightened up and began to check my horse for damage. By some miracle he was unharmed. As was I. Looking around, I spotted greenery thirty yards away and started to walk, tugging his reins until he lifted his head. For a long minute, he stared at me, then harrumphed and moved one leg forward. Then another. And we walked to where a small pool lay under the sparse bushes. I tipped the contents of my water bottle over myself, then re-filled it and finally let Steely walk into the shallow water. He lowered his muzzle to drink, before beginning to kick the water up at himself. I joined in, splashing him to cool his sweating flanks. Once we were both satisfied, I sat against a straggly bush to think.

Chrystal hadn't followed me away from the ambush. I had to assume she'd been taken captive. Or worse. But I wasn't going to think about that.

I should be making my way back, finding out what was happening and making a plan to free her.

But then, why should I? She'd brought me along on this trip as entertainment. I wasn't important to her - just some company on the trail and a plaything when it suited her. She was more concerned about her gadgets than me. If she'd been the one to escape, she wouldn't have hesitated - just left me to my fate while she went after her bloody calendar. Why was she obsessed with finding it? A lump of stone, carved with indecipherable symbols by a people who'd died out thousands of years ago. If it even existed!

And there was a legend about it. So what? Anyone could make up a story. If enough people heard it, believed it and told it to others, it became a legend. That didn't make it true. It was all just mumbo-jumbo.

Like the æther.

Like a heart made of a gemstone.

I shook my head. This wasn't getting me anywhere. I should get back to civilisation, find my way home by some means - *did cruise ships recruit staff for a single voyage?* That would be a cheap way to travel. And I knew something about the way those ships worked now.

I had a plan. All I had to do was find a town, where I could sell Steely and make my way home. To a place where I knew the rules and wasn't surrounded by strange gadgets and weird people who seemed to think modern science was getting it wrong.

Weird people like Chrystal.

I whistled to Steely as I stood up. He came willingly, ready to go, as if he'd already forgotten his scare. I decided to start out walking with him, just to be sure he'd got over that mad dash. I checked my saddle bags were fastened securely, filled my bottle again where the water looked cleanest and turned a slow circle.

Our hoofprints were clean on the dusty ground, so we followed them back to the point where Steely'd stopped. I could see our trail leading back, away from the sun. So that must be northwest. The only civilisation I knew of was back south and east, so all I had to do was keep walking in that direction. Sooner or later we'd hit a road or see a town. But I hesitated. *Was I sure I wanted to do this?* Desert Chrystal when she might be wounded - or worse? Resolutely, I tugged on Steely's reins and began to walk south.

After a few yards, a picture came into my mind. Chrystal, unconscious on the ground, bleeding from some dreadful wound and too weak to stand.

Bleeding.

Blood!

Suddenly I remembered it had been days since she'd asked me to give her blood for the Chrystal. I was so used to providing what she needed, I no longer paid it any great attention. But I realised she hadn't asked since the night before we left the last motel. She must have been feeling the need for it by now - and I'd been so terse this morning, maybe she didn't want to mention it.

I quickly mounted Steely, my lips tight. I turned his head back northwest and flicked the reins to get him moving.

Steely was the first to notice anything. His ears went up and he started pulling to the left. I resisted, tugging him back onto the right track. But he insisted and I let him have his head.

Perhaps he'd smelt water and we could both get a drink. He walked towards a small copse, but instead pushing through in search of a stream, he stood and whinnied. The trees rustled and parted. I held my breath, half-ready for Steely to turn about and flee again, but he stepped forward, blowing soft noises through his nose. To greet Cinnamon. The pinto stepped out of the sheltering trees, looking dusty and shaken. She was favouring her off front hoof and I slipped off Steely's back to investigate.

Fortunately, it was only a stone, quickly removed with my knife. The two horses were nuzzling and whiffling at each other like a pair of lovelorn teenagers, so I gave Cinnamon a quick once-over. She was fine, apart from the dust and I moved on to check her saddle. It looked intact - except the straps that had held the ætheric sender had been cut. Cleanly. Someone had used a very sharp knife. And that someone had Chrystal!

I pulled on Steely's reins to get his attention and remounted. Leading Cinnamon, we started off along our back trail. My heart was pounding as I tried not to picture all the possible disasters involving Chrystal. She could be lying unconscious, wounded, bleeding, dying of thirst...

When I closed my eyes, I could see the cut straps on the mare's saddle. I tried not to picture the damage a knife that sharp could do to a human body. And failed. The pictures grew more intense as we trotted back along the trail of hoofprints on the dusty ground.

My whole body hurt, as if all the aches I'd been earning for days now hit me all together. I slumped in the saddle, too tired to sit up. I was sore all over, the sun on my back was too hot and I took a T-shirt from my saddle bag to rig a mask against the dust from the horses' hooves. Everything was harder than when the two of us were together. Cinnamon would stop to crop grass whenever she had chance and Steely kept swinging his head to check on his mate.

Lulled by the monotonous soft clop of hooves and the heat, I sank into a sort of trance, just tugging on Cinnamon's rein when she stalled. I don't even know how long it was before I noticed the birds. They must have been there for a while, but I didn't realise it until we were walking past. A dozen or more scruffy bundles of black feathers, cawing noisily to the side of the trail.

I jerked upright, ignored Steely's protest and pulled his head to the side. We left the trail, climbing the bank on one side. From the top, I could see something in the dip beyond and was dropping from the saddle before I could think.

Chrystal lay on the ground. Hank's Stetson covered her head as she huddled in the sparse cover of the bank. I wasn't even sure if she was breathing. I rolled her onto her back, seeing caked dust on her closed eyes. I held her head while I trickled water from my bottle into her cracked lips. The water ran out again, soaking my leg and pooling on the ground. Frantically, I checked for her pulse and then noticed the Chrystal.

It was pale, washed-out green, like anaemic new leaves. I'd never seen it so insipid.

Reaching for my knife, I cut a clumsy wound in my thumb, dropping the knife as I tried to aim the flow at the corner below the gemstone. I'd fed it before, but always neatly, with a syringe of blood that could deliver in exactly the right place. I fumbled in my panic and hot blood splashed from my thumb, staining my clothes as well as hers. I checked her face where she lay in the crook of my right arm. Still no response. I checked for her pulse again - still nothing.

After what felt like hours, I lowered her to the ground. I took the T-shirt from my face, wrapped it around my still-oozing thumb, and went to find the horses, unsure what else to do. My brain and hands went through the checks automatically - girth tight, water bottle on its hook, saddlebags secured. The birds still flew around, cawing but keeping their distance. I didn't know what they'd do with Chrystal's body. *There! I'd managed to think the word!* And hesitated. Common sense said I needed to find help, to get her - *body* - onto Cinnamon's back. Loyalty told me I should try to find the cave she'd been so desperate to reach. I wavered, wishing the birds would shut up, with their constant cawing.

Especially the one that was croaking my name.

I spun round, unbelieving. But Chrystal's lips were moving. Her eyes, so pale I could barely see their colour.

"Sam?" barely intelligible, hardly even audible. I grabbed my water bottle off Steely's saddle.

Chapter 42

In which a cave is sought

Chrystal recovered quickly, the gem in her chest back to its normal dark, dark green once we'd cleaned off the rest of my blood. Her eyes were soon almost black again, too. She had a few knocks and bruises where she'd been pulled from Cinnamon's back, but nothing more serious. If she hadn't needed blood for her Chrystal, she would have been fine. If I hadn't deserted her just when she needed me. But then, if I'd been taken captive, perhaps things would have been more serious. Or maybe...

"They took the map," she interrupted my train of thought.

"Oh. So we're lost?"

"Perhaps not. I believe I can remember enough to locate the correct mesa, although we would still need to find the cave."

"Are you sure?"

She shook her head. "No, not certain. It is possible that the horses may be sensitive to the stone's whereabouts, but I would prefer not to rely on that and we cannot rely on any information from The Professor reaching us, either."

I remembered the cut straps where the ætheric sender had been taken from Cinnamon's saddle and suppressed a shiver.

"Sam? You are hurt?"

I realised she'd misinterpreted my tremble. I shook my head.

"No, I'm fine. Can you ride?"

In response, she clicked to Cinnamon, mounted the mare and smiled down at me, pale but determined.

"Well, shall we go?" she asked.

The horses had rested while I tended Chrystal and they

seemed eager to move on. We must have been a sorry sight, two dusty horses, their riders' clothes torn and splattered with blood. But I think we were all keen to get to our destination, to see this thing through to the end.

Chrystal navigated with less trouble than we'd expected, turning to follow a ravine that cut across the line we were following. I hoped she really did remember the route, as I could hardly tell one spot from another. Cinnamon and Steely were content to walk side-by-side, whiffling to each other and I took advantage of the chance to quiz Chrystal.

"Isn't it time you told me exactly what we're doing?" I began.

She looked at me.

"You were going to tell me more about this legend. And I think now would be a very good time, don't you?"

Chrystal took a deep breath.

"The legend is very old, I do not know how old. But the Earth is said to run on cycles of almost four hundred years. To be precise, it is three hundred and ninety-four years, plus a few months. When a cycle ends, there are actions necessary to ensure that the new cycle begins correctly. The current cycle is ending and we need to locate the appropriate place for us to begin the new one."

"And how do you know about this?"

"I believe it is fairly well known amongst scholars in certain fields of study. There has been talk even in the modern society of scientists that the Meso-American calendar is about to end."

I grunted in agreement. I had indeed heard something about this - I think there was even a film about the world ending in 2012.

"And these scholars have told you where to find the calendar?" I asked.

"They told me where to find the map, and I have been studying the Olmec languages, as much of it as is written. But there is no map in the modern sense, as you know. The last cycle ended in 1618, and written records from that time are very sparse."

I was nodding along with her explanation. I still wasn't sure I believed all this, but Chrystal obviously did and I wasn't about to argue.

"And what do you have to do to start the next cycle? You said something about a sacrifice..."

"The legend is both clear and obscure. There must be a blood sacrifice, made by *the one with no heart and the greatest heart,* but it does not give more details about the way this must be achieved."

I pulled back on Steely's reins and he stopped, but turned to look at me quizzically.

"Does it mean you have to die? Is that what this is about?" I gasped.

"I do not know. That is one reading of the legend, but there are other viable interpretations," she said.

"You're going to risk your own life? For a fairy story?"

"It is a legend, Sam. That means there is an element of truth in it. But I do not know what that truth may be. Only that the scholars believe it must be taken seriously."

"Do you want to die?"

She sighed.

"No, I do not wish to die. Even after all these years, life is still sweet. But if it is necessary, then I can hardly complain that I have not had more than my share of days on the Earth," she said slowly.

"But - how will you know? Has this happened before? What about the last time - when was it?" I asked, all in a rush.

"The last time was in 1618 and the Tibetan who first advised me of the need for me to act told me that the

Meso-Americans made a particularly poor attempt at making the sacrifice then - and the time before that."

"Poor attempt?" I could hardly believe she was being so calm about the whole thing.

"Yes. They thought the one with the *Great Heart* must be their ruler or a priest. Those men slew hundreds of people, hoping their sacrifice would suffice."

"And what makes you think you can do it where they couldn't?"

"We believe that if the right person makes the sacrifice, it will not be necessary to shed so much blood."

"Good job - since there's only two of us. So why didn't we bring more people?"

"I had hoped to pass unnoticed, in case there are more people like Farran determined to prevent our reaching the cave. But now I am wondering if I should have requested the Tibetans to travel with us. Or maybe The Professor."

I didn't answer. I would have been happier to have a platoon of soldiers with us, but it was too late for regrets.

"So how did they find you?" I asked and suddenly realised something. "Was this why they gave you the Chrystal in the first place?"

"I do not believe so," she twitched Cinnamon's rein to guide her round a treacherous-looking patch of ground. "I believe they gave me the Chrystal Vitalis to save my life. This was several generations ago and the men who acted that day could not have foreseen a need more than 150 years in their future."

"So they just gave you the stone and then had to come looking for you to save them?"

"Not to save them. Or at least, not just the Tibetans. The legend speaks of terrible disasters afflicting the whole Earth if the cycle of order does not begin again."

"Mumbo-jumbo!"

She didn't answer, just faced forward, watching the trail ahead of Cinnamon's hooves.

"I mean, who's meant to be behind this? Who says you have to die to stop the world from exploding? Or whatever?"

"There are forces greater than ours, Sam. We do not have to know their names to believe in their actions," she said.

"What - like stories about gods?"

"Call it what you will - it is a manifestation of the Laws of Nature. Would you argue the existence of the force of gravity, for example?"

"Well, no. But..." I stopped. *Could* I prove that gravity existed and that this calendar legend was untrue?

Chrystal reached the top of a hill we'd been climbing and reined Cinnamon to a halt. I turned to ask her why and then saw the mesa standing in front of us. Both horses pricked up their ears and seemed eager to move on.

"Is that it?" I breathed.

She nodded. "I can feel the calendar - it sings to my Chrystal. It is like the blood-link but not the same."

The mesa wasn't as high as some we'd passed, but had the same solid, timeless look. There was a track down the hill which led to one side and Chrystal guided Cinnamon that way. Steely and I followed behind.

We found a cave very quickly, but it only went a few feet into the rock, with no sign of a tunnel to take us deeper. Back outside, we remounted the horses and walked slowly around the whole mesa. There was nothing else even remotely like a cave entrance and we soon arrived back at our start point.

"We must have missed something," I said.

"I cannot see how," replied Chrystal. She turned Cinnamon in a tight circle, staring out over the wild lands. I clucked to Steely and began walking him around the rocky outcrop again. When I got back to the cave, Cinnamon was cropping the sparse grass. Her rider was nowhere to be seen. It was my turn to look all around, even at the rock face rising sheer above me. No sign. I slipped off Steely's back and, swallowing hard, stooped to enter the cave again.

Little sunlight penetrated the cave, but enough to show it was empty. There wasn't anything to hide behind and the cave wasn't big enough for me to lie straight, even at its widest point.

"Chrystal?" My shout bounced off the rock walls, but there was no answer.

"Chrystal!" I called again, beginning to panic. She couldn't have just vanished.

My eyes had begun to adjust, and I took a slow walk around the little cave, pressing on the walls and reaching my fingers into every crevice to see if it opened out.

A sound behind me made me jump and I spun round to see Chrystal landing close to the far wall. She straightened up and smiled at me.

"We are going to need our lights and the rope from your pack," she said.

"But - where were you?" I asked. "Why didn't you answer me?"

"I was examining some carvings. I believe I may have found the calendar stone," she said, ducking out through the door. "But I will need the lantern to make certain of my identification." I started to follow and then stopped, deciding it made more sense to stay inside, rather than dazzle myself in the sun. Chrystal came back almost immediately and passed me a clockwork torch. She had the coil of rope slung over one shoulder and she walked up to the wall she'd dropped down only a moment before. She braced one booted foot against the wall and reached up. I couldn't see what she used as handholds, but she pulled herself up and scrambled through an opening I couldn't see.

As she disappeared, I began to wind my torch, throwing all my fear at this small space into the work of cranking its little handle. I was still winding when the rope slid down the wall, looking like a snake in a tree. I didn't wait for instructions, but pushed my torch into my shirt, grabbed the rope with both hands and began to climb. I rose quickly and was soon scrambling up a shelf to where Chrystal stood, drawing the rope towards her, the lantern at her feet shining on the walls. She dropped the rope back through the hole, where it hung from the knot she'd tied around a massive boulder.

"Wow!" I was so surprised to see this extra cave that I forgot to be afraid of the restricted space. The rocks had been painted with pictures of animals and human figures, like the cave paintings I'd seen on telly.

"Indeed," said Chrystal. "But we need to move on. The stone is this way."

She ducked down to crawl though a low break in one wall and I steeled myself to follow.

As I straightened, the first thing I saw was a patch of light cast by the light in Chrystal's hand on the massive carved stone. I played my torch over it, too. It was more than three metres across, half a metre thick, perfectly circular and carved with more of those strange symbols. My hand followed the torch beam, almost involuntarily drawn to the work of that ancient artist. I poked my finger into one of the carved figures but couldn't reach the back of it. The calendar rested at an angle, propped against a wall over a hole that stretched deeper than my torch could reach. I swallowed hard and focused on the carved stone.

"It's beautiful," I whispered. The room felt like a church, some sort of sacred space I would contaminate if I spoke aloud. And I was afraid to hear my words echo back from the blackness beneath the rock.

Chrystal didn't reply. She was poring over the carvings, touching them lightly as she shone her lantern across the stone's face. I was so fascinated by her rapt concentration that I didn't hear anything until a sarcastic voice behind me said,

"Move away from the stone, Ladies."

Chapter 43

In which a pirate approaches

The two pirates crouched in the shadow of a boulder, the dark one looking through a pair of very modern-looking field glasses. In front of them a trail of hoofprints led towards a mesa standing in the centre of a wide hollow. The two slid backwards until they were out of sight, then Farran gestured to Donne and they crept around the shallow basin. After a few hundred yards, Farran checked over the ridge again, beckoned and led the way down the low hillside under the sparse tree cover.

As they reached the last tree, Farran bent gestured to his companion.

"Stay here. I can manage two women on my own," he said. He handed his field glasses to Donne, checked his weapon was secured on his back and sprinted across the open space, making for the two horses standing near the foot of the mesa. The grey stallion spooked at his approach and took very little persuading to run away from the outcrop, the pinto mare following. Farran unslung the weapon from his back and edged into the little cave he could see at the foot of the mesa. His blond companion stayed where he was, watching but keeping his distance.

Once inside, Farran paused while his eyes adapted, hearing the women's voices and seeing their torchlight seeping through a hole in the cave's roof. They'd even left a rope hanging there for him. Cautiously, he tested his weight on it and began to climb hand over calloused hand.

Chapter 44

In which a pirate confronts Chrystal and Sam

I turned to see Farran pointing an odd-looking gun at us. I'd never seen anything like it and had no idea how it worked, but it left me in no doubt that I was at the wrong end of a weapon. The torchlight glinted dully off a long barrel with a metal tube coiled around it. The end that rested against the pirate's upper arm was bulbous and looked like part of an animal. Farran gestured with it and I moved to the side, away from Chrystal where she stood by the stone.

"You too," he barked at her. She turned to face him, but kept one hand on the stone.

"Move!"

She smiled slowly. "An ætheric disruptor cannon, Farran? How very destructive. But we all know you cannot use it on both of us at the same time." She took a wide step to her right, forcing the pirate to swing his weapon to cover both of us.

"Stand still," he snapped, stepping backwards to keep us both in sight.

Chrystal took another step to the side. "Move? Stand still? Which is it, Farran?"

Realising I could help Chrystal, I took a step away from her. Farran swung his weapon slightly my way, then back onto Chrystal. Would I get close enough to attack him? Could I get his weapon away before he shot her? I took another step.

"Stop there, ginger girl," said Farran, sounding more in control. "You come round in front where I can see ya or I shoot your friend."

I paused. He'd hit on the flaw in Chrystal's plan - he didn't need to cover us both, just to threaten one of us and hope that would keep us both in check.

Unfortunately, he was right.

But Chrystal wasn't so easily out-manoeuvred.

"If you kill me here, by the calendar, you fulfil the prophecy, pirate. Is that what your master sent you to do?"

Her taunt struck home and he swung his weapon back to point at me, cruel smile on his face. I edged a little further away, almost reaching the hole through which we'd all entered.

"Are you so sure of your shot, Farran?" Chrystal asked softly. "If you strike the cave walls, you could bring this whole complex down. And you do not strike me as the type to martyr himself."

She had edged a little closer - one more step and she'd be able to reach the pirate. If I could just distract him for her.

Before I could think about what I was doing, I launched myself across the cave, grabbing for the weapon pointing at my chest. In slow-motion I watched the pirate duck away, the barrel of his gun swinging down to meet my head as we collided.

And everything went black.

Farran swung the barrel to meet the redhead as she ran at him, her hands curled like a she-tiger's claws. He grinned at the satisfying shudder of tempered brass meeting weak flesh but had no time to savour the familiar feeling. The other woman was on his back, pulling at his bandanna, trying to throttle him. He dropped the now-useless weapon and grabbed at the fabric, tearing it out of her grip.

He broke away from her, scrabbling for the torch where one of the women had dropped it and drawing a wickedly curved knife at the same time. He spun to meet his adversary as she tried to engage him again. He swung wildly, felt the knife blade bite into flesh and stepped back, breathing hard. Blood dripped from the serrated edge as he pointed the torch at her and scooped up his brass cannon.

She was half-crouched, tying his bandanna around her left thigh and pulling it tight. Then she straightened up, favouring the bleeding leg as she stepped towards him.

"So what are you going to do, Farran?" she asked hoarsely. "Kill me and restore the balance or risk firing into the walls and crushing yourself under tons of ancient rock?"

The pirate threw his gun, narrowly missing her head as he dived low, striking her injured leg with his shoulder. She yelped but did not fall, stepping away from the pirate and nearer the calendar stone. He lurched to his feet, knife in hand and ran towards her. She fended off his assault with her right arm, metal clanged on metal and Farran fell against the calendar. For a brief second he teetered over the hole in the ground, blood dripping from his knife onto the ancient calendar.

The stone seemed to turn itself, leaving him unsupported as it fell into the chasm, the pirate's cries echoing back as he followed it down.

The earth held its breath, the cries stopped suddenly and a shudder shook the cave.

Chapter 45

In which Sam and Chrystal rely on each other

I felt a hand roughly shaking my shoulder, but ignored it. There was pain as well and I didn't want to wake up and face that. I kept my eyes closed, hoping whoever it was would go away.

"Samantha!" Chrystal's voice. "You need to wake up. I cannot carry you out of the cave system."

I opened my eyes reluctantly. I'd been right about the pain - I felt bruised all over. Then I remembered we were still in the cave and my dark-adapted sight tried to focus on the rocky walls above me.

"Can you stand?" she asked, more solicitous this time.

"I, I think so," I replied. "But I'm kind of shaky - the walls look like they're moving."

She laughed without humour. "They are moving. This whole cave complex is falling down, Sam. We must get out of here!"

With that, she pulled me to my feet and supported me while she tied her rope about my waist. She handed me the torch and helped me to the hole we'd climbed up through.

"I will lower you to the entrance cave," she said. "You must fend yourself off the walls and then retreat from the cave. I fear it is about to collapse."

I wasn't going to argue. I'd never liked caves and one that was trying to collapse around me was more than I could cope with! I did my best to help as she let my still-groggy body down into the lower, smaller, cavern where I landed on my hands and knees. The rope followed me down and I crawled out dragging it behind me. After a few yards, I heard Chrystal drop to the ground. She pulled me half-upright, tugged my arm over her shoulders and ran with me. I could hear rocks grinding over each other, crashing and shattering behind us and filling the air with sharp dust. The ground started to slope upwards and Chrystal lowered me into a sitting position, my back to a tree. So I had a grandstand view of the collapsing mesa.

Chrystal walked off and came back carrying one saddlebag and a single cooking pot.

"It appears that our campsite had been raided," she said by way of explanation. "I gathered up everything that remained. Fortunately it includes the medical supplies pouch."

When the dust finally settled, I could see that a quarter of the outcrop had been smashed as if by a giant hammer. A huge dent cracked it, loose boulders and jagged rocks lay all around and there was no sign of the cave. The whole area looked like a bomb had gone off, leaving shrapnel and destruction. Trees had been knocked over by flying rocks and there wasn't a living thing in sight.

Except one figure.

I squinted against the sun, then raised my hand to shade my eyes. There was definitely someone moving at the other end of the dusty bowl.

"Chrystal?" She'd been sorting through the items from our little first aid kit.

"Yes?"

"There's someone over there," I said, pointing.

I could see him more clearly now. A small figure in a black coat, brown trousers and a red hat or something. With the glint of metal in his hand. He was half-running, half-staggering away from the mesa, heading in the opposite direction from us.

"I see him," said my companion. "One of Farran's men, I expect. He will be no danger to us now."

"Are you sure?"

"The prophecy is fulfilled. The calendar has turned and the new cycle is beginning," she said.

"But - you're still alive!"

"You sound almost disappointed, Sam-of-the-boy's-name. Would you rather I had died in that cavern?"

"That wasn't what I meant! I thought your prophecy said it needed your blood and you had to die..." I couldn't go on.

"It may be that Farran's death sufficed. He had my blood on himself when he fell, so mayhap that satisfied the calendar's requirements."

"I still don't understand how this prophecy thing works," I complained. But she sat down, her left leg sprawled out in front of her and I noticed the blood soaking her jeans.

"You're injured!"

"The wound is bloody, but not life-threatening, I believe," she said. "If you will assist me...?"

I helped dress the injury as best we could. She stood on it and seemed satisfied.

"That will have to suffice while we walk out of here," she said. "But in the meantime - I have a gift for you, Sam."

"A what?" I don't think I could have been more surprised if she'd sprouted wings and offered to carry me home.

She bent to pick up something lying in the undergrowth. It was Farran's gun and she held it out by its strap.

"I believe you were beginning your own collection of weapons that have failed to kill you," she said with a smile. I accepted it and looked more closely at the weapon than I'd been able to when it was being used to threaten me. My initial impressions were confirmed, although I still couldn't see how it worked. I looked quizzically at Chrystal, who seemed to understand my unspoken question.

"I have locked it against accidental usage," she said. "I will instruct you in its use when we have the leisure to do so."

I slung the gun onto my back, where it bumped comfortably against my backside. What had Chrystal called it when Farran had threatened us with it? An *ætheric disrupter,* or something like that. Chrystal gathered up what little we had and draped the saddlebag over her shoulder.

"Now. Which way to the nearest road?" she asked. "If we are fortunate, we may encounter our horses before too long."

She took my hand to help me up the rest of the slope and we kept our fingers meshed as we walked away, our backs to the lowering sun.

Chapter 46

In which a wave passes and further sacrifices are made

The screen display in the wooden bureau was undivided, showing a single large picture - an aerial view of Mid-America, its outline yellow against the cold grey-blue of ocean. Five figures gathered around it, Geb, Sobek, a pirate whose waistcoat strained at its buttons and two soldiers.

The pirate reached for a switch and flicked it.

The pre-recorded display looked unchanged for a few seconds, then the picture wavered, as if seen through a pond with a pebble thrown in. A disturbance began in the centre of the screen and spread outwards, in a series of growing circles. They spread to the edges of the display and off-screen, passing through land and ocean as if they were the same.

"And that was when?" hissed the snake-headed figure, standing where he had the best view of the screen.

"Less than ten minutes ago, Your Eminence. The wave has not reached us yet," said the fat pirate.

As he spoke, a strange disruption passed along the hall, as if the rock flexed and then relaxed again. The screen flashed a pattern of green interlocking lines and went dark.

Geb pushed his hood back onto his shoulders.

"Then she has succeeded," he said. "The calendar has turned and the new cycle begins."

No-one answered him. One of the soldiers eyed the nearest door and the very human electric light that shone through it. His companion kept his eyes on the floor.

"How has she done this?" hissed Geb.

No-one answered him.

A strident burrrr *sounded on the wooden bureau. The pirate looked to his master for permission and then lifted a headset. He listened for a moment, and said,*

"It's Donne. He says the cave has collapsed. He says Farran died when it happened. He's the only one left."

"And the women?"

Relaying over the communicator, he replied,

"They, too, are dead. No-one could have escaped when the mesa collapsed."

"And so the prophecy is fulfilled."

"Yes, Your Eminence."

A small voice sounded from the headset in the lackey's hand.

"He asks how he should return, Your Eminence. He says their craft is destroyed and Farran had their weapon with him when he entered the cave. Shall we send another pod to collect him?"

The tall man straightened and shook his snake-head.

"We will not waste another soldier to fetch him. Tell him to make his own way back here. If he dares." As Geb spoke, an odd musical sound rose behind his voice. A hiss that rose and fell just at the edge of hearing.

The pirate with the communicator nodded and relayed the message, switching off the headset whilst the man at the far end shouted his fear and terror.

"They took only a few wafers with them, Sire," said the taller soldier. "Without ætheric transportation, he will not be able to return in time for his next dose."

The snake-man stood to his full height and dropped his cloak. The musical hiss grew louder and he began to sway. Sobek's crocodile jaw fell open and he backed away, edging around the wooden bureau but keeping his eyes on Geb.

The three humans stood, swaying in time with the snake-man, their terrified eyes on his reptilian face as the huge fangs dropped into place. The first soldier fell quickly, without a cry as the massive dose of venom swelled his body and closed his throat.

Geb turned to the fat pirate, holding his arms and biting his neck almost tenderly. The man screamed and writhed on the floor, buttons flying from his waistcoat as his fast-swelling body began to turn black.

The final man broke free of the trance, turning towards the door as Geb's fangs sank into his shoulder. He fell to the floor and began to crawl away then fell onto his back, clutching at his crotch as the poison took hold. His mouth opened with a high-pitched keen that echoed around the room.

"Sobek," said Geb, standing over the stricken soldier.

"Your Eminence?" The crocodile-man stayed behind the wooden bureau as he spoke.

"Silence him, Sobek. And tell the kitchens there is blood for their wafers."

Appendices

In the course of this book, Chrystal has been using technologies that may be unfamiliar to many readers and these appendices are intended to clarify some of these issues and discuss other matters arising from the novel, together with suggested search terms to explore some of the ideas further on the Internet.

The Æther.

Many Victorians believed in the existence of something called The Æther, which is basically as Chrystal describes it on page 55 – a substance which underlies all matter in the universe and is present even in a perfect vacuum. Its properties vary according to the source consulted, not least because no-one ever proved its existence. One explanation was based around the fact that sound needs matter to travel through (in space, no-one can hear you ring an alarm clock), so there must be some form of matter which similarly carries light. For many years its existence was a subject of debate, and many people claimed that it was finally disproven by Albert Einstein's work in the early 20th Century. Except he didn't actually disprove its existence, merely came up with a mathematical way of describing reality that doesn't *need* the concept of æther to work.

Modern subatomic research, including work at the Large Hadron Collider in mainland Europe, is currently facing something it cannot explain. As most readers will know, atoms are made up of a dense nucleus, composed of neutrons and protons, with electrons orbiting around it. The next step was the discovery of elemental particles that make up the neutrons, protons and electrons. These are called Quarks, Hadrons, Leptons, etc. and they are known as the Standard Model (including the last-to-be-discovered Higg's Boson). But so-called solid matter is still largely empty space between these incredibly tiny particles. Research over the last sixty years has shown that this supposedly empty space is "lumpy" or "grainy". It is described as having a texture like a mass of bubbles so is usually called Quantum Foam, and research is being conducted into its precise nature. Now, correct me if I'm wrong, but isn't that yet another level of matter, underlying all the matter in the universe? Doesn't that sound a lot like the Victorian description of Æther? What a beautiful thought. Æther theories have also been proposed as explanations for so-called Dark Energy. These are exciting times for physicists and the deeper they look into the fundamental laws of the universe, the more it looks as if there may be an æther waiting to be discovered.

Now, as Chrystal herself explains on page 49, using disturbances in the æther as a power source is by definition limited, as it's utilising wasted energy from other forms of generation. But it would be nice to collect this and make use of it.

Suggested search terms: "luminiferous æther" "quantum foam"

Chrystal's glass-moving wand.

The concept of quantum foam forms the basis of wormhole theory – that matter could be passed through this foam as a short-cut to another point in the universe. Or maybe somewhere else entirely. Modern Science has failed to work out a way to make use of this theory – but passing through the foam is obviously going to be rather uncomfortable for a living creature. It is likely to be pretty difficult for solid objects, too, as you'd need to re-arrange it at the other end. Perhaps with a kind of 3D-printer.

But we could pass matter through a wormhole if it was pliable and we don't care what shape it comes out in. A liquid would be a good place to start.

Many people think of glass as a solid, but some theorists claim it remains liquid throughout its life – it's just a very slow-moving one (sometimes called an amorphous solid). This is implied by close inspection of large sheets of glass which have been fixed in window frames for hundreds of years. The glass is noticeably thicker at the bottom than it is at the top – just as treacle oozes slowly downwards, the glass has flowed over the years into this un-even form.

So we may be able to pass a liquid through a wormhole and glass is just a very slow-moving liquid. All that Chrystal's wand needs to do is to speed it up and suck it into a wormhole back to the "birdcage" in her workshop. Simples!

Note: There is some debate as to whether this is due to glass flowing or to unevenness caused by the manufacturing process. I am no expert in these matters and this is not a textbook - it's a work of fiction. Chrystal chooses to make use of the more esoteric interpretation and damn that modern science!

Suggested search terms: æther, wormhole (try it in an online encyclopaedia), "Behaviour of antique glass"

The Character of Chrystal

Chrystal is a fascinating character to write about. I fell in love with idea of someone from the Victorian era surviving to the present day and spent a lot of time thinking about the changing moral code over the intervening decades. What would a person who'd lived all those years be like? Would they retain the societal mores of their upbringing? Would they adopt modern thinking about relationships?

Or would they have their own set of morals, based partly on the relative ephemerality (is that even a word?) of any prospective partners? I think Chrystal has a bit of all of these characteristics.

She is very much a Victorian woman. To her, good manners are not second nature - they are her first nature. Her place in society is something she takes for granted too, and people in the 21st Century respond to this. Ever thought someone was "trying too hard"? Chrystal is the opposite - she doesn't "try", she just *is.* At the same time, she gives off clear signals of what she expects from others, which people seem to find simultaneously reassuring and a little weird. As her chronicler, I've found that she is good company, doesn't presume on a relationship which is essentially business and that her word can be trusted completely.

Quite refreshing, really.

Chrystal has kept many characteristics and interests from her early years. In common with many Victorians, she is fascinated by fossils and has a deep fascination with / mistrust of the culture of Ancient Egypt. Maybe there are reasons for that which have been lost in the intervening decades.

There is evidence of lesbianism and female bisexuality in the 19th Century, including some references to the appropriately-named *female marriages,* although these would not have been a marriage in any legal sense. In many ways,

Victorian Society was more forgiving of individual preferences than we are in the 21st Century. Our modern view that they were very straight-laced is more accurately a reflection of the early 20th Century than it is of Victoria's reign. I side with the view that there have always been "ladies who prefer ladies" and all other possible variations on that theme. Born in 1824, Philomena was 27 years old at the time of her attack and miraculous rescue. An unmarried woman of that age may have been unusual, but there are records from those years which mention unmarried women in that age group. Maybe she was an unusually modern thinker from the outset and made a conscious choice not to marry, preferring her own company and that of short-term relationships to marriage.

In the twenty-first century, Chrystal has shown herself eager to have relationships with both men and women, although her memoirs are quite discrete about the details. As her chronicler, I get the impression that she's basically bored. In all those years, she's really "been there, done that, got the corset" - and who can blame her for trying new things when she gets the chance?

So, why did the Tibetan delegation intervene to save her? Maybe they recognised something of the iron determination in this "cat who walks by herself" who was able to make a most unladylike attempt at self-defence. Whatever the reasons, Chrystal is remarkable in many ways and this is obviously one of the reasons she has survived and remained undetected by the wider population. Take a long look at any Steampunks you meet, especially those with quirky speech patterns. Maybe it isn't just an affectation – maybe this is the way they learned to speak as a child a long, long time ago.

Naturally, Chrystal has changed somewhat over the years, adapting so as to keep herself as inconspicuous as possible in an evolving society. But her unique viewpoint has allowed her to select which changes she wishes to embrace and which ones she prefers to ignore.

I'm not about to recommend any Internet search terms on these subjects. Not unless you really want an education in such matters!

Chrystal′s Stash

Why the Stash?

When economists talk of the Great Crash of 1929, they're talking about history, something they studied at University.

Chrystal was there. She's seen a few lesser ones, too.

In times of economic uncertainty, the cautious put their money into gold bullion and works of art. It's widely accepted that these are the safest investments for anyone who doesn't trust banks.

Chrystal is very wealthy, having accumulated money over a lifespan those economists cannot even dream of. She's kept this wealth in the form of items she can buy that will be easily translated into cash when she needs it. Yes, she has accounts with a few banks - but her savings are stored in a cave in a geologically stable area of mid-Wales. And a few other places, but she hasn't given me those details.

No, even Chrystal doesn't have a lifespan that's significant in geological terms. But there's no point storing works of art long-term in an earthquake zone.

So what's in the stash? We hear of precious artefacts, paintings, sculptures, jewellery and other items that are believed to be "in private hands". Which simply means they been bought by someone who doesn't want to put them on display in a museum or gallery. And occasionally they resurface.

We've already seen Chrystal selling the Maxberg Archaeopteryx, but there were a lot more boxes when Sam went to visit. Tantalising...

The Maxberg Archaeopteryx

A missing fossil.

Archaeopteryx was a species of very primitive bird, with many reptilian characteristics as well as birdlike ones such as feathers and hollow bones.

Very few fossils of archaeopteryx are known and the so-called Maxberg fossil was only the third one found. Discovered in 1956, it was exhibited in the Maxberg Museum in Germany for a while. Casts and x-rays were taken of it, but it was never properly cleaned or scrutinised as closely as many people would have liked. The owner refused to sell it, as he didn't want to pay tax on the income and he refused access to it after taking it home from the display in 1974. No-one saw it after this and it was not in his house after he died in 1991. The whereabouts of this important fossil remain unknown. Its value would be incredible, were it to come to light.

Suggested search terms: Archaeopteryx, Maxberg, Eduard Opitsch (the owner's name).

The Bad Guys

One of the joys of writing longer fiction (i.e. this novel) is that I get to spend more time with my baddies. I subscribe to the view that no-one except a psychopath truly believes that they are evil - they merely have desires and aims that are in a different direction to the heroes (or heroines). Which meant I had to work out exactly what my Bad Guys are trying to do, in more depth than I had with previous baddies.

So - Geb and his motley crew of pirates and other malcontents. Who are they and what have they got against Chrystal?

Well, Geb was once worshipped as a deity. In Ancient Egypt. Geb was the Earth god, associated with Nut, the Sky goddess. And one of his forms was that of a gigantic, snake-headed man. He's different to the others in his stronghold, in that he seems to be the original god worshipped five thousand years ago. He looks like a living Mummy with leathery skin and emaciated limbs. Some of the others - Renenutet and Sobek for example, may be descended from the original figures that were worshipped by the Pharaohs. The exact details aren't clear yet.

Geb isn't actually bad, he just wants to restore the balance of power between order and chaos (Isfet and Maat). Things have been pushed too far in one direction, thanks to human activities. Ever since the Meso-Americans started creating calendars that tracked the turning of the Earth, our planet has been getting less chaotic. Everything Is measured and counted - we know how long a day is (and they *are* getting longer), we measure how much rain or sunshine we get each year and Geb thinks we are seeing ourselves as gods because we can measure all this.

That offends him deeply. He was always the defender of the balance, stepping in when his compatriots threatened to push it too far in either direction. He may not be as powerful as he was millennia ago - but he's learnt a few tricks over the years and he's not above using 21st Century human technology when it suits him.

Being a snake-headed deity, Geb produces a venom which is fatal to humans. All of the symptoms described in the text are documented to occur from the venom of other poisonous creatures.

The pirates and other humans in Geb's army are men discontented with the world they live in. A few were criminals before they came to him. Many were just roamers or dropouts, looking for a chance at a better life. But once they come and taste Geb's *wafers,* they cannot leave him. The drug contained in them is addictive both physically and psychologically. It causes the soldiers to burn more brightly and exaggerates their aggressive tendencies, but the fire which burns more brightly burns itself out all the faster...

Suggested search terms for more info on aspects of Egyptian mythology:

Ennead of Heliopolis, Isfet and Maat, any of the names mentioned above.

Corvidae

The crow family, the corvidae, are one of the most widespread on Earth. Intelligent, usually gregarious and highly adaptable, there are members of this clan on every continent except Antarctica. As well as crows of various types, this includes jays, ravens, magpies, rooks, choughs, jackdaws, picathartes, nutcrackers and treepies. Legends abound in human civilisations about birds as intelligent as people - even our collective nouns reflect an underlying assumption that we're not talking about your average bird-brains: a scold of jays, a congregation of magpies, a chattering of choughs, a parliament of rooks, a train of jackdaws, an unkindness of ravens, a murder of crows - terms that imply a degree of intelligence or even malice! Corvids have long been associated with pagan beliefs, the occult and are often seen as harbingers of bad news. Is it just that many of them have black feathers? But we don't see the blackbird in the same light. Maybe our ancestors knew how bright these dark birds are.

Studies by human scientists have documented corvidae using tools to get at food and recognising themselves in mirrors. Crows in Japan have learned that walnuts break open if they're left on a busy road - and that the traffic will stop and allow a bird to collect its spoils if the nut was left on a pedestrian crossing. Their brain/body mass ratio is about the same as chimps and dolphins, only slightly less than it is for humans.

But why do they attack Chrystal? Presumably they can tell they're something different about her. Is it the Chrystal itself they object to? Can they tell that she's older than a human has a right to be? Or do they remember something about a person with a gemstone heart that we don't know?

There's a lot of information about these fascinating avians on the internet. Look for videos and be amazed at some of the puzzles a birdbrain can solve.

Suggested search terms:

Corvidae, intelligent crows, crow tool-use, bird mirror self, crow walnuts Japan, any of the names listed above.

The Meso-American Calendar

There has been plenty of publicity over the ending of the so-called Mayan calendar at the end of 2012. Contrary to the popular myth, this was never meant to prophecy the apocalypse or anything dramatic at all. It was merely the end of a cycle that the calendar counts and the Mayans would have expected to begin counting again just as we do on January 1 each year. Although they may have had rituals surrounding the ending of one calendar and the start of the next.

The Mayan calendar was based on a much earlier one, laid out by the Olmec civilisation thousands of years earlier. And the much-photographed Mayan calendar stones were similarly copied from others. The stone that Chrystal locates is presumably the original that requires a sacrifice to be made at the turning of each cycle. Where such a thing may be located is unknown to modern research, but it's always possible that an older civilisation has records that go back beyond even folk memory.

This is a fascinating subject for research, and if a reader wishes to know more, I'd suggest search terms of: Mesoamerican Long Count Calendar, Mayan calendar rock.

Of course, there's going to be the problem of feeding the master calendar stone when this current cycle comes to an end. But none of us will be around in 374 years to worry about it. Although Chrystal might!

Friends of Chrystal Heart

Finally, I have the happy duty of acknowledging the kind, generous people who contributed when I crowdfunded for this novel. Thank you all, from the bottom of my heart.

Andy and Steph Sutton
Antique Keys
Awr-Glas Cwrfu
Bluehook
Bob Cockshott
Bushel
Captain Emilia Etherheart
Cole E. Optera
David De Silva
David Hunter
David Ord and Soo Abram
Dewi Cas-Gwent
Dim Sunnie
Doktor Steam
Esme Moore
Eugenie Summerfield
Evelyn Grainger
Exeter Tim
Fay & Martyn Maillardet
General Factotum
Gwen Hufer
Ice Lightning
Jack Goodwin
Janet and Jon Mier
Janet Thomas
Karen and Sue
Kenny Halley

Kraken Rider
Maggie Hampton
Major Major Major Minor
Marie Irshad
Marit Meredith
Natalie Caswell
Neula & Kim Kaos
Organ Morgan
Pacific Green
P.D.Williams
Phil and Jenny Larke
Phil Anthropist
Prof. Magnim, Vizerus Temporis
Professor Plumbum
Robert Darke
Sandy Kay and Stewart Dyer
Sir Peregrine Storm Esq.
Steamed Punk
Steph and Deb Faulkner
Sue F
Sunny A
Susan Hooper
The Dragon Whisperer
Tommy Cook
Vogon Musicians
William Wedge

Chrystal and Sam's story will be continued in
Chrystal Travels